WOLF HAVEN

ALSO BY ANTHONY M. STRONG

THE JOHN DECKER SUPERNATURAL THRILLER SERIES

Soul Catcher (prequel) • What Vengeance Comes • Cold Sanctuary
Crimson Deep • Grendel's Labyrinth • Whitechapel Rising
Black Tide • Ghost Canyon • Cryptic Quest • Last Resort
Dark Force • A Ghost of Christmas Past • Deadly Crossing
Final Destiny • Night Wraith • Wolf Haven

THE CUSP FILES

Deadly Truth • Devil's Forest

THE REMNANTS SERIES

The Remnants of Yesterday • The Silence of Tomorrow

STANDALONE BOOKS

The Haunting of Willow House • Crow Song

WOLF HAVEN

A John Decker Novel

ANTHONY M.STRONG

WEST STREET

Wolf Haven
West Street Publishing

Cover art and interior design by
Bad Dog Media, LLC.

ISBN: 978-1-942207-56-6

For Nick and Tony Shaw…
Two of the good guys!

PROLOGUE

THE CHAIN-LINK FENCE towered above them in the darkness, illuminated by the twin spears of Justin Keaton's headlights.

Jordan Norris leaned forward from the back of the car and stuck her head between the front seats. She pushed the cascading locks of her blonde hair back over her shoulders and peered up through the windshield. "What are we doing here?"

Paige Adamson, who was sitting next to Jordan, stared at the scene in front of them and wrinkled her nose. "If you brought us here to make out, you're out of luck. It's not going to happen."

Chris Pierce, Wolf Haven High's star running back, who occupied the front passenger seat, looked around at the girls. "Don't worry. There's plenty of time to make out later. We're going to have some fun first."

"Um, this is your idea of fun?" Jordan scowled. "It's a construction site."

"Who said romance was dead?" Paige sat back in her seat with a huff and folded her arms.

"Not just any construction site." Chris released his seatbelt, then tugged at his door handle and climbed out of the car. He waited for the others to join him, then looked up at the partially completed road that ran off across the swamp into darkness on huge concrete piers. Beneath it, standing to one side in the shadow of the highway, was a rundown shack with a sagging porch and a bowed roof. "This is Annie Doucet's old land."

"Seriously?" Now it was Jordan's turn to fold her arms. She gave Justin a defiant stare. "This is *not* how I wanted to spend my night."

"Me either," said Paige.

"Would you two quit complaining?" Chris went to the back of the car and opened the trunk. He took out a couple of flashlights, handed one to Justin, and kept the other for himself. He snapped it on, then started toward the fence. "What else have you got to do?"

"I can think of so many things, and none of them involve poking around a haunted old shack in the middle of the swamp." Jordan reached out and snatched the flashlight from Justin's hand. "You could at least have brought enough of these for all of us."

Chris shrugged. "It was all I could find."

"Then maybe you should've said where we were going." Paige took her phone out and turned the light on. "My dad has flashlights all over the house in case of a power outage."

"What, and ruin the surprise?" Chris walked to the fence and stopped at a spot where the chain-link had separated from its post and was curled back. He pulled the fence back further to make a hole big enough for them to pass through, then turned to the others. "After you."

"Great. We're really going to do this?" Jordan let Justin step through before glancing at Paige. "Maybe we should stay here. Let the guys have their fun, then they can drive us home."

"Are you kidding me?" Paige glanced around the pitch-black landscape surrounding them. Tall pines stood to their left, the start of the Piney Woods that covered thousands of square miles across that part of the state. Beyond the cabin, murky swampland stretched into the distance, broken here and there by the ghostly silhouettes of bald cypress trees dripping with Spanish moss. She shuddered and turned her attention back to the construction site in front of them. "I'm not staying out here on my own. It's too creepy."

"Creepier than that?" Jordan nodded toward the dilapidated cabin.

"Everything out here is creepy. The quicker we get this over with, the sooner we can leave." Paige ducked through the hole in the fence. "You can stay if you want to. I'm going with the guys."

Chris looked at her, still holding the fence back. When she didn't move, he shrugged and ducked through, leaving Jordan by herself.

She watched her friends depart, striking out across the open expanse toward the cabin. Behind her, the car was a haven of safety. She almost turned and climbed back in, locked the doors. But then she truly would be alone, and that might be worse than anything. Muttering under her breath, she pushed through the fence and ran to catch up with the others.

The cabin was even more dilapidated up close than it had looked from the other side of the fence. Most of the windows were broken out, with only one left intact. Shingles had come off the roof and littered the ground in front of the slouching porch. A faded sign nailed to one of the porch posts still advertised the means of Annie Doucet's meager existence.

TAROT READINGS.
PALMISTRY.
POTIONS.

The sign was barely readable, but it was enough to send a shudder down Jordan's spine. Annie Doucet was long gone, shot to death by Wolf Haven's previous sheriff, but it hadn't stopped the rumors. That she was a witch who had transformed herself into a wolf—the legendary Cajun loup-garou—and terrorized the town, murdering anyone associated with the road that had robbed the old woman of her property. Which was why a brand-new highway leading out to the interstate now loomed over the ramshackle cabin that Annie had once called home. The stories were ridiculous, of course. But enough folk swore they had encountered the beast—people like Ed Johnson, who ran the County Line Saloon—to keep everyone whispering about the monster that had brought death down upon Wolf Haven.

"Hey!"

A hand landed on Jordan's shoulder. She snapped back to reality, realizing she had zoned out for a moment. It was Chris. "Sorry, I was miles away."

"Come on," he said, climbing the porch steps.

The cabin door stood open. The others were already inside. She hurried to join them.

The cabin was just as bad on the inside as she had imagined it to be. She was standing in a small living room with a moldy couch gently falling in upon itself and the remains of an old cathode ray tube TV that had toppled off its stand and lay smashed on the floor. Floral wallpaper had peeled away from the walls to reveal the cracked plaster beneath. They weren't the first to visit the cabin since Annie's demise. Someone had sprayed graffiti across the walls. Probably more than one person, judging by the way each act of vandalism overlaid the previous to create a chaotic and almost unreadable hodgepodge of insults directed at the dead woman. She picked out the words Witch, and Got What You Deserved, along with a crude representation of a wolf with what looked like blood dripping from its mouth.

"Nice," Paige muttered under her breath.

"See! This is why I didn't want to come here. It's creepy." Jordan glanced around. Beyond the living room was a tiny kitchen with cabinets barely hanging on the walls. One upper cabinet had come away completely, or maybe someone had torn it off the wall. There was a gaping hole where the stove should have been. The fridge was still there, its doors open, and interior walls lined with black mold. A dark corridor led to what she assumed must be the bedrooms.

Chris was at the door on the left, staring into the room wide-eyed with disbelief. "Hey guys, you've got to see this."

"What?" Justin started toward him.

"See for yourself. It's nuts."

Jordan started across the living room. The floorboards beneath her feet were rotten and bowed. They shifted under her weight and for a moment she thought she might fall through, but then she reached the corridor and stepped into the bedroom behind Paige and Justin.

What she saw made the breath catch in her throat.

Unlike the rest of the shack, this room looked like it had been frozen in time. There was an iron framed bed standing against one wall, complete with sheets and a thick comforter. A three-drawer dresser stood against the opposite wall. There was a hairbrush sitting upon it with strands of hair still visible.

Jordan shook her head and backed out of the room. "Okay. That's too much."

"It's just an old hairbrush," Justin said, laughing. "What's the big deal?"

"It's weird, that's what," Jordan replied. "That room is like a museum."

"Maybe this is Annie's old bedroom," Paige said in a voice barely above a whisper. "It's awesome."

Jordan had wandered down the corridor and stuck her head into the door on her right, shining her flashlight into the space beyond. "That wasn't Annie's room," she said. "This one was."

"How do you know that?" Chris stepped back into the corridor.

"Look for yourselves." Jordan stepped into the room and stared down at the floor.

Paige came through the doorway and stopped in her tracks. Her eyes flew wide. "Holy crap."

There were only two pieces of furniture in the room. A

rusting bedframe leaned against one wall. Another dresser, this one missing its drawers, stood nearby. The paint had flaked away to reveal rotten wood beneath. But this wasn't what had drawn Jordan's attention. It was the pentagram drawn in chalk on the bare floorboards, and the clumps of wax—the melted remains of candles—that surrounded it.

"Nope. Too much." Paige backpedaled into the corridor and vanished into the darkness.

"Hey, I thought you were good with this stuff?" Justin called after her.

His only response was the sound of the front door opening, then slamming closed again.

"We should go after her," said Chris, backing up.

"Yeah." Justin looked down at the pentagram, then turned and stepped from the room.

Jordan swung the flashlight around, half expecting the old witch to come lunging at her out of the darkness, but she was alone. Casting one last glance toward the pentagram and the melted candles, she hurried from the room.

Chris and Justin were already out on the cabin's front porch, looking around.

"I don't see her," said Chris, peering off into the darkness.

"Maybe she went back to the car already." Justin stepped off the porch.

"She couldn't have gotten back there that fast."

"Where is she then, genius?" Justin stood with his hands on his hips, looking around. He shouted her name.

There was no reply.

"I don't like this." Jordan wished they had never come out here. She should have known that Chris and Justin weren't taking them to Sullivans Pond to make out and drink wine. There was always a way about them when they were up to no good. The knowing glances. The cryptic replies. She wished they would just grow up. Act like young adults instead of idiotic teens.

"Paige. Where are you?" Justin called out again. His voice was snatched by the December wind and whisked away.

"Maybe she's hiding," Chris said. "Getting her own back at us for bringing her here."

"That's ridiculous. She's not hiding." Jordan took a step forward, felt something sticky under her shoe. She pointed the flashlight down and saw that she was standing in a pool of dark red viscous goo. No, not goo. Blood. Jordan sucked in a quick breath as the implication dawned upon her. Then she screamed.

Justin turned toward her, startled. "What the—"

His exclamation was cut off by a movement in the darkness. A shifting of the shadows off to his left. He looked toward it, startled.

Chris swung his flashlight around, briefly capturing a fast shape, muscular and hairy, before it vanished into the darkness again.

"There's something out there," Jordan said. She motioned to Justin. "Get back up here."

Justin hesitated, glancing around nervously, and started back toward the porch. He'd barely taken two steps before there was another flash of movement, barely perceptible against the darkness. Then, even as he turned toward it, Justin was gone. Snatched up and dragged away. A moment later, there was a high-pitched scream, swiftly cut off.

Jordan whimpered.

Chris waved the flashlight around, its beam bouncing off piles of construction materials, a tractor-trailer parked near one of the highway piers, and a bright yellow backhoe. "What the hell was that?"

"I don't know." Jordan willed herself to move, but she was frozen in place. "We have to get out of here. Fetch help."

"We can't just leave them here."

"You can do what you want." Jordan's legs finally obeyed her. She crossed the porch and hurried down the steps. "I'm going."

Chris lingered a second, then changed his mind. He started after Jordan, who was already sprinting across the open space between the cabin and the fence. "Wait for me."

Jordan reached the fence and ducked through the hole. Breathless, she turned, expecting to see Chris right behind her.

But he wasn't there.

Instead, she saw his flashlight lying abandoned on the ground.

"Chris. Where are you?" she called in a hoarse whisper.

There was no reply.

"Chris?" Jordan stared off into the darkness, praying that he would appear. That he had just tripped and dropped the flashlight. But she knew better. She was on her own now. Vulnerable and alone.

And as if to prove it, a shape detached itself from the blackness. It padded toward her on all fours. Large and muscular, covered in coarse black hair. A beast that observed her with burning yellow eyes. And in that moment, Jordan knew what she was looking at.

The loup-garou.

She stifled a scream, turned, and ran for the car, then jumped behind the wheel even as she fumbled to lock the door. It was at that moment she realized that she didn't have the keys. They were in Justin's pocket.

Jordan looked up, stared through the windshield.

The creature had pushed through the fence. It stood ten feet away from the car, staring back at her.

Then, to Jordan's horror, it raised itself up on two legs, lifted its gaze to the heavens, and howled.

ONE

AT 10 AM the morning after returning from Boston, John Decker strode across the expansive lobby toward a long, sleek reception desk of steel and polished wood construction, behind which sat a woman of diminutive stature with bobbed black hair, a thin nose, and wireframe glasses. At his approach, she looked up, a flash of recognition passing across her face that soon turned to surprise.

"Mr. Decker. I didn't think we would have the pleasure of your company again," she said, her expression quickly changing back to one of stoic indifference.

"Me either," Decker replied, glancing around. Only two weeks ago, he had resigned from the clandestine organization known as Classified Universal Special Projects, and now here he was, once more, standing in their island headquarters off the coast of Maine. "I have an appointment."

"With Adam Hunt?" The receptionist turned her attention to a flatscreen monitor on the desk and tapped away at the keyboard.

"No." Decker shook his head. "With the director."

"Oh. I'm not sure that—" The woman stopped herself. She

looked up at Decker. "That's most unusual. The director doesn't normally take appointments."

"She does for me."

The receptionist looked down again. "I don't see it on the schedule."

"That's because I've only just arrived back from Boston. I called ahead and told her I was coming, then caught the first ferry over to the island. It's an urgent situation. Please, feel free to check."

"There won't be any need for that." A fresh voice boomed out.

Decker turned to see Adam Hunt striding toward him.

"Are we back in your good books, or have you come here to berate us some more?" Hunt asked.

"Neither." Decker thanked the receptionist and walked to meet his erstwhile boss. "Does this mean you'll be sitting in on my meeting, after all?"

"I *am* the Assistant Director of CUSP. It's my prerogative."

"I was hoping to speak with Mina in private."

Hunt pursed his lips. "I was hoping that today would be dull and uneventful. And now, here *you* are. Given how we parted ways, I have to assume that you've gotten yourself into a situation you can't handle on your own." Hunt shot Decker a mirthless smile. "We don't always get what we want."

"Fair enough." Decker shrugged, then followed Hunt when he turned and made his way toward a security station on the other side of the lobby near the elevators that rose into the restricted areas of the building.

"Phone and wallet," Hunt said, nodding toward the guard sitting behind the desk. "Weapon too, if you have one on you."

"No weapons," Decker replied, removing his phone and wallet from his pocket and handing them to the guard. "Is this really necessary?"

"Standard procedure for visitors." Hunt stood with his arms folded. "You don't work for CUSP anymore, remember?"

"Whatever." Decker turned toward the elevators. "Can we hurry this along? What I have to say is urgent."

Hunt observed Decker for a moment, then shrugged. He used the key card to summon the elevator and then stepped aside for Decker to enter. They rose three floors in silence, then stepped out into a sterile white corridor that could have been in any of a million office buildings around the globe. Seconds later, they stepped into a conference room with a large oak table in the middle surrounded by plush leather chairs.

Mina was already there, sitting at the opposite end of the table.

Upon their entry, she stood. "John. It's good to see you."

"Likewise," Decker replied.

"Please, sit down."

Decker took a seat on one side of the table while Adam Hunt settled on the other.

Mina waited for them to get comfortable before speaking once more. "I feared you might never talk to us again."

"That was the plan," Decker answered in an even voice. "Circumstances dictated otherwise."

"Interesting." A look of intrigue flashed across Mina's face. "Would this have anything to do with your recent trip to Boston?"

"You know about that?"

"You might not work for CUSP anymore, but that doesn't mean we haven't kept tabs on you."

Decker stared at Mina. "I don't appreciate being surveilled."

"You make it sound so dramatic."

"I was thinking underhanded."

Hunt leaned forward. "John, it's nothing personal. Like any organization such as ours, we have protocols that need to be followed when a person leaves our employ. We have to make sure that—"

Decker waved him off, eager to get to the crux of his visit.

"It's not important, but what I've come here to discuss with you is."

Mina raised an eyebrow. "Then perhaps you should get to the point."

Decker slipped a hand into his pocket and removed the letter that Nancy had found inside the Charles Dickens' first edition of *A Christmas Carol*. He slid it across the table toward Mina and waited while she read it. When she was done, Mina handed it to Hunt, who gave it a quick glance before looking up at Decker.

"Is this for real?" He asked.

"Yes." Decker nodded.

"One of Charles Dickens' most famous books was based upon a real supernatural experience he had in Boston?"

"A Christmas Carol. Yes." Decker nodded again. "And not just Charles Dickens. The house, and the spirits contained within, are still there. At least, if you need them to be."

"Are we to assume that you and Nancy found this house?" Mina asked.

"A more accurate description would be that it found us." The visions he had experienced within that ghostly house were still fresh in Decker's mind. He hoped to settle one of them and change its outcome on this visit. For the other, he would have to travel back to a place he never thought he would visit again. Wolf Haven, Louisiana. He looked at Mina and Hunt. "I saw something inside that house that you need to know about. It's life or death."

"Do go on," Mina said, leaning forward with her elbows on the desk.

Decker took a deep breath, then he told them everything. How he came to terms with his mother's death and finally learned the truth of what happened back then. How the events of the past had turned Annie Doucet into a teenaged killer harnessing the power of witchcraft. And how she had become the loup-garou. And later, how she exacted her revenge on his parents by transforming once again into the wolf and killing his mother. That had led to the final confrontation between Decker and the old woman at the high school during a raging hurricane. A confrontation that had lost Decker his job as the town sheriff and led him to CUSP in the first place. But that wasn't all of it. There were also the events that he saw in his future, and of those closest to him. The events in Italy that led to the deaths of Colum O'Shea and one of his team at the hands of a harpy, and Decker's own deadly confrontation with the loup-garou in Wolf Haven. A creature that had returned and was already on the loose even as they spoke.

When he was done, there was a moment of silence. Hunt and Mina exchanged glances.

Finally, Hunt cleared his throat and spoke. "You couldn't possibly know about the situation in Italy."

"Then the ghost was right. There is a harpy." Decker tried to hide his disappointment. He had hoped that by some miracle, the visions he saw in his future were wrong.

Hunt nodded. "It's a possibility, but we're still monitoring the situation. We haven't decided whether to intervene yet."

"But you will," Decker replied. "And unless something changes, it won't go well, which leads me to one inescapable conclusion."

"And what would that be?" Mina asked.

Decker hesitated a moment before answering, then he took a deep breath. "I have to come back to CUSP."

TWO

THERE WAS a moment of silence as Mina and Adam Hunt absorbed Decker's statement. Then Mina spoke. "You think that coming back to CUSP will save Colum's life?"

"Based on the vision showed to me by the Ghost of *All Things Yet to Come*, you'll send Colum to Italy at some point in the next couple of weeks, and he will die at the hands of that harpy. Unless I'm here to stop it, that is."

"Except that you've told us what will happen," Mina said. "You don't need to come back. We can choose to make a different decision now."

"That won't work." Decker shook his head. "Given your unique circumstances, you should know better than anyone that you can't escape destiny. The vision was clear. If I'm not around to handle the situation, Colum will die, and I suspect that any actions you take to stop that outcome will fail. One way or the other, he will face the harpy and lose."

There was another brief silence before Mina spoke again. "Is this what you really want? To come back to CUSP?"

"It's not a question of what I want so much as my duty. I have no choice."

"And Nancy?"

"She's not happy, but she understands."

"And the other thing you told us about?" Hunt said. "The situation in Wolf Haven?"

"The loup-garou," Mina added.

"I'll need to deal with that first, of course. But we have time. According to my vision, you don't send Colum to Italy for almost a month after first learning about the situation there. I'll deal with the loup-garou, then take care of the harpy."

"Except that you saw the wolf kill you." Mina didn't look convinced. "You were right when you talked about destiny. Like you said, I should know. What if you return to Wolf Haven and die there, leaving us with no choice but to send Colum to Italy, anyway?"

"I don't think that will happen." Decker had already thought of this and came to the only suitable conclusion. "If it was my destiny to die in Wolf Haven—if it was inevitable—the ghost would not have shown that vision to me. Anyway, it's irrelevant. Colum is safe for now, and the situation in Wolf Haven is immediate. It requires my attention. Once I've taken care of the loup-garou, I'll return and resume my old position with CUSP. Assuming that you're both agreeable, of course. After that, we can talk about the harpy."

"We'd love you to come back, naturally," Mina said.

"That goes without saying," Hunt interjected.

"But not when you come back." Mina smiled. "I think it would be best if we reinstate you immediately."

"That won't change anything," Decker said. "I still have to go back to Wolf Haven. I've made the arrangements already. I have a flight out of Manchester tomorrow afternoon."

"I'm not trying to change your mind about Wolf Haven," Mina said. "I'm trying to keep you alive long enough to be useful to us again. What do you say?"

"I think there's only one thing I can say."

"Good." A slight smile touched Mina's lips.

Hunt extended an arm. "Welcome back."

"Thanks… I think." Decker took Hunt's outstretched hand and shook it. "Does this mean I can get my phone back now?"

"It means more than that," Mina said. "You can cancel that commercial flight and take the jet. It will be more comfortable and much quicker."

"There really is no need. The flight is already paid for and I'm sure it can't be canceled at such short notice. I'll be fine."

"Nonsense." Mina shook her head. "You're taking the jet and that's an order. I also expect you to keep us appraised of the situation on the ground there. If you run into trouble and need help, we're here."

"Might I remind you this isn't an official CUSP investigation."

"But you *are* an official CUSP operative again as of about a minute ago. We can't afford to lose you a second time."

"Fair enough," Decker said. "I'll cancel my flight and take the jet. Will there be anything else?"

"Actually, yes there is," Hunt said. "Nancy."

"What about her?" Decker was confused.

"You're not married yet," said Mina. "I feel like it's our fault, given the circumstances. And here you are about to face one of your oldest enemies—"

"An enemy that killed you in your vision—" Hunt continued.

"And you've done nothing to address the situation."

"I agree, but it's not like I've had much opportunity since returning from Boston, and the situation in Wolf Haven cannot wait. I'll take care of it as soon as I get back."

"Not good enough." Mina stood up. "There's plenty of time to rectify the situation. Go home. Tell Nancy to get ready. Both of you come back here at 4 PM. We'll handle the rest."

"Are you serious?" Decker could hardly believe what he was hearing.

"Oh, yes. I'm deadly serious." Mina put her hands on her hips. "There's no way I'm letting you put yourself in danger again before we put this right. Nancy's been through enough already. By the time you get on that plane tomorrow afternoon, you'll be a married man."

THREE

MINA WAS as good as her word. Decker returned to the mainland and fetched Nancy, who was both surprised and excited by the prospect of tying the knot on the spur of the moment. It was, she said, the antithesis of their last attempt to get married, which had gone horrendously wrong on Singer Cay when Decker was lost to the past, along with a much younger Mina. Now, she had little appetite for months of planning and a large wedding. With Decker's impending departure for Wolf Haven, and the inherent danger contained within that trip, she was happy to formalize their union regardless of circumstance.

That was why, at 6 PM that evening, the two of them stood in a small stone chapel contained within the nineteenth-century mansion that formed one wing of CUSP's headquarters on an island off the Maine coast. The old mansion, originally built by a railroad magnate, now contained living quarters, guest suites for visiting dignitaries, an executive dining room, and, of course, the chapel.

There were only a few people present at the ceremony, which was officiated by Adam Hunt, just like the previous one on Singer Cay. By a stroke of luck, Rory McCormick was already on the island for a debriefing related to a recently completed mission in Egypt, and he brought his girlfriend, Cassie Locke, along for the trip. The two had been staying in a guesthouse on the mainland while Rory shuttled back-and-forth to the island, and had now relocated to one of the suites in the mansion for the night. Another surprise guest was Nancy's daughter, Taylor, who had made the journey up from college in Boston thanks to a town car sent by Mina to collect her. The only disappointment was that Colum O'Shea could not make the ceremony since he was in the middle of an assignment halfway around the world. An assignment that Decker was relieved to learn had nothing to do with a harpy in Italy. But Celine Rothman—who Colum had been dating for several months—*was* in attendance, and this time her presence was planned.

An hour later, after exchanging their vows and finally completing the task they had begun almost a year earlier on Singer Cay, Nancy, Decker, and the rest of the wedding party retreated to the executive dining room for a wedding reception that included a three-course feast, an open bar, and a band that played until midnight. After that, the pair retreated to the mansion's penthouse suite for the night. It was a scant substitute for a true honeymoon, but it was enough, at least for now.

FOUR

ERNIE WILLS, manager of the new Pinch-A-Cent discount grocery store that had opened the year before on a tract of land outside of Wolf Haven that had once been a mosquito infested swamp, made his way from the stockroom at the back of the store toward his office near the front past the public restrooms and the staff lounge. It was almost ten at night and he was the only person left in the building. In fact, he was probably the only person left in the entire shopping plaza, which also included a coffee shop, seafood restaurant, and several units that were not rented yet, all built in anticipation of the new Wolf Haven interchange off the nearby interstate that would be completed the following year. These would soon be joined by a gas station and travel center, and a national fast-food hamburger chain that was slated to open the following summer. There was even talk of a hotel being built to give weary drivers somewhere to lay their heads when they wandered off the highway.

Ernie couldn't help a derisive snort at that thought. It was ludicrous. There were already more than enough hotels lining every offramp from Alabama to the Texas border, and he truly doubted that many motorists would find enough interest in Wolf Haven and its surroundings to detour from their journey in such a remote location when there were better places to stop. Even the grocery store was hardly a sure thing. It had been open for almost a month and was already struggling to attract customers from town who were so stuck in their ways that they preferred to shop in the smaller supermarket that had served Wolf Haven for as long as anyone could remember even though the prices were higher, and the selection was smaller. Ernie wondered if he would still have a job by the time the interstate offramp opened and hopefully brought in new business. In his estimation, the faceless corporate entity that owned not just this store, but another thirty-five locations across the South, had miscalculated in their zeal to beat the larger supermarket chains to this backwater corner of Louisiana.

Shaking his head, Ernie strolled through the fresh produce section, noting how the lettuce looked a little wilted, and the fruit over ripe. Another reminder that there were not enough customers to ensure a swift turnover of stock. Still, it wasn't all bad. His employment contract guaranteed him a fat severance package if the store went belly up and the company didn't offer him a suitable position somewhere else. And maybe that wouldn't be a bad thing. He'd been working in retail for the last thirty years, mostly for the same company, and had relocated three times to take the helm at new stores. This last move had been tough. Wolf Haven was nothing more than a backwater speck on the map and was just far enough away from New Orleans to make the drive untenable.

Ernie reached the front of the building and stepped past the restrooms into the corridor leading to the staff lounge and offices. He pushed open a door marked STAFF ONLY and ducked into the small room beyond, then went to a bank of switches, most of which he turned off. When he exited, the store was dark, save for a few lights at the front that illuminated the lobby where lines of stacked grocery carts waited for the following day's shoppers, and the registers.

After checking that the sliding doors leading out to the

parking lot were locked and that the store's alarm system was engaged, Ernie turned back toward the corridor.

It was then that he heard it.

A faint noise, like shuffling feet from somewhere among the aisles.

He froze, listening. There shouldn't be anyone left in the store. Even the other employees had gone home for the night.

The sound came again.

"Hello?" Ernie called out. "Is anybody there?"

He received no answer.

"Store's closed." Ernie stepped past the registers and looked around, but saw nothing. "If you meet me at the front, I can let you out."

Again, nothing.

Ernie swallowed. Maybe it was just his overactive imagination playing tricks. After all, the store was pretty creepy at night with the lights off. He glanced toward the front of the store and the mostly empty parking lot beyond. He could see his car there, waiting in a pool of illumination under one of the pole mounted LED lights that were dotted throughout the space.

"The hell with this," he muttered under his breath, and took a step back toward the corridor and the staff entrance.

From deeper in the store, there was a sudden crash. The sound of breaking glass as something hit the floor and smashed.

Ernie swiveled around with wide eyes. "What the hell?"

Another crash and tinkle of glass.

"Dammit." Ernie hurried toward the aisles, following the sound, even as he reached for his cell phone to dial 911. Was there an intruder in the store? Had they been hiding until the staff went home and then snuck out to rob the place? That made no sense. There were surveillance cameras throughout the building, and they would surely be caught. And why bother for nothing more than loaves of bread, packages of deli meat, and cartons of eggs? It was a lot of risk for little reward. There was no money to be had. The day's takings were already in the night safe, and any would-be thief would require an oxyacetylene torch and several hours just to get into it.

Then another thought occurred to him. Rats. There had been a similar problem at one of his other stores. The vermin would come out at night and run along the shelves, knocking things off and chewing through packages.

A shudder ran up Ernie's spine.

He hated rats, with their fat black bodies, beady red eyes, and hairless pink tails.

And when he turned onto the pasta aisle, he found his proof. Several jars of marinara sauce had fallen from the shelf and lay broken beneath, the red sauce spilled across the linoleum tiles like a thick crimson lake. Chunks of glass, the remains of sauce bottles, emerged from the mess like small, shattered islands.

Ernie cursed under his breath. He was tired and hungry. The last thing he wanted to do was grab a mop and bucket from the stockroom and spend the next thirty minutes cleaning this mess up. But what choice did he have? If he left it there, flies would be swarming over it by morning. Then again, that would also be true if it had happened after he had left the store. And tomorrow he could tell someone else to clean it.

Making up his mind, Ernie turned away from the aisle and back toward the registers.

Then he saw it. A creature standing several feet away near an end cap full of *buy one, get one free* store-brand soda. At first, he thought it was a big dog, maybe a stray, that had snuck in through the loading bay doors earlier in the day. But then he realized his mistake. It wasn't a dog. It looked more like—Ernie could hardly believe his eyes—an enormous wolf.

Which was impossible because there were no wolves in Louisiana, and even if there were, how would it have gotten into his store?

Ernie took a step back.

The creature padded forward on thick, muscular legs. Then, even more impossibly, it reared up and stood before him.

Something snapped in Ernie's mind.

A scream welled up in his throat even as he turned to run.

At that moment, the wolf pounced.

FIVE

WHEN DECKER ARRIVED at the airport a little after noon the next day, there was a surprise for him. Mina's daughter, Daisy, was waiting near CUSP's private jet, standing at the bottom of the airstairs.

"Did your mother send you to see me off?" Decker asked as he approached the plane.

"Not quite." Daisy said in her crisp British accent, which she hadn't lost despite so many years in the United States. A faint smile played across her face. "I'm coming with you."

"The hell you are." Decker was already reaching for his phone.

"If you're going to call my mother, don't bother. It won't make any difference."

"I don't need a chaperone," Decker said, not bothering to hide the annoyance in his voice. "And certainly not one who's barely old enough to drink a beer."

"Really?" Now it was Daisy's turn to sound annoyed. "Do you remember when we first met, Mr. Decker?"

Decker nodded. "The Christmas party your father took me to in the English countryside."

"That's right. A party that took place in the winter of 1911."

Decker remained silent.

Daisy pressed her point. "Then tell me, other than the fact that I stopped aging in my early twenties, which was hardly through my own choice, how am I barely old enough to drink beer?"

"Okay, you've made your point." Decker dropped his bag at the bottom of the airstairs and watched as a man in blue overalls scooped it up and headed toward the aircraft's open hold.

"Have I, though?" Daisy folded her arms. "Despite my youthful appearance, I have more life experience than you will ever achieve. I was born in the late 1800s. I've lived through the entire 20th century. I've seen everything from the first radio receivers and mass-produced automobiles to the discovery of antibiotics, the invention of instant coffee, crossword puzzles, and even the bra." She looked up at the aircraft behind them. "And of course, I saw humanity take to powered flight for the first time."

"None of which gives you the experience to deal with a loup-garou," Decker said, even though he knew he was about to lose this argument, too.

Daisy did not disappoint him. "I've also been at my mother's side for a century while she ran The Order of St. George and then Classified Universal Special Projects. But you already know all of this. You were there at the beginning. And I don't just mean when you and my mother got thrown back into the past during your wedding on Singer Cay. My mother would not be practically immortal—would not have passed that ability on to me in turn—had you not allowed her to become embroiled in your investigation of Jack The Ripper after he was released from his century-long sleep in that basement under the townhouse in Hays Mews. In fact, had my mother not crossed paths with Abraham Turner that first time, had she not almost died at his hands, I daresay this conversation would not be happening because I would not exist." Daisy took a long breath. "But I'm here whether you like it or not, and I have more experience dealing with the supernatural than you could ever hope to achieve."

"That still doesn't mean I want a partner," Decker said, even as he realized that his protestations were futile. "The situation in Wolf Haven has nothing to do with CUSP. It's personal."

"And you saw a vision of your own death when you were in that house in Boston."

"One possible future. Unlike many of the events that occurred to Mina and me in the past, this one is not set in stone."

"But it is a possibility, just like your claim that Colum will die if we send him on his own to deal with the harpy in Italy."

"Yes." Decker couldn't argue on that point.

"Which is why we can't take the chance. We need you alive." Daisy watched the jet's ground crew close the hold and begin final preparations for their departure. "And so does Nancy. She's been married to you for less than twenty-four hours. Have you even told her what the Ghost of *All Things Yet to Come* showed you?"

"Not all of it," Decker admitted.

"Meaning you kept quiet about seeing your own death at the hands of the loup-garou."

Decker nodded. "Telling her would change nothing."

"I'm not sure she would agree with that sentiment under the circumstances."

"Maybe not. But I can't see the point in worrying Nancy about something that might not even happen. What the ghost showed me was only one possible future."

"And one which we are going to avoid at all costs," Daisy said, turning toward the stairs. She climbed them, then turned around at the top and looked back down toward Decker. "I'm coming to Wolf Haven, whether or not you like it. Now, are you going to hop aboard this plane so we can leave, or would you rather stand around on the tarmac and watch me take off without you?"

Decker stared up at Daisy, marveling at how much of her

mother's looks and personality she had inherited. It was precisely this stubbornness that had gotten Mina involved in their investigation of Abraham Turner in the first place.

"Well?" Daisy raised an eyebrow.

"Fine. If you want to come, then I can't stop you." Decker started up the airstairs, even as Daisy turned and disappeared into the dark interior of the jet. Fifteen minutes later, they were barreling down the runway and taking to the air.

Next stop... Decker's past.

SIX

DECKER OBSERVED Daisy sitting across the table from him on CUSP's private jet as it skirted the Canadian border and the Great Lakes, soaring at 40,000 feet above New York State on their way to New Orleans, and Wolf Haven beyond.

Daisy sat with her eyes closed. She looked almost as if she were asleep, except for her the fingers of her right hand, which toyed with a small charm hanging from a chain around her neck. A silver ornament representing a snake coiled around a pyramid that Decker recognized as the crest of Classified Universal Special Projects. If she was aware of his gaze, she did not show it. At least until she took a deep sigh, and said, "Is there something I can do for you, Mr. Decker?"

"I was just thinking how much you look like your mother," Decker said, shifting his gaze to look out of the window across the cloud tops that stretched into the hazy blue distance. "The two of you could be sisters. I'm surprised that I didn't see it more clearly back in 1911, at least until Thomas Finch admitted his secret to me."

"You saw what you expected to see." Daisy opened her eyes and looked at Decker. A slight smile played across her lips that swiftly vanished, to be replaced by a look more akin to yearning.

"I miss that time in my life. Back when I was still aging like a normal person, and I didn't know the truth of my existence."

"I can understand why you would feel like that," said Decker.

"It's funny, but I used to wonder exactly what my father did for a living. He never spoke about it at home. He always said it was just a boring government job. Paper pushing. I never believed that. He kept such odd hours and had such a strange way about him."

"He was trying to protect you."

"It didn't work." There was a sudden hard edge to Daisy's voice. "He lied to me for the first twenty-five years of my life. Hid my real mother from me. Let me think that I had a normal family. If I hadn't stopped aging, he probably never would have told me the truth. Neither would Mina."

"They cared about you," Decker said. "But I understand your anger."

Daisy shook her head. "You misunderstand me, Mr. Decker. I'm not angry. Maybe I was once, a very long time ago, but I've had over a century to make my peace with the situation and my mother. She told me why she hid my true origins and why she walked away from my father. Let him marry another woman. She was worried that her enemies would become our enemies, too. That she was vulnerable because of who she was… what she was. She didn't want to put us in the middle of that. To endanger our lives any more than necessary."

"I know," Decker said. "She told me as much."

"Not that it worked. If the vampires ever found out that she had passed her curse onto me, they would redouble their efforts to find us. My mother is unique in that she's a hybrid, with one foot in both worlds. I'm even more unique because I possess not only my mother's longevity but also my father's human traits."

"What about the urges?" Decker asked. He knew very well that Mina had struggled with an inner darkness. A basal desire passed on to her from Abraham Turner to extend her life even further by stealing that of others. She had resisted this inner darkness, just as she had resisted finding the amulet that had once belonged to Turner and was now inexorably linked to her. He wondered if Mina's will would have been so strong had she possessed Turner's amulet, which was a vital link in the exchange of life force between victim and vampire. Thankfully, the amulet had been entrusted to a guardian for safekeeping and had waited through the ages in a lead box wrapped in gold leaf that shielded it not just from Abraham Turner, who had been entombed in a London basement, but also from Mina.

"I don't share her urges," Daisy said. "Possibly thanks to my father's contribution to my genetic makeup. Like I said, I'm even more unique than my mother. For example, I haven't actually stopped aging. I just age at an incredibly slow rate, although I have no idea how long my life will really be. I suspect I inherited whatever lifespan Mina possessed at the time of my conception. One day, perhaps many long centuries from now, I will be an old woman."

"And you're okay with that?"

"Yes. I'm lucky not to share the totality of my mother's afflictions. It has taken all of her willpower not to be led astray by her inner demons. I'm not sure that I would have such strength, especially with that amulet still out there."

"Speaking of the amulet, I have a question," Decker said.

He had remembered something from their encounter with Abraham Turner that didn't make sense. "Back at the start of all this, before Mina inherited Abraham Turner's powers, a woman named Stephanie Gleason brought the amulet to us when we were in London. She claimed that she was its guardian, that it had been passed down through the generations of her family. When Turner escaped his century-long entombment, she followed her great-great-grandfather's instructions and sought us out so that the amulet could be better protected."

"And that man was Thomas Finch," Daisy said.

"Yes. Which is what puzzles me. Since you're his only child,

31

either Stephanie Gleason is your direct descendent and Thomas Finch entrusted the amulet to you, which I find unlikely given the circumstances, or she was lying about her ancestry."

Daisy hesitated a moment before replying. "She wasn't lying, but she isn't my direct descendent, either. I made the decision not to have children after I discovered my true nature. I've also avoided long-term relationships. Watching someone that I love age and die while I stay the same doesn't hold much appeal to me, especially after seeing my mother go through that exact experience with my father. She never admitted it, but I could see how much it affected her, even though she had pushed him away decades before."

"If Stephanie Gleason is not your direct descendent, then who is she?" Decker asked.

"The descendent of my half-brother. My father had a child with another woman when he was very young, before he met my mother. It was that son who was eventually entrusted with the amulet and passed it down through his bloodline. He took the amulet and vanished with it at my father's request to ensure that Mina could not find it if her urges ever became too much. After that, no one in my family ever spoke of my half-brother and I never met him, nor any of his descendants. They took their task seriously and stayed in the shadows, at least until Stephanie Gleason brought the watch with the amulet inside to you in London after Abraham Turner escaped."

"I see." Decker wondered if Daisy was going to elaborate further on the events of her unusual life, and how it had affected her, but she settled back into her seat again and closed her eyes. Apparently, she was done with the conversation.

Decker shifted in his own seat and turned his gaze once more to the window, and the thin air beyond. It wouldn't be long before they arrived at their destination, the place where his own strange journey had begun. And he couldn't help but wonder, why was the wolf back now, and what did it want?

SEVEN

FORMER DEPUTY CHAD HARDWICK was sitting in the Wolf Haven Sheriff's Office with his chair reclined, feet up on the desk, and a cup of coffee in his hand when the door opened, and his former boss walked in. He jumped up quickly, swinging his legs down and almost spilling his coffee.

Decker's old dispatcher, Carol Lawson, looked up from her computer when Decker stepped into the building. A wide grin spread across her face. "John. It's so good to see you again."

"You too, Carol," Decker said, approaching the counter with Daisy at his side. After taking off from Portland, CUSP's jet had flown them southwest toward the Gulf of Mexico. A little over two hours later—much faster than a commercial airliner—they were back on the ground and cruising along the runway at Louis Armstrong International Airport. From there, they had collected a rental car and drove an hour northwest across Lake Pontchartrain to Wolf Haven. Now, he stood in his old office, overcome by a sudden sensation of familiarity that felt just a little off. It was like no time had passed since he was last there, and yet in other ways, it felt like such a long time ago.

Chad was at the counter now, his gaze alighting on Daisy even as his mouth curled into a lopsided half smile. "Who's this attractive young lady? Did you come to your senses and trade up from Nancy, or is this a daughter we don't know about?"

Decker resisted the urge to grab his old deputy by the lapel and shake some manners into him. "Neither."

"I'm John's associate," Daisy said in a light voice. "And you must be Chad Hardwick."

"That I am." Chad paused. "British?"

"Once. A very long time ago." Daisy glanced at Decker, then back to the sheriff. "I've heard so much about you."

"All good, I hope." Chad ran a hand through his hair and grinned.

"No. Not really." Daisy looked around the office and wrinkled her nose. She eyed the space on the other side of the counter. "We've come a long way at your request, Sheriff Hardwick. Are you going to keep us standing here forever, or shall we get down to business?"

"Right. Of course." Chad lifted the hatch and waited for Decker and Daisy to step past the front counter and into the back of the office. He glanced toward a door on the other side of the room marked *Interview 1*. "We can go in there to talk."

"Lead the way," Decker said, starting toward the door.

But before he had taken more than two steps, Carol slid from her seat and intercepted him, pulling Decker into a tight hug. She released him and looked up into Decker's face. "Things haven't been the same around here without you."

"That much, I believe," Decker replied, casting a quick glance toward Chad before turning his attention back to Carol. "We'll catch up later, okay?"

"Sure. I look forward to it." Carol lingered a moment, then turned and went back to her chair.

Chad picked up a folder from his desk and crossed to the interview room, then stepped inside.

Decker followed behind and waited for Daisy to join them before closing the door. There was a desk in the middle with two chairs on one side and one on the other. A classic interrogation room setup. He quickly took a seat on the side with two chairs, the one where the interviewers would normally sit.

Daisy sat down next to him, leaving Chad to take a seat on the other side of the table, where the suspect would normally reside.

The ex-deputy lingered a moment before sitting down, even as a scowl flashed across his face, but then he settled on the chair and cleared his throat. He looked at Decker. "I want you to know, I would never have bothered you with this if…"

If you thought you could deal with it on your own, Decker mused silently. He suspected that the last thing Chad wanted to do was turn to his old boss for help. It wasn't like they were exactly on speaking terms. The man had stabbed him in the back, refusing to verify Decker's version of events at the hearing that took place after Annie Doucet's bloodlust filled rampage in the high school that resulted in the death of the town's mayor, Beau Thornton. And in some ways, he didn't blame Chad. It was a crazy story. Who would ever believe that an old woman had transformed herself through witchcraft into a Cajun werewolf and went on a killing spree as revenge for the town taking her land to build a spur road from the interstate? But at the same time, Decker knew that there was more to Chad's betrayal than just fear of ridicule. His old deputy had been happy to watch Decker lose his job and had stepped into his boss's shoes before they even had time to cool. Now he sat on the other side of the desk, doing his best not to look uncomfortable.

Decker leaned forward. "Just to be clear, my return has nothing to do with you. I'm here because there are still people in this town that I care about, like Carol. If it weren't for that…"

Chad squirmed in his chair. "Come on John, don't you think it's about time we put what happened in that high school behind us? After all, it turned out fine in the end. You landed on your feet. I heard you went federal—got a job with some black-ops government agency."

"That's not quite what happened," Decker said, not bothering to elaborate.

Now it was Daisy's turn to talk. "This is all very interesting, but irrelevant. How about you fill us in on what's been happening around here?"

"Right." Chad nodded. He placed the folder on the desk and pushed it across to Decker. "The first attack was several nights ago. Bunch of teenagers who went out to Annie Doucet's old place to fool around. It's become something of a macabre attraction, especially among the local high schoolers. They dare each other to go there and break into the house, even though it's falling down and pretty much a construction zone now. We've even had some problems with people doing rituals out there."

"What kind of rituals?" Daisy asked.

"The kind where you draw pentagrams on the floor and burn black candles." Chad shook his head. "I don't get it. After everything that happened, why won't people just let it go?"

"Because that's not human nature," Decker said, pulling the folder toward him. "You said *the first attack*. Does that mean there's been more than one?"

"Ernie Wills, manager of the new Pinch-A-Cent grocery store. Something killed him after he closed up last night. One of the cashiers found his body this morning when she showed up for her shift." Chad shuddered. "Poor guy was torn to pieces."

"How do you know these attacks were the work of a loup-garou?" Daisy asked.

Chad sat back in his chair. "Easy. We have an eyewitness to the first attack. A survivor. The creature killed her three friends but left her alive. I don't know why."

"Eyewitness testimony is notoriously unreliable," Daisy said. "A terrified young woman who just watched her friends die and knows the history of that cabin... maybe she saw what she expected to see."

"I don't doubt what she saw," Chad replied. "She was very sure of herself. But it's not just that. The second killing in the grocery store was caught on film. They have security cameras all around the store. Damned thing killed the manager right in front of one. It captured everything in gory detail."

"Interesting." Decker sat forward. "Can we see that footage?"

"Sure. I have a copy on my laptop." Chad drew in a long breath. "But I warn you… it's pretty graphic."

EIGHT

THEY HUDDLED around Chad's laptop, and he played the security footage. Because the store was new, the cameras were full-color and high-resolution. They showed everything in gory detail. At first, all they saw was the store manager wandering the aisles, apparently looking for something.

Chad paused the video. "We found several broken bottles of marinara sauce in one of the aisles. Looks like the creature knocked it off to lure its victim deeper into the store."

"He was the only one in the building?" Decker asked.

"Yes. Apart from the creature, of course. It was after closing and the rest of the staff had already left for the night. It wasn't unusual for the manager to do a tour of the store and check everything was in order and locked up before going home."

"How come he wasn't found until this morning?" Daisy asked. "Why didn't anybody miss him earlier?"

"There was no one *to* miss him," Chad replied. "He'd been with the grocery chain for a long time but had only recently moved to this area. He lived on his own and had no significant other. He was something of a loner, by all accounts. Kept to himself outside of work."

"And ended up dying the same way," Daisy said. "All alone in a strange town with no one to even care that he's gone."

"I care," Chad said. "Wolf Haven is a quiet place. A peaceful place. Things like this don't happen here."

"Except that they do," Daisy retorted, glancing toward Decker. "I've read the file on what happened the last time you had a loup-garou running around."

Chad was silent for a moment, his lips pressed tightly together, then he said, "How about we continue?"

He reached down and pressed play.

The video started again.

Both Decker and Daisy leaned forward, their eyes fixed on the screen.

The store manager disappeared down an aisle. Thirty seconds later, he reappeared with a scowl on his face. For a moment, it looked like he was going to head toward the front of the store. Then he turned as if his attention had been drawn by something offscreen. The annoyance on his face turned to horror even as a large shape padded into view.

Decker tensed. It was hard to make out too many details from the camera's high vantage point, but it showed enough to dispel any doubt in his mind about the perpetrator of the recent killings. Because the creature slinking toward the store manager was all too familiar to Decker. The last time he had seen it was during a raging hurricane at the town's high school. Back then, it had tried to kill Nancy's daughter Taylor, and it had almost succeeded. But this couldn't be the same creature, because Annie Doucet, who had transformed herself into the beast to exact revenge on those she thought had wronged her, was dead. Decker had killed the beast and stood over her lifeless body after she reverted to her true form.

Next to him, Decker heard Daisy draw a sharp intake of breath. He realized that he had zoned out for a moment.

The video was still playing, except that now it showed a gruesome scene. The store manager was down with the beast straddling him. There was no sound on the clip, but Decker could see that his mouth was open, no doubt in a tortured scream, which was quickly cut off with one swipe of the creature's paw that opened a wide gash in his neck.

Blood spurted across the floor.

Decker had seen enough. He looked away.

Chad turned the video off. "Like I said, not for the faint of heart."

Decker didn't reply. Something was nagging at him. When he realized what it was, he nodded toward the laptop. "Can you play that clip again from when the creature walks into view?"

Chad nodded and replayed the video.

A moment after the creature appeared, Decker tapped his hand on the table. "Pause it right there."

"What are you looking for?" Chad asked, staring at the frozen image.

"The creature. Look at what it does when it steps into view."

Daisy leaned forward, her eyes narrowing. "It looks up at the camera."

"Precisely."

"Like it knows the camera is there," Chad said with a tinge of excitement in his voice. "That it's being recorded."

"It wants us to watch that man die," Decker said. "And it wants us to know what killed him."

"Okay." Chad looked perplexed. "I think you're reading a lot into one casual glance."

"Is he, though?" Carol said from her perch at the front desk. She stood and approached the group gathered around the laptop. "Think about it. We couldn't figure out why the creature only killed three of the four teenagers out at Annie Doucet's old shack. It had plenty of opportunity to kill that girl, and yet it walked off and left her there huddling terrified in the car."

"It wanted a witness," Daisy said.

"Exactly." Carol looked down at the image on the screen. "Just like it wanted a witness to the attack in the grocery store."

"Except that this time, the victim was alone," Chad said.

"Which was fine because it knew the camera was there. The creature lured that man to a specific spot where it was sure the attack would be recorded."

Chad glanced up at Carol. "The question is, why?"

An image of the beast in the vision shown to him by the ghost back in Boston flashed through Decker's mind. Of those terrible jaws closing around his neck. Killing him. "There's only one reason I can think of. To bring me back here."

Chad was silent for a moment as he pondered this. "Even if you're right, that still doesn't answer the question of why. You've been gone from Wolf Haven for so long. What motivation could anyone possibly have to murder four innocent people just to get you back here?"

"That's what we need to find out," Decker said.

"There's something else we need to find out, too," Daisy said. "And if we do, it might go a long way to answering the first question."

"Which is?" Chad asked.

"How." Daisy looked around the group. "Annie Doucet was a witch. She used her spell book to transform into the beast. How many people around here would have access to that kind of knowledge?"

"And the desire to use it," Carol added.

"Not very many." Chad glanced across the room toward the evidence locker. "And we have Annie's spell book locked up tight."

"You sure of that?" Decker asked. He remembered going out to Annie's cabin with Chad the day after the hurricane blew through and searching it. The spell book had been there, open to the page upon which was written the incantation that had turned Annie into the wolf. And there was more. The ingredients for a potion and a copper bowl containing the dregs of that same elixir that Annie had swallowed to bring about the change. They had gathered everything up and entered it as evidence, not that it had done much good. Now, those same items should still be there, sitting on a shelf out of harm's way in the evidence locker.

"Of course I'm sure," Chad said. "After all the trouble that it caused, you think I'd let that spell book out of my sight?"

"How about we find out?" Carol said, starting toward the door. She pulled a set of keys from her pocket and unlocked it, then stepped into the darkness beyond. A moment later, a light clicked on to reveal metal shelving that held cardboard boxes containing the evidence of every crime that had ever occurred in Wolf Haven.

Decker stepped into the room with Chad and Daisy at his heel, just as Carol located the box marked *Annie Doucet* and pulled it from the shelf. She placed the box on a metal table sitting in the middle of the room and removed the lid. Then she turned to look at them. "It's not here."

"What do you mean, it's not there," Chad said, pushing past her.

"Exactly what I said." Carol met Decker's gaze. "The spell book is gone."

NINE

CHAD STARED down into the box with a look of dismay on his face. "There's no way the book can be gone. I put it here myself after we collected the evidence at Annie's cabin." He looked at Decker. "You know that. You were there."

"I was," said Decker. "But who knows what has happened here since I left Wolf Haven."

"Don't blame this on me." Chad shook his head. "That book should still be there."

"Is it possible that there's a second evidence box?" Daisy asked.

"No." Chad pointed to the front of the box and the label. Beneath the case number and Annie Doucet's name was 1/1 written in black marker. "See?"

"Who has access to this evidence locker?" Daisy looked at Carol, perhaps hoping for a less hostile reception.

Carol shrugged. "Just me and the sheriff."

"You don't have a deputy?"

"Not since John left. Plus, the evidence locker is always kept locked. It's protocol."

"And it wasn't either of us who took the book," Chad said quickly. "Before you point fingers."

"No one's pointing any fingers," Decker said. "But someone came in here and took that spell book and I'm guessing it's the same person who's been rampaging around town and killing people, although to what end I can't fathom."

"When's the last time you were in here?" Daisy asked Carol.

"Couple of weeks ago. It's not like we get much crime around here, present circumstances accepted. Some of these boxes go back to the 1960s."

"And you didn't notice it missing then?"

"No." Carol shook her head. "Why would I? We've had no reason to even look in that box for well over a year. It wasn't like there was a trial, or anything. Annie Doucet was dead, and it was pretty obvious that she was the one killing people. The investigation wrapped up quickly. After that, there was just the inquest where John lost his job..." Carol threw Decker sheepish glance. "Sorry."

"It's fine. All in the past." Decker turned his attention back to the box. "If what you're saying is true, the book could have been taken anytime of the last twelve months."

"I suppose."

"Although in all likelihood it must've been taken at night when the office is closed," Decker said.

"Because there's someone here all day," Carol said. "Either Chad or me."

"You close the sheriff's office?" Daisy looked surprised.

"Sure. We don't have enough staff to man it twenty-four hours a day."

"What happens if someone has an emergency after hours?"

Chad cleared his throat. "The call gets routed through to the State Police and they respond. If it's something serious, they notify me."

"Like those teenagers who got themselves killed out at Annie Doucet's place?"

"Right. Although it was the next morning before we got the call. The survivor sat in the car most of the night. She was afraid to move and didn't have the keys. In the end, she walked back to town at dawn and called 911."

"She couldn't have made that call earlier?"

"No. There's no cell service out in the swamp," Chad said. "At least not yet. I'm sure there will be as soon as the road out to the interstate is finished. Anyway, the call went to the State Police, and they alerted me. Honestly, it was a good thing they were there. It's not like I could have dealt with a crime scene like that on my own."

Decker nodded and looked at Carol. "You still keep the keys to the evidence locker in your drawer when you go home?"

"Sure. Just like I always did."

"That's not very secure," Daisy said.

"It's as secure as it needs to be, young lady," Carol said. "We're a small town. With the exception of werewolves running around and killing people once in a while, nothing much happens. The last murder we had in Wolf Haven, at least committed by a human, was back in the late 90s and any evidence related to a crime of such significance would end up in the State Police evidence locker since they would be the ones taking charge of the investigation."

"But the Annie Doucet evidence was stored in here."

"Yes. It was treated more like a wild animal attack than a string of murders. John and Chad investigated it, at least until…" Carol let the words trail off.

"Until I got fired," said Decker. "By that time, the investigation was pretty much over, and no one had much interest in listening to the truth."

"Which is what I told you would happen if you started spouting off about werewolves and witchcraft," Chad said.

Decker glared at Chad. "Maybe if you had backed me up, even a little—"

"Okay, boys." Carol stepped between the two men. "This isn't the time or the place."

Decker dropped his gaze. "I assume the camera that monitors the front desk still works."

"It does," said Carol. Her eyes widened. "If someone came in after hours and took those keys, it will have recorded them."

Chad nodded. "And that camera has a direct line of sight to the evidence locker door as well. We'll have our perpetrator caught red-handed."

"There's only one problem."

"What?"

"We only keep the footage for a month before it gets wiped. Video files take up a lot of space and cloud storage isn't cheap. If the keys went missing before that, we're back to square one."

"I'm willing to bet the spell book was stolen right before the killings began," Decker said. "After all, why take it only to do nothing with it?"

"Especially as the risk of discovery gets greater the longer the book is missing," Chad said.

Carol replaced the lid and put the box back on the shelf. "I'll start going through the footage this evening. I can access the cloud files from my laptop at home."

"Good." Decker stepped toward the door. "Keep me informed of your progress, and if you find anything, let me know right away."

"Of course." Carol waited for everyone to leave the evidence room, then closed the door and locked it. But instead of returning the keys to her desk drawer, she pushed them into her pocket. When she saw Decker looking at her, she grimaced. "Yeah, I know. Better late than never, right?"

TEN

WITH NOTHING FURTHER TO DISCOVER, and finding Chad's company grating, Decker decided it was time to leave.

Out on the sidewalk, he turned to Daisy. "I still have a place in town and there's a spare bedroom going for free if you want it."

"Actually, I booked into a guesthouse for the next week. The Oaklawn. Kind of sounds a bit more like a cemetery, but it was the only accommodation I could find. The room looks nice enough, if a little outdated."

"I know it well," said Decker, trying not to sound too downbeat. "Claude and Olivia Cormier have been running the place for at least thirty years. Took it over from his parents. Unless they've put some money into it since I left town, outdated is an understatement. The rooms don't even have en suite bathrooms."

"I'll be fine," Daisy said. "I've stayed in worse."

Decker had no doubt of that. "Well, if The Oaklawn doesn't cut it, the offer of a room is still there."

"I'll keep that in mind." Daisy glanced back toward the sheriff's office. "I swear, that creature wanted to be seen. It's almost like it was sending a message. What do you make of it?"

"I don't know," Decker replied. If there was a message in the killings, he couldn't decipher it. Annie Doucet was long dead, so it wasn't her still looking for revenge. Instead, someone had taken the spell book from the evidence locker and was using it to transform into the wolf. To start the terror all over again. But there were only a few people who knew it was there, and even though he disliked Chad, Decker couldn't see his former deputy doing such a thing. Same went for Carol. So who was it? Maybe the answer, at least to the human identity of their loup-garou, was waiting in the security footage from the camera that monitored the front desk. But Decker wasn't going to hold his breath. The person who stole the spell book knew where to find it, which meant they might also have known about the camera. He wasn't optimistic. "But I know one thing. The loup-garou isn't done if history is anything to go by."

"I agree," Daisy said. "It will attack again if we don't stop it first."

"Then let's hope Carol finds something in that footage, because we don't have much else to go on." Decker took a step toward the car that they had rented at the airport. "Let's get you checked in at the guesthouse. We can meet up later for dinner. Maybe around seven?"

"Sounds good." Daisy nodded. "Is there anywhere decent to eat in this town?"

"Only one place that I know of," Decker replied, and he wasn't looking forward to going there.

ELEVEN

FIFTEEN MINUTES after dropping Daisy off at The Oaklawn and seeing her inside with her luggage, Decker pulled up in front of a neat two-story Acadian residence with a trimmed yard on a leafy road off Main Street. This was his family home—the same one that he had grown up in and where his father had descended into madness after his mother's death. After he was fired as the local sheriff and he and Nancy decided to put some distance between themselves and Wolf Haven, he had kept the place even as Nancy sold her own home and the diner.

He wasn't sure exactly why he kept it. Perhaps it was because selling this last vestige of their connection to Wolf Haven meant that Chad and his cronies had won in running them out of town. Or maybe he just didn't want to deal with the accumulated ephemera of his parents' lives. Those possessions of his mother's that his father refused to divest himself of under the guise of sentimentality, and everything that his father had left behind, like the boxes of notepads and other paperwork chronicling his father's obsession with finding the creature that robbed him of his wife.

Decker had moved all of this into the garage when he moved back from New York—cardboard boxes full of the past that were stacked almost to the ceiling. It was all still there now, and Decker was about as inclined to take care of it now as he had been before.

Decker parked in front of the garage and made his way to the front door, pleased to see that the yard service he had hired to tend to the grounds in his absence was doing a good job. He pulled a set of keys from his pocket and let himself inside, noticing the musty air that assaulted his nostrils, heavy and thick. It wouldn't hurt to open some windows to air the place out and maybe even pick up a couple of air fresheners when he went to the grocery store to stock up on supplies.

But that could wait.

Decker dropped his travel bag on the floor and the keys on a small side table next to the door, then stood for a moment, taking in the silence. It felt strange to be back. He gazed at the stairs, could almost see his mother coming down them, dirty laundry in hand. Could almost hear his father calling out from the living room for her to bring him a glass of iced tea.

When he looked toward the study, which was really just a small room off the hallway behind the stairs, another less domestic memory sprang to mind. Sheriff Robbie Decker locking himself in that room and filling notebook after notebook with his crazy theories, desperate to find an answer to his wife's death.

Ironically, Robbie Decker was closer to the truth than he would ever know. Annie Doucet, transformed into the loup-garou, had murdered Decker's mother as the last act in a sequence of events that had begun years before when they were teenagers.

All of this had been revealed to Decker by the ghosts in the house on Boston Common. He hadn't even had time to absorb it before his phone rang and Chad told him the loup-garou was back. Now, standing in his childhood home, Decker couldn't help a pang of sorrow. How different would his life have been if Robbie Decker had never become entangled with Annie Doucet? But there was no point in dwelling on things that couldn't be changed. He took a deep breath and closed the front door, then turned on the hallway light to chase the shadows away.

Going to the kitchen, Decker plugged in the fridge and ran the taps to clear the pipes of standing water. He was about to retreat back into the hallway and grab his bag to take it upstairs when his phone rang.

It was Chad.

Decker's gut tightened. There was no way Carol could have watched all the security footage yet. He glanced at his watch. It was five o'clock and outside it was already dark. Had there been another attack?

But he needn't have worried.

"Hey, I know you're probably settling in," Chad said when Decker answered, "but I was wondering if you wanted to grab a beer. You know, for old time's sake."

"There are no old times," Decker replied, trying his best not to sound peeved. "At least, none worth reminiscing over with you."

"Come on, don't be like that. We have to work together, at least in the short term." There was a momentary pause on the other end of the line before Chad spoke again. "I'm extending an olive branch here, John. The least you can do is meet me halfway."

"Fine." If he had to work with Chad, they might as well settle their grievances, or at least declare a temporary truce. "Where and when?"

"County Line Saloon in thirty minutes?"

"I'll be there," Decker replied. Then he added, "But you're buying."

TWELVE

WHEN DECKER ENTERED THE BAR, Chad was already there, sitting at the counter with a mug of frothy beer in front of him. He had changed out of his uniform, and now wore a pair of blue jeans and a light gray polo shirt. There were only a few other customers in the place. Two young men playing pool, and an older couple sitting at a table near the back, hunched over in conversation. A country song Decker didn't recognize was playing.

Ed Johnson, owner of the County Line, was leaning against the back of the bar with his arms folded. At Decker's approach, he pulled himself straight, a wide smile breaking across his face. "Well, look who it is. The best sheriff this old town ever knew."

Chad pulled a face. "Hell Ed, I'm sitting right here."

"Don't remind me." Ed turned his attention to Decker. "What'll it be, John?"

"You have an IPA on draft?"

Ed nodded. "Sure do. Local brew aptly named Swamp Monster."

"I'll give it a go." Decker settled on a stool next to Chad and watched Ed grab a glass from under the bar and turn toward the beer pumps.

"You can put that beer on my tab," Chad said, a sour note in his voice. He turned to Decker. "I sure do appreciate you coming down here to clear the air. I sensed some animosity back at the sheriff's office. Figure it'll be better all round if we're not at each other's throats over the next few days since we need to work together."

"Makes sense," Decker said. The truth was that he'd thought about it on the way to the bar and concluded that he didn't care much about Chad either way. After everything that had happened—almost getting stuck in the past and being separated from Nancy forever, not to mention almost losing his life on the Titanic—holding a grudge against Chad seemed like more trouble than it was worth. "And you don't need to worry. Life's too short. How about we start fresh?"

"I'd like that." Chad's face brightened noticeably. "And I really am sorry about what happened."

"Yeah, so you keep saying." Decker watched as Ed finished pouring his beer and placed it on the bar top in front of him. He lifted it and took a sip, then nodded his appreciation. "This isn't half bad."

"Thought you'd like it," Ed said. He glanced between the two men. "I'll give the pair of you some privacy. Looks like you have a lot of catching up to do."

"Appreciate that, Ed," Chad said, then turned to Decker once the bar owner had retreated to the other end of the counter and turned his attention to a Saints game playing on a wall-mounted TV. "I hear that you and Nancy Cassidy are still together."

"Actually, we're married." Decker held up his left hand to show Chad his ring. "Tied the knot right before I came here."

"No way. Congratulations." Chad gripped Decker's hand and pumped it vigorously. "Me too. Well, not married, but engaged."

"Really?" Decker couldn't imagine any woman putting up with Chad long enough to get engaged to him. "Anyone I know?"

"Probably not. She moved to town after you left. Her name is Keira."

Decker didn't know what to say. "What happened to that woman you were dating back in the day. The part-time server at the diner. What was her name?"

"Holly. Didn't work out," Chad said without elaborating. "But it was all for the best. I love Kiera. We're perfect together. And she has a 16-year-old son, Ben, so I get an instant family in the bargain."

"Wow."

"Yeah. Nice kid. Respectful. He's been showing some interest in the job, so maybe he'll become a cop one day. Even hangs out with me at the sheriff's office sometimes after school." Chad took a swig of his drink. "But enough about me. I want to hear about this job of yours."

"There's not much to tell." Decker had no intention of going into the details of his work at CUSP with Chad. "I work for an agency that handles situations outside the normal expertise of standard law enforcement."

"Like?" Chad raised an eyebrow.

"Like I'm not at liberty to say."

"Come on, John, you can't tease me with vague references to situations outside the expertise of regular law enforcement and not tell me something. I ask you, what does that even mean? Like you're some sort of spy? Or a fancy government analyst?"

"I never said that I work for the government. And regardless, I can't discuss it."

Chat frowned. "Can't or won't?"

Decker said nothing. He simply picked up his beer and took a drink.

Chad's shoulders slumped. "At least tell me about that young woman you showed up here with. Does she work for this maybe-maybe not government organization, too?"

"She does, yes."

"And she decided to accompany you here to deal with a

loup-garou. A trip that I'm pretty sure isn't within your official roster of duties."

"She did. And I have the full backing of my organization regarding any action that I take here... Just so that we're clear."

"Huh. That really piques my interest. The last time you tried to convince someone that werewolves were real, it didn't go so well. I guess that either the people who run this organization of yours are particularly gullible, or the situations they deal with are more unusual than even your cryptic comments would lead me to believe."

"Let's just say that they like to keep an open mind." Decker finished his beer and motioned for Ed, who was still lingering at the other end of the bar, to pour them a pair of refills. "And I think you'll find Daisy to be an invaluable asset. She has a lot of experience. This isn't the first time she's dealt with something like this."

"Experience? She looks like she's twelve." Chad picked up his beer and downed the last of it, then pushed the mug across the counter in anticipation of another. "I assumed she was your trainee or something."

"Nothing of the sort," replied Decker with a smile. "Now, since we've cleared the air, how about we enjoy our beers and talk about something other than work?"

THIRTEEN

AFTER DECKER LEFT THE BAR, he called Daisy and told her to meet him in the lobby, then walked over to the guesthouse where she was staying. It was a little after seven, and he figured they could grab a bite to eat.

As he walked, he thought about his conversation with Chad. The former deputy—now sheriff—was about as insufferable as ever and Decker wondered if the panicked call that he had received back in Boston was less about Decker's expertise with such matters as it was about securing a scapegoat should things go south like they had the first time around. After all, Chad would not want to lose his job the same way Decker had. This was one of the reasons that Decker was loath to discuss his current employment. Not that it mattered. Even if he had wanted to fill Chad in, he wouldn't have been allowed. CUSP had a strict policy on such matters, and for good reason.

Reaching the guesthouse, Decker stepped into the lobby and approached the registration desk where Olivia Cormier sat with a book in her hand and reading glasses perched on her nose. A tangle of white hair, along with her age-lined face, made the Oaklawn's proprietor look older than Decker knew she was by a good decade. The wrinkles that marred her skin were probably the result of Olivia's smoking habit, which had been at least a couple of packs a day when Decker was still living in town and might be more now judging by the ashtray full of cigarette butts next to the old desktop computer that served as a reservation system.

"John, what a pleasant surprise," Olivia said at his approach. "I didn't know you were back in town."

"Just a flying visit," Decker said, leaning on the counter and glancing around. "An associate of mine checked in this afternoon."

"That must be Daisy. She's the only person who checked in today. In fact, there are no other rooms booked until tomorrow night. It's been a quiet week."

"Business slow?" Decker asked.

"Isn't it always?" Olivia forced a smile. "Things were different back in the day when Wolf Haven still had some industry. When Claude's parents ran this place, they used to get a lot of folk staying here who had business with the old lumber mill out on Stark Road or the sugarcane growers. Of course, all of that is gone now. Still, maybe when that road from the interstate is finished, we'll get some tourists coming through. Not that there's much to see in this backwater town, especially with New Orleans right down the road."

"You might be surprised," Decker said. Back when the idea for the spur road was first floated by the local development board, Nancy had believed that it would reinvigorate the local economy, that travelers looking for the real small-town Louisiana would find their way to Wolf Haven. Decker hadn't been sure, but he hoped she was right, especially after the amount of blood that was spilled over that road.

"We'll see." Olivia looked around as a slender figure appeared at the bottom of the staircase.

It was Daisy. She crossed the lobby toward them.

As before, Decker was taken aback by her stunning similarity to Mina. He wondered how Thomas Finch's wife had taken it when her stepdaughter stopped aging and her true mother stepped into the picture. After raising the child as her own, it must have been hard to see Daisy discover her true identity. He also wondered how difficult that transition must have been. It wasn't every day that you found out your entire past was a lie and that the inherited supernatural powers of a vampiric creature coursed through your veins. Considering all that she had been through, Daisy had ended up surprisingly normal. Although, as he reminded himself, more than a century had passed since then, giving her ample time to make peace with her lot.

"You look positively lost in thought," Daisy said as she drew close to Decker.

He shook the musings off. "Not at all. Just waiting for you. Hungry?"

"Ravenous."

"Me, too." Decker bade Olivia farewell, and they left the guesthouse. Outside, he turned to Daisy. "There aren't many places around here to eat. A Chinese restaurant that mostly does takeout. Same with Sammie's Pizza on 4th Street. We could pick something up and go back to my place."

"Greasy takeout food?" Daisy shook her head. "Is there anything else?"

"There is one other option," Decker said. An establishment he knew all too well. "Cassidy's Diner. It's the only sit-down restaurant in town. And I warn you, it might not be any less greasy than Chinese food."

"Cassidy's?" The look on Daisy's face told Decker that she recognized the name. "Maybe takeout food won't be so bad after all."

"It's no big deal." Decker hoped his response sounded genuine. "I'm not in the mood for mediocre fried rice or cardboard pizza. Cassidy's is fine."

"You sure about that?"

"I'm sure." Decker grinned. "Unless you want me to cook my famous seafood gumbo."

"Why is it famous?" Daisy asked. "Is it really *that* good?"

"No. It's really *that* bad. Nancy told me that if I ever make it again, she's leaving me."

"I think I'll pass."

"A wise choice," Decker said with a chuckle. "I don't have anything in the house to make it with anyway."

"Then Cassidy's it is." Daisy took off walking toward Main Street.

As they drew close to the restaurant, Decker couldn't help but wonder what Nancy would say about their destination, especially since the restaurant that had been in her family for three generations looked nothing like how he remembered it, at least from the outside. The woodwork, which had been painted a light sage green for as long as he could remember, was now a gaudy firetruck red. The neon signs that had hung in the windows advertising home-cooked comfort foods like po'boys, shrimp and grits, red beans and rice, and jambalaya, along with freshly brewed coffee, were gone, leaving the windowpanes stark and strangely empty. Also gone was the family name above the door. Instead of Cassidy's, the establishment now bore the moniker Main Street Grill. It made Decker sad to see the eating establishment that had been a fixture in Wolf Haven for decades changed forever. He could only imagine what Nancy's reaction would have been.

Daisy must have noticed the look on his face. "Still want to eat here? We can always drive to the gas station outside of town and pick up a couple of sandwiches."

"I'll pass on that, if it's all the same with you." Decker pulled the restaurant door open and let Daisy enter first, then followed her inside.

The interior of the diner was as different as its façade. The retro tabletop jukeboxes that had adorned the booths were gone. Even the red leatherette benches and chrome rimmed tables had been replaced with regular restaurant style tables and chairs. The black and white checkerboard pattern tile floor had been switched to dark wood planks. The counter was still there, although the stools had been removed. It looked nothing like he remembered, and he almost turned around and walked back out. But Daisy was already skirting a sign that asked patrons to seat themselves and had selected a table near the window where she settled.

Decker hesitated a moment, overcome by a sudden sense of lost history, then shook the feeling off and joined her. He had barely sat down, when a familiar voice boomed out across the dining room.

"John Decker. As I live and breathe."

Decker turned to see Jerome, the cook who had been a fixture at the diner for as long as he could remember, coming toward them.

"I heard you were in town," the cook said with a grin, arriving at the table. "This is the one place I never thought you'd come."

"Yeah, well, there aren't exactly a lot of dining options in Wolf Haven," Decker replied, looking around at the decor. "And boy, am I glad to see you. At least the food will still be good."

"Figured you'd not be too pleased with what the new owners have done to the place." Jerome grimaced. "But after what happened, they didn't want the association with…"

"With the Cassidy name," Decker said, unable to keep the anger from his voice. "None of it was her fault. If anyone should be blamed, it's me. Cassidy's has been an institution in this town for decades. It still should be, even if Nancy isn't running it."

"Yeah. I know, trust me. Tried to tell 'em, but they wouldn't listen." Jerome glanced toward the menus sitting on the table. "See anything you like?"

"Haven't looked yet."

"Well, good. If you don't like the new décor, you're going to hate the new menu." He reached into the pocket of his apron and pulled out an oblong card. "Try this, instead."

Decker took the card. It was another menu, smaller than the one in front of him on the table. At the top, it read CASSIDY'S CLASSICS. Beneath was a list of familiar dishes that included jambalaya, red beans and rice, gumbo, and a shrimp po'boy. He looked up at Jerome. "Is this for real?"

"Sure is, my man." Jerome's grin widened. "Just because we aren't called Cassidy's anymore, doesn't mean that everyone has forgotten what this place used to be like. New owners ain't here much. They live in Baton Rouge. Own three other restaurants, each about as uninspired as the next. They don't know a whole heap about this community, and to be honest, I don't think they care. New menu has about as much character as a plank of wood. All hamburgers and hotdogs. Ham and eggs. Pancakes with fake syrup. There ain't even any chicory in the coffee. Might as well be eating at Denny's. Which is why I keep this little unofficial menu on hand for those who still yearn for the good old days."

"I could hug you right now." Decker was overcome by a swell of gratitude. The old diner wasn't entirely gone, after all.

Jerome laughed. "Please don't. Just leave a good tip. That's all I ask. And maybe get rid of that dang loup-garou, just like you did before."

"Goes without saying." Decker looked back down at the menu. "Your po'boy still good as ever?"

"What do you think?" Jerome folded his arms.

"Sold." Decker handed the menu over to Daisy.

She didn't even look before saying, "Make that two."

FOURTEEN

THEY LEFT the Main Street Grill a little over an hour later. Decker walked Daisy back to her accommodation and arranged to meet up with her the next morning before heading to his car.

When he arrived back at his house, Decker was struck by how cold and empty it felt. Not like his home at all. Maybe it was finally time to dispense with the last vestiges of his past and sell the place, he mused as he made his way down the hallway toward a door near the stairs leading to the garage. Regardless of what happened over the next few days, Decker suspected this would be the last time he visited the town where he had grown up. It wasn't *his* town anymore and there was nothing left for him here.

Picking his way through the old furniture and other assorted junk stored in the garage, Decker made his way to an old desk at the back, upon which sat a file storage box that contained the collected results of his father's obsession with his mother's death.

He had gone through the contents of this box looking for answers once before, back when Annie Doucet was terrorizing Wolf Haven, and had found nothing to help his investigation. He didn't expect a different outcome this time around, but with no idea why the loup-garou was back, or who had stolen the spell book from the evidence locker, it was worth a try. Maybe there was some clue he had overlooked before. A nugget of information in his father's fevered ramblings that might help them stop the creature before someone else died. And it gave him something to do other than wander the silent house until it was time for bed.

Pulling the lid off the box, Decker took out notebooks full of his father's handwriting—at first neat, then becoming scratchy and frantic as he became trapped by the wild theories that had finally filled his head to the exclusion of everything else. Except his theories weren't wild fantasies, at least not all of them. Sheriff Robbie Decker had theorized that a loup-garou was responsible for the death of his wife, Lily. Maybe it was because he had seen the creature once before at the Kickoff Kegger party in the woods when he was a teenager. Having slaughtered most of his friends, the wolf version of Annie Doucet had let him live, perhaps because she still harbored feelings toward him. Robbie Decker had kept quiet about his experience, which was probably just as well, because no one would have believed him. But later, when his wife was so brutally attacked and killed in the woods, the memory of his encounter with the wolf had obviously resurfaced. The one thing he didn't know at the time—couldn't possibly know—was the creature's true identity. If he had, it would've done nothing to save his wife, but Annie Doucet's murderous rampage decades later might have been avoided.

Decker now found himself in a similar situation. The creature currently terrorizing Wolf Haven was not Annie Doucet. It was whoever had stolen the spell book. Stopping this creature would save lives not just in the present, but perhaps in the future, too. Once, many years before, when he was a detective in New York, Decker had taken a course with the FBI at Quantico. One of the things he learned was that once a person killed for pleasure, they did not stop. Serial killers, although rare, were consistent. He had to assume that the same is true of a supernatural killer. The basic psychology did not change, as Annie Doucet had proven when she turned time and again to the spell book and the wolf to solve her problems.

Sitting down in a rickety office chair next to the desk, Decker went through the notebooks. He set aside the oldest of them, those that were filled with more mundane theories, and focused on the later volumes, where mentions of the loup-garou became more frequent. But as he read, struggling at times with his father's increasingly messy handwriting, he was overcome with the same sense of futility as the last time he had gone through them. There was nothing here of any use. The writings contained in his father's notebooks were just desperation-tinged speculation, with no hard evidence to back up his theories.

Decker gathered the notebooks back together without bothering to go through the last of them, was about to return them to the box, when a photograph fell out and landed on the desk in front of him. It was a crime scene photo taken in the woods on the day his mother died. There were at least thirty other photographs similar to this one in an envelope inside the box. Decker had looked at them the last time he went through this stuff but hadn't lingered on the photos because of their content and the memories they invoked. This one, though, was not with the others. It had been clipped to a page near the back of one of the notebooks. Upon closer inspection, he could see the top of the paperclip poking out.

He put the notebooks down and stared at the photo. It was black and white, clearly taken at night with a flash because the police officers and paramedics gathering around the body that Decker knew was his mother were rendered in stark relief. But there was someone else there, too. A figure standing on her own between the trees, as if they didn't want to be noticed. A woman with porcelain features, clad in black so that she merged almost entirely with the background.

But Sheriff Robbie Decker had noticed her, at least after the fact. He had taken a pen to the photograph and circled her, writing three short words on the picture's white border.

Who is she?

Decker suspected that if he looked inside the notebook from which the photograph had come, he would discover that his father never found an answer to that question. But there was no need to look at the notebook, because despite the grainy nature of the image, and the size of the figure, Decker could narrow down the face staring back at him to one of two people.

It was either Daisy or Mina.

Decker stared in disbelief. What the hell was CUSP doing at the scene of his mother's murder? And not just CUSP, but either its founder or her daughter. Decker wanted answers. He reached for his phone, was about to dial Daisy's number, when it rang.

It was Carol.

Decker answered, pushing aside a glimmer of frustration.

"I'm not catching you at a bad time, am I?" Carol asked, picking up on the strain in his voice.

"No. I'm fine," Decker replied. "Is this about the camera footage?"

"Yes. But it's not good news. I figured the best place to start would be the two weeks before the first killing, so I pulled up each date. The camera is motion activated and records short clips, so it's not like I had to sift through twenty-four hours of footage. At first, everything was normal. No sign of anyone going near the evidence locker. But then, about six days before those teenagers were killed at Annie Doucet's old shack, there was something weird. The camera was activated at around 11 PM, when the office should have been empty. At first, I couldn't see what triggered it—everything looked normal—but when I went back and looked again, I saw a shadow move across the far wall. Then, ten seconds in, the recording cuts off abruptly. Normally, I wouldn't find that strange. The camera has caught shadows moving before. There are all sorts of reasons, like someone walking past outside or headlights from a passing car.

But here's the thing, the camera is supposed to record clips of thirty seconds in length. This one was interrupted mid recording."

"Meaning that the camera malfunctioned," Decker said, "or someone unplugged it."

"I doubt it malfunctioned," Carol said. "When I checked the files for the next day, it recorded me arriving at work, so it was working again by the next morning."

"How is that possible?" Decker asked. "If it didn't malfunction, then wouldn't the camera have captured the perpetrator coming into the building just like it recorded you?"

"Yes, if they used the front door. But there's a rear entrance out of the camera's field-of-view. Our thief could enter that way, then walk through the office and unplug the camera without being seen. Once they had the book, they could plug it back in and leave the same way."

"And no one would be any the wiser."

"Except they didn't count on casting a shadow that activated the camera," Carol said.

"Not that it does us much good," Decker replied. "We're still no closer to knowing who it was."

FIFTEEN

THE BLACK ESPLANADE stood parked at the curb in a patch of darkness between two streetlamps, and far enough away from John Decker's home that Wolf Haven's old sheriff wouldn't easily notice it.

Behind the wheel was a stocky man named Harlan Van Cleve, who had spent eight years serving in the Marines, until they drummed him out with a dishonorable discharge. His current employer was less picky.

Harlan looked down and flicked a piece of imaginary lint from a suit as dark as the vehicle within which he sat. A suit that did little to hide his bulging frame. His bald head and the scorpion tattoo above his right ear further added to his thuggish appearance.

Satisfied that the suit was free of unwanted material, he turned his attention back to the house and stared through the windshield, watching as a light went on in one of the downstairs rooms. A moment later, he saw a figure in the window, which he assumed to be Decker. He pressed back in his seat, shrinking into the darkness lest he be seen, but the figure didn't linger, instead pulling a set of curtains across with a quick swoosh and cutting off the view inside the room.

Harlan reached toward the center console of his vehicle and picked up a cell phone. He dialed the number and waited, then pressed the phone to his ear when the recipient of his call answered.

"Hey, it's me. Decker is in for the night."

He listened to the response, then nodded.

"You want me to go in?"

Another short pause as the person on the other end of the line talked.

"Are you sure? He's right there and I have the element of surprise." Harlan's free hand roamed absently to the weapon concealed under his jacket. A Sig P226, the favored handgun of U.S. Marines for over thirty years, and still his own personal favorite despite the ignominious way he had left that organization.

Another pause.

"All right. You're the boss. We'll do it your way."

Harlan listened for a few moments more, then ended the call. He sat for a while longer, studying the house and lost in thought, then he put the phone back down, started the SUV, and pulled away from the curb. He only switched his headlights on when he had turned at the end of the road and was out of sight.

SIXTEEN

AT 10 PM Daisy stood at the window in her room at the Oaklawn and stared out into the night. Her accommodation faced the rear of the building, which overlooked a garden area with a small lawn and a couple of picnic tables where guests could enjoy a continental breakfast courtesy of the establishment when the weather permitted. But it was the vast expanse of swamp beyond the garden that interested her. She could see the faint glow of headlights moving in the distance, following the thin strip of asphalt that made up the interstate. Somewhere out there, she knew, was the still unfinished road that would someday soon connect to Wolf Haven. Nearby, abandoned and being left to collapse into the ground, was the shack that had belonged to Annie Doucet until Decker shot her dead in that high school corridor.

Daisy stepped away from the window, her mind on the three teenagers who had lost their lives at that shack. And then there was the fourth girl, who huddled terrified and alone in her boyfriend's car for the rest of the night, wondering if the beast would return and do the same to her.

In Daisy's experience, supernatural creatures rarely left people alive to tell their tale, and especially not creatures as

69

violent as the loup-garou. An image of the beast killing the supermarket manager right under the silent gaze of the store security camera ran through her head. There was no doubt about it. The creature was announcing its presence. But why?

Her thoughts returned to Annie's shack. This was where everything had begun so long ago, and even if it wasn't the same creature, the loup-garou had a connection to that place. Maybe that was why the beast chose it as the location where it would kill its first victims. Which meant that the teenagers were not targeted for who they were, but because they were in the wrong place at the wrong time.

A sudden desire to see the shack for herself overcame Daisy. And what better time to do so than at night when she could experience it the same way as those teenagers. The problem was that she didn't have any transportation. The rental car was parked at Decker's home across town, and she doubted he would go along with her plan to drive out to the shack in the middle of the night. He would say that they should wait until morning. Daisy didn't want to wait that long.

Making up her mind, Daisy left her room and headed downstairs to the lobby. There was no one at the registration desk, which wasn't surprising given how late it was, but there was a front doorbell style pushbutton screwed to the desk with a small sign saying ring for service.

Daisy pushed it and waited.

After five minutes passed, she considered pushing it again, but as she reached for the button, a door opened behind the desk and the woman who had checked her in earlier appeared wearing a pastel blue dressing gown. Daisy recalled that her name was Olivia.

"Can I help you, honey"? she asked, stifling a yawn.

"Sorry. I didn't mean to wake you," Daisy replied. "I was wondering if there is a local taxi company anywhere hereabouts."

"Bit late to be taking a cab ride, isn't it?" Olivia observed her with watery eyes. "Is there something wrong?"

"Oh, no. Everything's fine. I just need to go somewhere."

"You're checking out?" A look of surprise passed across Olivia's face.

Daisy shook her head. "No, I'm not checking out. I'll be gone for an hour. Two at most. I promise not to disturb you again. I'll be quiet when I come back."

"Make sure that you are." Olivia rummaged through a holder full of business cards and selected one, which she held out to Daisy. "Here. This is about the only taxi company that will pick you up at this time of night. They're not local, so you might have to wait a while, and it won't be cheap, I'm sure. Especially at this time of night."

"Thank you." Daisy took the card. There was only one other thing she needed. "I don't suppose you have a flashlight I could borrow?"

Olivia furrowed her brow. "A flashlight? Look, young lady, I don't know what you're up to, but whatever it is, I'd advise you to wait until morning. I'm sure you've heard about the recent animal attacks. I'd hate for you to run into whatever killed those poor people."

"You don't need to worry about me. I can take care of myself," Daisy said.

Olivia observed her for a long moment, then she nodded. "You know what? I bet you can. There's something different about you. I get the impression that you've lived more years and battled through more adversity than your youthful countenance suggests."

Daisy was momentarily stunned. "I, um, I don't know what would make you think that."

"I have a gift. I can read people. See down into their souls, and yours is old. But it's more than that. It's like there's something else inside of you. A force. Actually, more like an entity. Practically ancient... and evil." A flicker of terror passed across Olivia's face. "I'm sorry. I hardly ever talk about my perceptions of people, especially when they are so outlandish. I'm probably just tired. Ignore my ramblings." She reached beneath the counter and produced a large silver flashlight. "Here. Take this. Leave it on the counter when you're done."

"Thank you." Daisy took the flashlight with a shaking hand.

"You're welcome," Olivia replied, then she turned and hurried back through the door without another word.

SEVENTEEN

THE TAXI SHOWED up twenty minutes after Daisy called the number on the card. She told the driver where she wanted to go, showing him the location of Annie Doucet's shack on her phone because she didn't have an address.

After putting the coordinates into his GPS, the taxi driver looked at her with a suspicious frown. "That's the middle of nowhere. Nothing but swamp and mosquitoes. You sure you want to go out there so late at night?"

"I'm sure," Daisy replied.

The taxi driver glanced briefly at the flashlight clutched in Daisy's hand, then shrugged without commenting and eased forward, swinging the steering wheel. "Whatever. You're the boss."

Pulling away from the guesthouse, he pointed the vehicle toward Main Street. They rode in silence. Daisy watched the landscape roll past beyond her window. The small downtown area was practically deserted. The only establishment still open was the local tavern, which went by the name of the County Line Saloon, although there were no vehicles parked in either the small lot on the side of the building or the street out front, which meant it was probably a slow night. Further afield, as they left

Wolf Haven behind, a gas station came into view, but its lights were dark, and the pumps were empty.

Ten minutes later, they arrived at the coordinates provided by Daisy. The skeletal outline of the unfinished road from the interstate stood silhouetted against the starry sky. Beneath it, under the massive supports that held the elevated roadway above the swamp, was a smaller, squat outline that Daisy knew to be the now abandoned shack. Further away, she could see construction equipment, including a backhoe, at least three dump trucks, and a crawler-mounted crane. Surrounding it all was a chain-link fence. Darkness lay like a shroud across the landscape, with only the pale light from a crescent moon to see by.

The taxi driver stared through the windshield in obvious disbelief. "You sure this is the place, lady?"

"I'm sure," Daisy replied, although she couldn't help a twinge of apprehension as she followed his gaze. She took a deep breath to calm her nerves, then reached into her pocket and handed the driver thirty dollars in cash before reaching for the door handle. "My business here shouldn't take longer than fifteen minutes. Twenty at most. I'd like you to wait and then take me back to town."

The driver pressed his lips together even as his brow furrowed. "I don't know. I can't afford to get into trouble. You're not doing anything illegal here, are you?"

"No, I'm not." Daisy reached into her pocket again and produced a slim black wallet within which were credentials identifying her as an FBI agent. It was fake, of course, but would hold up to scrutiny nonetheless thanks to genuine contacts within the agency, including the deputy director, who had turned to CUSP on more than one occasion to help with cases that were beyond their expertise. She flashed the credentials and quickly returned them to her pocket.

"You're FBI?" The cabdriver didn't sound convinced. "You look like you're barely out of your teens."

"Don't let my apparent youth fool you," Daisy said, pushing the passenger door open. "I'm older than I look. Will you wait?"

The driver studied her for a moment longer, then nodded. "Sure. Whatever. It'll cost you, though. Fifty bucks plus the cost of the ride back. But no longer than fifteen minutes. This place is creepy, and I'd rather not be sitting out here all night."

"It's a deal. Just don't go anywhere." Daisy climbed out of the cab and swung the door closed, then started across a muddy expanse crisscrossed by deep ruts left by construction vehicles, snapping on the flashlight as she went.

When she reached the fence, Daisy shone the flashlight to the left and right, playing the beam across the metal links and looking for a means of entry. She found it ten yards distant at a spot where the fence had come away from a post and was peeled back upon itself. This was, no doubt, the spot where the doomed teenagers had gained access days before.

She squeezed through the gap, careful to avoid snagging her clothes on the sharp metal prongs of the fence, and then made her way to the shack. Before climbing the steps onto the porch and heading inside, she glanced over her shoulder to make sure the taxi was still there. The twin beams of the vehicle's headlights lanced the darkness. Faint music reached her ears. The driver must have turned the radio on to distract himself while he waited. Satisfied, Daisy ducked inside the cabin and pulled the door closed.

A pungent odor of decay assaulted her nostrils. She swung the flashlight around. The beam played over an old sofa, an even older TV, and a coffee table thick with dust. Further away was a cramped kitchen with a refrigerator that probably dated back to the seventies. The door to the freezer section was missing, the space beyond nothing but a deep, dark hole.

Daisy wrinkled her nose and moved further into the cabin, picking her way toward a corridor at the rear. There were three rooms leading off the narrow hallway. A bedroom that looked like it was stuck in a bygone era, with outdated furnishings. It was almost as if someone had gotten up, walked out, and never came back. From what she knew of Annie Doucet, Daisy surmised that this must have been her mother's room, kept as a shrine by her daughter.

She pulled the door closed and moved on. The room at the end of the corridor was a bathroom. The last door revealed another bedroom, but this one contained a surprise. What little furniture remained—an old bedframe and a dresser—had been moved aside, and a pentagram scrawled on the floor in what looked like white chalk. Burned and melted candles surrounded the demonic symbol. A couple of crushed beer cans and an empty vodka bottle thrown into the corner of the room suggested that this was more the work of bored teenagers than disciples of the occult.

Daisy stood and looked at the pentagram for a moment, then turned and left the room before making her way back through the shack to the front door. She exited onto the sagging front porch, descended the steps onto the dirt lot in front of the cabin, and looked around. This was where the killings had taken place, outside in the open. But there was no sign of any disturbance now except a few patches of disturbed ground and a piece of crime scene tape that had gotten caught on a nearby bush and now flapped in the wind. She glanced up at the towering construction project that overshadowed the shack. The unfinished road deck—held above the swamp by huge concrete piers—that ended abruptly in a fifty-foot drop. More empty piers continued on past the fence, waiting for the road to be built atop them. Soon, once they finished the road, there would be nothing left of Annie Doucet's old home except memories and half-truths whispered by frightened teenagers during sleepovers and camping trips.

Daisy dropped her gaze, disappointed that there wasn't more to see, and started back toward the hole in the fence.

It was then that she noticed it.

A small white object half buried in the dirt.

She stopped and bent down, plucked it from the soil, her heart beating a little faster as she realized what it was.

Then she froze, her ears picking up a sound from somewhere behind her. Stealthy footfalls, as if someone or something was sneaking up on her.

She risked a furtive glance sideways, saw that the taxi was still sitting there with its lights on beyond the fence. It was too dark to see inside, but the music was still playing. Why hadn't the driver blown his horn to warn her of whatever was sneaking up from her rear? Was he sitting there, lost in a world of his own, listening to the 80s rock that provided a surreal backdrop to her creepy surroundings? Or had he fallen prey to whatever was out here and would never listen to anything ever again?

Daisy tensed.

She steeled herself for whatever was going to come next and straightened up, turning quickly and dropping into a fighting stance, arms raised, to confront her attacker.

"Whoa. Easy there, lady." The taxi driver stood ten feet away, a look of alarm on his face. "I was just coming to get you. Time's up. This place gives me the creeps, and I'd like to get out of here."

Daisy let out the pent-up breath that she'd been holding. It wasn't a monster, after all. No Cajun werewolf out on the prowl looking for victims. It was just a nervous cab driver who didn't want to be out in the swamp at night.

"Sorry, I didn't realize how much time had passed," she said. "I'm done here. We can go."

"Good." The taxi driver turned and started back toward the hole in the fence.

Daisy followed behind, with the object that she had found clasped in her hand. She looked down at the curved, three-inch long claw nestled in her palm and felt a rush of satisfaction. This hadn't been a wasted trip after all. Not in the least.

EIGHTEEN

AFTER DECKER SPOKE TO CAROL, he sat at the desk in the garage, lost in thought. CUSP had been in Wolf Haven back at the time of his mother's murder, yet as far as he knew, they hadn't intervened. Had made no attempt to stop it. His first reaction had been to call Daisy and ask her what she knew. But upon reflection, he decided it was better to wait. He wanted time to think. Get everything straight in his head before he confronted her.

Rising from the desk, he left the garage, went to the kitchen, and made a late supper of a ham sandwich and a glass of milk. He had stopped briefly at the small grocery store on Main Street after dropping Daisy off at her guesthouse and picked up the basics. Eggs and bacon for breakfast, coffee, milk, bread, deli ham, and bottled water. It would be enough to keep him going for a few days. If they ended up staying longer, he would need to stock up on a larger selection of easy foods, probably at the larger grocery store out near the highway. Assuming it had opened back up by then, since the manager had met an untimely end there thanks to the loup-garou, and it was currently a crime scene.

He took his supper to the kitchen table and sat there to eat.

Afterward he called Nancy. It was ten o'clock, and an hour later in Maine, but she was obviously waiting for his call and answered on the first ring. They chatted for thirty minutes and then said their good nights. Afterward, Decker tidied up, turned out the lights, and climbed the stairs to his bedroom on the second floor. After making up the bed with clean sheets from the closet, he climbed in and was soon asleep.

———

At some point later, the incessant ring of his phone on the nightstand pulled Decker from a deep and dreamless sleep. He reached out and fumbled for the handset, almost knocking it onto the floor in his haste. It was one o'clock in the morning and the room was swathed in darkness.

According to the caller ID, it was Chad.

Still half-asleep moments before, Decker snapped fully awake. There were few reasons for his old deputy to call at such an hour, and he feared the worst. Had there been another attack?

He answered with a terse, "What's happened?" even as he was swinging his legs off the bed and reaching for his pants. "Is it the loup-garou?"

"Hey, relax. It isn't the beast." Chad cleared his throat. "It's the sheriff's office. Someone broke in. Carol had the good sense to install a second camera and hide it after she discovered the tampered recording. One of those modern ones that links to a phone app. She set it up to trigger automatically if there was motion, and wouldn't you know it, she got a notification about thirty minutes ago. Someone activated the camera. It recorded them entering the building and going to the evidence locker. They had the spell book, John."

"They were putting it back?"

"That's exactly what they were doing. Carol emailed the recording to you. You should look at it, then call me back."

"Okay, give me a minute," Decker said, then he hung up and

went to his email. Sure enough, there was a message from Carol with a video attachment.

He opened it and watched the recording.

A figure stepped into view, dressed in black and wearing a hoodie pulled over their head. Under one arm was a thick volume that Decker knew to be the spell book. The figure moved furtively through the dark office, making straight for the front counter and the original camera. As before, the intruder unplugged it, then turned toward the evidence room, digging into their pocket, and pulling out a set of keys. Soon the door was open, and the figure vanished inside. Moments later, the intruder reappeared again, head bent low and face not visible. After closing and locking the evidence room door, the figure turned and hurried back through the office and out of view. This time, they did not have the book. The video finished a moment later.

Decker watched the recording a second time, then called Chad back. "Our book thief appears to have gotten cold feet and put it back."

"Yeah. Looks that way." Chad's voice was flat and emotionless. "Although they could easily have copied the page with the incantation first."

"Which means the attacks might continue."

"If we let our nocturnal visitor go free, which I don't intend to do."

Decker wondered how they were going to stop them, considering that the intruder concealed their face and he was pretty sure they were wearing gloves. He was about to say as much when he realized something else. "Keys. The person who broke into the office had a set of keys."

"Yeah." There was a strange tone to Chad's voice.

"How is that possible when only yourself and Carol have access to the evidence locker?" Decker asked, suspecting that Chad knew more than he had let on so far. "And another thing. The intruder must have possessed a key to the back entrance because the sheriff's office has an alarm system, which would have gone off if anyone broke in."

"You don't think I know that already?" Chad said, sounding miserable. "The only explanation is that the intruder stole my keys, had duplicates made, then returned them before I noticed."

"And just how would that happen, exactly?" Decker asked. "Are you saying someone broke into your house and stole your keys, then broke in all over again just to put them back?"

"No. I wish that were the case, but I'm afraid this is an inside job."

"I don't understand."

Chad sighed. "I recognized our intruder the moment they stepped into view. I've seen that jacket with the hoodie before. And the way he walked… there's no doubt. It's my girlfriend's son, Ben Donelson."

NINETEEN

DECKER'S CALL woke Daisy a little after one thirty. She groaned and rolled over in bed, noticing the time on her phone as she reached for it. A shudder of dread rushed through her. Why would he be calling in the middle of the night?

She got her answer a few moments later when she answered. After a brief conversation, she jumped out of bed, pulled on the same clothes she had been wearing the day before because they were close at hand, and then rushed out of the room and downstairs.

When she reached the sidewalk in front of the guesthouse, the rental car was waiting at the curb with Decker behind the wheel. She climbed in, noting that Decker wore a holster containing a Glock pistol, the standard service weapon of CUSP. Her own gun, a Sig Sauer P365, was concealed under her shirt in a form fitting shoulder holster.

They rode the short distance to the house where Chad's girlfriend lived, although the turn of events that had roused Daisy from her bed were running through her mind the whole way there. They'd only been in town for less than twenty-four hours and it appeared that the case was solved, thanks to Carol's quick thinking. That was, she mused, something of a record even if it wasn't an official CUSP case.

When they arrived, Chad was already there, standing at the curb next to his patrol car with his hands pushed deep into his pockets and an expression somewhere between anguish and determination on his face.

"I sure do appreciate you coming out here to help with this," he said as they climbed from the rental vehicle and joined the sheriff on the sidewalk.

"You're welcome." Decker turned to look at the house where Chad's girlfriend lived. It was a narrow one-story building commonly referred to as a shotgun shack. The name came from the fact that if you opened the front and back doors, you could fire a shotgun clear through the house without hitting a single wall thanks to the unique interior layout designed to increase airflow through the structure in the days before air conditioning. These types of homes were ubiquitous in the south and especially Louisiana. "You ready to get this over with?"

"Not really, but I guess we have no choice." Chad pulled a hand from his pocket and produced a pair of shiny gold badges, which he held out to them. "But before we do, I must deputize the pair of you. This is going to get weird enough given the circumstances, without some slick defense attorney claiming an illegal arrest."

"This is a turnaround," Decker said, taking the badge. "Me being your deputy."

"It's just for a few hours, so don't sweat it," Chad said, but he couldn't help a grin despite his obvious sour mood. He took a step toward the house. "Let's get this over with."

They made their way up the path and mounted the steps to the narrow front porch. When they reached the front door, Chad lifted an arm to knock, then hesitated.

"You want me to do it?" Decker asked.

"Nope." Chad brought his fist down three times on the door, then stepped back.

For a minute, there was no response from within the building, then a soft glow appeared in the window to their left. The porch light flicked on above their heads.

The door opened.

An attractive woman in her late thirties with shoulder length dark hair and sparkling green eyes stood in the doorway. She wore a thin cotton robe tied closed over a lacy nightgown. Daisy assumed that this was Chad's girlfriend, Keira.

"Chad? What are you doing here?" Her gaze shifted to Decker and Daisy. "And who are these people?"

"I'll explain inside," Chad replied. "Can we come in?"

"Of course you can come in." Keira stepped aside. "You didn't even need to knock. You have a key."

"Which it wouldn't be appropriate to use in this instance." Chad stepped past her into a small living room at the front of the house. "This isn't a social call. We're here on official police business."

"That explains your companions and the unannounced visit in the middle of the night." Keira's gaze shifted between them. "Now, would one of you like to tell me what the hell is going on?"

"Where's Ben?" Chad asked. "In his room?"

"Where else would he be at this time of the morning?" Kiera narrowed her eyes. "I'm sure he's sleeping."

"He wasn't sleeping a couple of hours ago when he snuck into the sheriff's office to put back the book that he stole."

"What are you talking about?" Kiera glared at Chad. "Ben's a good boy, always has been. He wouldn't break into your office, and he certainly wouldn't steal anything."

"Yeah, that's what I thought, too." Chad sidestepped Kiera. "But it doesn't make it any less true. We have security footage that proves it was him."

"This is crazy." Kiera moved to block Chad from going deeper into the house. "You can't just come in here and take my son."

"I can when he's wanted for murder." Chad took his girlfriend by the shoulders and eased her out of the way.

"Murder? You said he stole a book."

"Yeah. But then he used the book." Chad started down the narrow corridor that ran from the front of the house to the back. "Trust me, Kiera, I don't want to do this, but I have no choice."

"You arrest Ben and we're over." Keira's voice trembled when she spoke. "Finished. You hear me?"

"Loud and clear." Chad came to a halt next to a closed door on the left side of the corridor. His hand rested on the butt of his gun in its holster hanging from his belt.

Daisy and Decker hurried to join him. Daisy wondered if Chad was going to pull his weapon, but instead, he reached out and turned the handle.

The room beyond the door was mired in darkness.

Chad waited a moment, listening for any sign of movement from within, then reached around the doorframe and snapped the light on.

Then he stopped and stared.

The bedroom was empty, the covers on the bed pushed back as if someone had jumped out in a hurry. Nearby was an open window, the curtains flapping in a light breeze.

Ben was gone.

TWENTY

DAMMIT." Chad raced across the room to the window.

Decker turned and pushed past Kiera, who was standing openmouthed in the doorway, then ran toward the front of the house. Without needing to be told, Daisy took off in the other direction toward the back door.

When Decker got outside, he took the porch steps two at a time and turned to the right, sprinting around the side of the house toward the open window, searching the darkness ahead of him for even the slightest movement as he went.

He scolded himself for not anticipating that Ben would run. It was a rookie mistake. He and Daisy should have let Chad go into the house while they circled around to cut off any potential escape routes. But this wasn't a hardened criminal they were dealing with. It was a sixteen-year-old kid. Even so, he should have known better. He had let Chad take the lead, allowed him to call the shots simply because he was now Wolf Haven's sheriff. But having a title didn't make someone good at their job, and Decker should have realized that regardless of his new position, the man was just as incompetent and self-absorbed as he had been when he was a deputy. He also didn't have the experience to handle a murder investigation. Add to that his personal relationship with the suspect's mother, and it was a recipe for disaster.

Decker should have stepped up. He only hoped that the boy had not made a copy of the incantation, that he wasn't intending to transform into the beast to defend himself, because if that happened, it could turn into an even bigger mess than it already had. And if someone else died, if the beast killed an innocent bystander, their blood would be on Decker's hands, no matter how much he tried to convince himself that Chad was ultimately responsible.

"John." Daisy's voice cut through the darkness between the houses. "Any luck?"

"No." He saw her coming toward him from the other direction, approaching the still open window. They reached it at the same time and came to a stop, chests heaving.

A moment later, Chad appeared, trotting toward them with a grim expression on his face. He must have jumped out of the window and taken off around the back of the houses, looking for the missing boy. Not that it had done much good, because he shook his head slowly. "He's gone."

Decker didn't reply. Instead, he turned and strode back toward the front door and entered the house to find Kiera standing in the living room like a statue, as if she couldn't comprehend exactly what was happening.

He went up to her. "Where would he go?"

"What?" Kiera stared at Decker blankly.

"Your son, Ben. Does he have somewhere that he goes? A special place, or a friend's house? Somewhere that he thinks would be safe."

"I don't know. I mean… He's a sixteen-year-old boy. It's not like he confides in me anymore." Kiera went to the sofa and sank down on it, burying her head in her hands. "This is a nightmare. Why would Chad think that my son is a murderer?"

"That's a long story," Decker said. "And I think it would be better if the sheriff explained it to you."

Kiera nodded. She looked up at Decker with tear-filled eyes. "Ben wouldn't hurt a fly. He's a gentle boy. Sensitive."

Decker sensed movement to his left. When he looked around, Chad was standing close by with his arms folded.

"I know this is hard, Kiera, but Ben might not be as gentle as you think he is. At least, not under certain circumstances."

"What you mean by that?"

"It's difficult to explain. Are you sure there's nowhere that Ben would go? A place where he could hide."

"I'm sorry, but like I said to your companion, I wouldn't know if there was. Ben keeps to himself, at least around me. You know what teenagers are like."

"Kiera, think." Chad went to the sofa and kneeled in front of his girlfriend, placing his hand on her leg. "This is very important. Lives may depend on it."

"I don't know." Kiera's voice rose in pitch, becoming almost a screech. "Why won't you believe…"

She trailed off, her eyes narrowing as if she were concentrating.

"What is it?" Chad glanced up at Decker, then back to Kiera.

"There is one place. I overheard him talking about it with one of his friends from school several months ago. It's an old hut in the swamp."

Chad patted her leg. "Can you tell us where it is?"

Kiera shook her head. "I just heard them talking about it. All I know is that it's a wooden hut on a small rise of land somewhere in the swamp. They found it when they were checking out the shack that belonged to that crazy old woman who wouldn't sell her land, so it can't be far from there."

"That's a hell of a lot of land to search," Chad said, standing up. "Especially in the swamp."

"Maybe you could search from the air," Daisy said. Until now, she had been standing near the front door and listening quietly. "Do you have access to a helicopter?"

Chad snorted. "I wish. The closest helicopter is in New

Orleans, and good luck getting NOPD to let us use it without going through a bunch of red tape. Not to mention how much it would cost the department, and I'm not sure we have that kind of money."

"It might not matter," Decker said, because he had remembered something from back when he was inside the house on Boston Common being shown his past by the ghost. An old ramshackle hut out in the swamp where Annie Doucet had hidden the spell book away from temptation. How many places like that could there be out in the bayou? He turned to Chad. "I think I know where Ben has gone."

TWENTY-ONE

"I HOPE you're right about this," Chad said as they pulled up in his police cruiser near the chain-link fence that ringed the road construction site and Annie Doucet's cabin. "Because if you're not, it just gives Ben more time to make his escape."

"If I'm wrong about this, we don't have any other clues to his location, anyway." Decker opened the car door and stepped out, flashlight in hand, then waited for Daisy and Chad to join him before starting along the fence line toward the unfinished road that towered over them.

The landscape had changed since the last time he was here. The trees had been stripped back and now the cabin, which had once sat at the edge of the swamp, overlooked land that had been filled to provide a more stable base for the concrete piers that held the road aloft. Heavy construction equipment sat between piles of construction materials, waiting to be used.

He paused under the shadow of the road, swinging his flashlight left and right for any sign of the path through the swamp that Annie had taken to reach the abandoned hut in the vision shown to him by the ghost back in Boston. He saw nothing. Either the swamp had swallowed the path in the years since Annie had hidden the spell book there, or the construction crew had obliterated it when they were preparing the land. Decker didn't think it was the former because Ben wouldn't have been able to find the hut if that were the case. The path must still be out there somewhere, pushed all the way back to the new boundary of the swamp beyond Annie's cabin where the road came onto dry land.

"You okay, there?" Chad asked, drawing level with Decker and peering out into the darkness. "Lost your way?"

"No." Decker made up his mind. "It's this way."

He took off again, letting the beam from his flashlight play across the ground ahead of them as he weaved through the construction site toward the edge of the swamp. And then he saw what he was looking for. A thin ridge of land surrounded by brackish water that meandered off into the gloom. This must be it. The path.

He waited for the others to catch up, then pressed on. The path was narrow and treacherous, only wide enough for them to move in a single file. The swamp fell away into darkness to their left and right, and it took all of Decker's willpower not to give in to his imagination. To a sudden conviction that a giant alligator would erupt from the water and drag one of them kicking and screaming off into the blackness.

Daisy must have been thinking the same thing. She glanced around nervously. "It's safe to be walking out here in the middle of the night, right?"

"Depends on what you mean by safe," Chad replied. He swung his flashlight out over the swamp, stopped when it picked up the shine from a pair of eyes jutting up out of the water beneath bony ridged brows.

"Is that what I think it is?" Daisy asked, a flicker of apprehension in her voice.

"Yup. And he's probably not the only one watching us," Chad said.

"You don't need to worry," Decker said, pushing his own irrational fear to the back of his mind. "Attacks on humans are rare. He's probably more afraid of us than we are of him. As long as we don't do anything to look like prey, we'll be just fine."

As if to prove Decker correct, the eyes sank out of view. A moment later there was a splash, and an armored tail briefly broke the surface of the water as the creature turned in the other direction and swam off into the night, leaving a rippling wake that soon dissipated.

"See?" Decker said. "Nothing to worry about."

"From that one," Daisy shot back, her gaze still fixed on the dark waters. "It's the alligators I can't see that worry me. How much further is this hut, anyway?"

"Not far." Decker pointed down the path ahead of them, where a low rise of land could be seen against the backdrop of cypress trees that dotted the swamp and the starry sky. Upon this patch of dry land was a small, squat wooden structure that leaned slightly to one side, with a sagging roof line and uneven walls.

"You think that's where Ben is hiding out?" Chad asked, clearly skeptical.

"Can you think of a better place?" Decker said in a hushed voice. He slowed his pace, realizing that they would be visible if the teenager was paying any attention. Assuming Ben was even there, of course. "No one would ever think to look for him out here."

"Except for you." Chad swatted at an insect that was flying around his face. "How did you even know it was here?"

"That's a long story," Decker replied. "And I'm not sure you'd believe me, even if I told you."

"Just for once, a straight answer would be nice." Chad scowled and scratched his neck where a bug had bitten him.

"Maybe I'll tell you everything one day when we have more time," Decker said, although he had no intention of doing so. "Right now, we need to focus on that cabin."

He turned off his flashlight and waited for the others to do the same, then advanced slowly along the path toward the low rise of land. When they reached it, Decker motioned for Chad to flank one side of the door while Decker took up a position on the other, with Daisy at his side.

Chad slipped his service weapon from the holster on his belt.

Decker did the same, unholstering his Glock. Then he motioned again, silently signaling that they would go in on the count of three. He dropped one finger, then another. But before he could finish the count, the door burst open and slammed back on its hinges with a resounding crash. Decker jumped out of the way to avoid being hit.

Then the loup-garou was among them.

TWENTY-TWO

THE CREATURE LANDED with a snarling growl and turned to face them. Chad took a step back, gun raised, finger curled around the trigger. Decker sensed Daisy to his right, circling around to cover the creature from the other side. She had a gun in her hand that he hadn't seen before. A small Sig Sauer pistol that she must have been carrying in a concealed holster. He leveled his own gun at the beast, praying that he wouldn't need to use it. Regardless of what the creature had done, there was a sixteen-year-old boy somewhere deep down within it. A boy who might not know that he was a killer.

The beast rose onto its hind legs and advanced, its attention shifting between Decker, Daisy, and Chad, as if trying to decide which of them to attack first.

"Ben. Don't do it," Chad said, his voice calm yet commanding. "Don't make me shoot you."

The creature glared at him, as if summing up his chances, then took another step forward.

"Listen to him, Ben," Decker said, moving to place himself in the creature's line of sight but maintaining a healthy distance. "You're outnumbered and outmatched. It's three against one and we are all armed. You might get lucky and kill one of us, but you won't be able to take all three of us out, and trust me, you aren't impervious to bullets. I know that firsthand. You're not the first loup-garou that I've encountered."

"He's right," Daisy said. "You need to do what we say before you end up dead. It's not worth it."

The creature stood unmoving, watching them with wary eyes.

Chad cleared his throat. "Think of your mother, Ben. What would she want you to do? How would it affect her if you never came home again?"

This had an effect. The creature took another step, but this time back toward the hut, arms at its side and head bent low. It crouched down, kneeled on the dirt in front of the door, then threw its head back and let out a long, anguished howl.

"John?" Chad glanced quickly toward Decker. "What the hell is it doing?"

"I think it's surrendering to us," Decker replied.

"It's doing more than that," said Daisy.

Decker looked back toward the beast and saw what she meant. The creature had dropped onto all fours. Its skin rippled and undulated, as if it had a life of its own. The beast tilted its head back, let out another howl, this one full of pain. Then, as they looked on, its face contorted almost like it was made of clay, molding itself into another shape even as its limbs twisted upon themselves and cracked as if the beast's very bones were breaking and reforming.

From somewhere off to his right, Decker heard Chad gasp.

Another cry, this one almost human, rose from the creature's mouth and was snatched away by the wind and carried away across the swamp. Except it wasn't a creature anymore. Its skin had turned from a mottled and leathery brown to a pale white. Its limbs had shrunk and lost the bulging muscles that made the creature appear so powerful. Instead of a bloodthirsty werewolf, they were now looking at the fragile form of a young man laying curled into a ball on the soft earth in front of them, his bare skin glistening with sweat under the bayou moon.

For a long minute, the boy didn't stir, then he moved, pushed himself up, and looked at Chad, his face streaked with tears. "Please don't kill me," he said in a small voice. "I didn't mean anything by it. I was just having some fun."

"Yeah, well, fun's over, son." Chad lowered his gun and slipped it back into its holster, before pulling a set of handcuffs from his belt. "And for your information, I'm not going to kill you. I'm arresting you for murder instead."

TWENTY-THREE

AT FOUR IN THE MORNING, Ben Donelson sat in a small interview room at the back of the sheriff's office and stared morosely into space. His hands rested on the table. His wrists were cuffed, but otherwise, he was unrestrained. Any resistance had vanished along with the wolf once he changed back into human form.

They had allowed him to get dressed before leading him back out of the swamp to the waiting police cruiser, then driven him back to town. But not before they searched the hut and found a copy of the incantation along with a sludge-streaked bowl. All that remained of the potion he had used to turn into the loup-garou. The photocopied incantation and the dirty bowl now sat on the desk in clear plastic evidence bags.

Keira Donelson, Ben's mother, sat next to her son. She looked at the page in the bag and shook her head. "That's all the evidence you have that my son committed four murders?"

"Along with eyewitness testimony and surveillance footage from the Pinch-A-Cent grocery store," Chad replied. He was sitting on the other side of the table with Decker to his right. Daisy and Carol were watching the proceedings from the front office on a video feed from a camera mounted on the wall near the ceiling.

"Eyewitness testimony and surveillance footage?" Keira let out a derisive snicker. "Don't make me laugh. All you have are the incoherent ramblings of a frightened girl talking about a monster, and what might as well be a scene from a badly made horror movie. That's not proof of anything."

"We can prove that your son made duplicates of the keys to this building. He then stole Annie Doucet's spell book from our evidence locker and used the incantation contained within to transform into a loup-garou. He even photocopied the relevant page before returning the book," Chad said. "The eyewitness testimony and surveillance footage prove that the loup-garou committed the murders."

"Good luck taking that to court," Keira said, shaking her head. She looked at Decker. "Didn't you already lose your job by claiming that a monster killed the town mayor?"

Decker said nothing, even though he agreed with her. There was no way they could ever charge Ben with anything other than stealing the spell book. But they couldn't let him go free, either. That was where CUSP came in. He had already floated his idea to Daisy, who had agreed to run it past her mother and Adam Hunt. Not that Keira would be any happier with *his* solution than she would with her son going on trial.

Keira obviously took Decker's silence as answer enough. She turned her attention to Chad. "You want to end up jobless and run out of town just like your old boss here? All you have to do is keep telling people my son turned into a werewolf."

"We all saw it with our own eyes, Keira." Chad shifted in his seat. "When he came out of that hut, he *was* the loup-garou. He changed back into Ben right in front of us. We were lucky he didn't attack us. If we hadn't been armed—"

"I had no intention of attacking you." Ben spoke for the first time, his voice strained. "I just wanted to scare you away so that you would leave me alone."

"That was never going to happen, son," Chad leaned forward and rested his elbows on the desk. "Not after you killed those people."

"I didn't kill anyone. You have to believe me." He looked around wildly, his gaze darting from his mother, then to Decker, and finally to Chad. "You know me. I could never do anything like that."

"Not as you are right now," Chad said. "But as the beast—"

"No." Ben sprang to his feet, toppling his chair, which crashed back onto the floor with a thud. "I admit that I made copies of your keys, then came in here and took the spell book. But I didn't kill those people. That wasn't me. I only turned into the wolf a couple of times, and all I did was run in the woods."

"Sit down, son," Chad said sternly.

Ben glared at him but made no move to retake his seat.

"I said sit down!"

This time, Ben did as he was told. He righted his chair and sat back down. Then he bowed his head. "I didn't do it. I didn't kill those people."

Chad sighed. "I'd like to believe you. I really would. But you might not even remember what you did after you transformed."

"I remember it well enough. I waited until mom was asleep, then climbed out of my bedroom window, took the book into the piney woods behind our house to a clearing near the edge of the swamp. I'd gathered the ingredients earlier that day and made the potion just like the book said, put it into a thermos flask. I took the top off, drank it, then recited the incantation. I didn't really think anything would happen, despite what everyone at school said about that witch who killed a bunch of people. How she transformed into the beast. I was just curious, that's all. But it *did* work."

"I didn't bother to get undressed that first time and practically shredded my clothes. Then I ran through the woods for a couple of hours. I chased a rabbit, but I didn't hurt it. I remember that clearly. After the rabbit went down a hole, I picked up the scent of a coyote. It was weird. My senses were so sharp. The animal must've been a mile away at least, but I was able to track it, anyway. I could smell where it had walked. And not just the coyote. Other animals too. They weaved through the forest almost like a roadmap. It was exhilarating. Eventually, I returned to the clearing and changed back. I had to walk home naked because my clothes were ruined, then sneak back into the house. I was lucky it was so late at night, or I probably would have gotten caught. I snuck out one more time and turned into the wolf again, but that was before the murders happened. Even if I didn't remember being the loup-garou, which I do, I would still know that I wasn't a murderer, because I was at home when both attacks happened. I was in bed, asleep."

Chad exchanged a glance with Decker, then turned back to Ben. "That's all well and good, but we only have your word."

"He was at home both nights when the murders happened," Keira said. "I can vouch for that."

"Which means nothing. He's just admitted to sneaking out on two different occasions without your knowledge."

Now it was Decker's turn to ask a question. "If it wasn't you that killed those people, why did you risk sneaking back into the sheriff's office to return the book right after the killings occurred?"

"Why do you think?" Ben looked at Chad. "I overheard you talking with Carol about the murders when I was hanging out in the office. About how they were committed by a beast like the one that killed all those people a few years ago. A loup-garou. I figured you would check the evidence locker at some point to see if the spell book was still there. I didn't want to be caught with it because I knew that you'd blame me."

"Or maybe you returned the book because you committed the murders and knew that it would incriminate you," Chad said.

"You're wrong." Panic flashed across Ben's face. "How can I prove that to you?"

Chad shook his head. "Right now, I'm not sure that you can."

TWENTY-FOUR

OUTSIDE IN THE CORRIDOR, Decker turned to Chad. "You realize that even if we get a signed confession from that young man, he'll never see a day in court, right?"

"You don't think I know that?" Chad ran a hand across his forehead, which glistened with sweat. "Going to the DA with a murder charge against a werewolf. The department would be a laughingstock. I'd end up jobless and drummed out of town quicker than you were." He swore under his breath. "What a mess. This is worse than the Annie Doucet incident. Regardless of whether anyone believed she was a loup-garou, at least there was proof—hard DNA evidence—that she was responsible for Mayor Thornton's death. And thanks to the bullet you put in her, there was no need to file charges."

"Didn't help me much though, did it?" Decker said, glancing toward the interview room door, behind which Ben and his mother still sat.

"No, it didn't." Chad leaned against the wall and pushed his hands into his pockets. "Look, I know I already said this, but I'm sorry I didn't support you back then. Honestly, I was just trying to save my own hide. It wasn't personal."

"Yeah." Decker brushed the apology aside. "How about we focus on the situation at hand?"

"I'm not sure there's much to focus on. Like you said, we can't charge Ben with murder, at least not if we want to look in the least bit credible. But it doesn't alter the fact that he killed those people, even if it was as the loup-garou."

"He's adamant that he didn't do it. Says he remembers every second that he was a wolf and that he didn't even transform on the nights of the murders."

"You believe that?" Chad raised an eyebrow.

"Just playing devil's advocate. Honestly, chances are that he's lying to us. After all, who else *could have* killed those people? We have an eyewitness basically described a werewolf, and video footage that shows the creature killing that grocery store manager. We also know that Ben stole the spell book, and we have footage of him returning it."

"Let's not forget, we encountered the creature tonight and saw it change back into Ben," Chad said. "There's no doubt that he was the loup-garou. Hell, it's not like there could be two of them running around. What are the odds?"

"A million to one." Decker rubbed his chin, lost in thought for a moment. "Unless he showed the book to someone else, like a friend at school."

"Nah." Chad shook his head. "Ben was terrified in there when we were questioning him. He thinks he's going to prison for life. If he'd let anyone else see that book, even so much as glance at it, he would have said so."

"Still worth asking."

"I agree. But I don't think it will get us anywhere." Chad scowled. "This is messed up. I can't just let him go, not after what he's done, but I don't have any evidence to lock him up, either. At least, none that I can actually stand behind. Put on a charge sheet. And whatever happens, I have a feeling that I've messed up my relationship with Keira. I can't imagine she's going to want to see me again after this. She must think I've lost my marbles."

"You don't know that," Decker said. "Look at me and Nancy. We're still together. She didn't run for the hills."

"Nancy's different. It's not even close to the same situation. Imagine what she would've done if you'd accused her daughter Taylor of being a werewolf." Chad's shoulders slumped. "What am I going to do, John? Where do I go from here?"

"You could let me take care of it," said a voice to their rear.

Decker turned to find Daisy standing a few feet away. He wondered how long she'd been there.

"And just who exactly *are* you and what do you do?" Chad pushed himself away from the wall. "Other than working for the same organization as John, which he's been frustratingly tight lipped about."

"I'm the person who takes care of situations like this so that you don't end up drummed out of town and jobless, as you so eloquently put it," Daisy said, removing a business card from her pocket and offering it to Chad.

He took the card and studied it for a moment before looking back up at her. "Classified Universal Special Projects. Never heard of you."

"That's how we like it. You're not supposed to have heard of us. Even that business card will self-destruct in thirty seconds."

Chad looked down at the card and for a moment Decker thought he was actually going to drop it, but then he looked back up, looking sheepish. "You were joking about the card, weren't you."

"What do you think?" Daisy took a step forward. "But I meant everything else. We specialize in situations like this, which is how I can make your problem go away while allowing you to feel like justice was served."

"And Ben? What will happen to him?"

Daisy glanced at Decker. "The same thing that would

probably have happened to Annie Doucet had she not died. We have a facility designed to handle people like Ben."

Decker's thoughts flew back to the photo he had found. To the figure standing in the woods at the scene of his mother's death. A figure that looked very much like either Mina or Daisy. He wondered if CUSP were also in Wolf Haven when Annie Doucet went on her rampage, despite Mina's claims to the contrary, watching and waiting to make sure everything transpired the way that it should. He hadn't brought the subject up with Daisy yet, but he was now even more determined to do so at the first opportunity.

Chad was staring at Daisy for a different reason. "A facility? You mean a prison, right?"

"Of sorts."

"And Ben won't get a trial?"

"I think you've already come to the obvious conclusion regarding that scenario," replied Daisy. "The court system isn't particularly well-suited to prosecuting supernatural creatures."

A flash of anger passed across Chad's face. "Ben's not a supernatural creature. He's a dumb teenager who did a stupid thing. And without that spell book, that's all he is. A regular teenager."

"And he also killed four people," Daisy countered. "Let's not forget that."

"She's right," said Decker, even though he wasn't sure that Ben belonged in a cell at The Zoo, CUSP's secure facility for creatures too dangerous to be left to their own devices. "You either let us handle this or you have to let him walk. And you said it yourself, regardless of whether he was under the influence of the loup-garou, he's still a murderer."

"Dammit." Chad slammed his fist into the wall. "I'm not letting anyone take Ben anywhere. Not until I have more information." Then he turned and stomped back into the interview room, slamming the door behind him.

TWENTY-FIVE

HARLAN VAN CLEVE sat in his black Esplanade and watched the sheriff's office from a side street off Main that provided a direct view of the building. He had been there for almost four hours. Before that, he had followed Decker and his companions as they drove out of town to an old hut deep in the bayou. And what he had witnessed there was startling. It also made their task in Wolf Haven that much harder.

The sheriff's office door opened, and John Decker stepped out with a young woman by his side. This was another wrench in their plan. He was supposed to have come to Wolf Haven on his own. Still, it wasn't all bad. Decker had rejoined CUSP, which would make it easier for them to gain access to their island headquarters in Maine when the time came. In the meantime, it was vital that Decker stayed in Wolf Haven, which meant giving him a reason to do so now that he thought that the creature terrorizing the town had been caught.

He picked up his phone and placed a call which was answered after one ring.

"Hey, it's me. We have a problem. I followed Decker, the girl, and the sheriff out into the swamp. You won't believe this, but some kid has been transforming into the loup-garou. They arrested him." Harlan shifted in his seat, rubbed his eyes. He'd been up all night and was exhausted. "If Decker thinks he's stopped the loup-garou, he'll leave town before we're ready to put our plan into action. We need to act fast, or this is going to slip through our fingers. Maybe we should just act now."

"Absolutely not. We can't afford for anyone to miss him." The man on the other end of the line sounded cool and collected, but Harlan was still glad he wasn't relaying the news in person. "Francesca won't be there until late tonight, and neither will I. Timing is crucial. We wait until then."

"But—"

"Watch him closely. Keep him there. Do whatever you need to. Understand?"

"Yes." Harlan nodded, even as he watched Decker and the young woman climb into a car parked outside the sheriff's office and drive off. "What about the girl?"

"We'll take care of her when I get there. She wasn't supposed to be here. She's a liability." There was a slight pause. "In fact, I have an idea about that. Listen closely."

Harlan did as he was told. When his boss finished speaking, a smile spread across his face. "That's genius."

"No. It's revenge."

"And the sheriff?"

"Let's leave him be for now. He's harmless, and his dislike of Decker might work in our favor."

"Understood." Harlan's gaze lingered on the red glow of Decker's taillights until they faded into the darkness and vanished. "Leave it to me. Decker and the girl won't be leaving town anytime soon."

TWENTY-SIX

AT SEVEN-THIRTY IN THE MORNING, Decker drove Daisy back to the guesthouse. A fine mist of rain hung in the air, slicking the road and leeching all trace of color from the atmosphere. As they drove, he took the opportunity to bring up a subject that had been weighing on his mind since the previous evening.

"I was going through my father's files last night, searching for anything that might help us with the loup-garou, and I found a photograph taken at the scene of my mother's death. The crazy thing is that I recognized someone in that photograph who shouldn't have been there. A figure standing near the tree line, observing the activity and trying their best to blend into the background. A person who looked an awful lot like either you or Mina."

Daisy was silent for a moment, her gaze fixed on the world beyond the car's windshield. "Your mother died decades ago. What does that have to do with the situation we're dealing with now?"

"Nothing." Decker glanced toward Daisy, noticed that she kept her gaze averted. "But it has a lot to do with the timeline that brought us to this moment. Mina assured me that she didn't interfere with my life before I met the younger version of her for the first time in Shackleton, Alaska."

"If that's what she told you, then she didn't. My mother is not a liar."

"I never said that she was, but that photograph proves CUSP was here in Wolf Haven at a seminal point in my life." Decker paused, waiting for Daisy to reply. When she didn't, he continued. "I don't know which of you it was, but one of you was here. I wonder how many other times you've been there in the background, watching my life unfold."

"It wasn't me in that photograph," Daisy said. "After the events at Blackthorne Manor during the Christmas party in 1911, I didn't have any interaction with you again until we met in the bunker on Singer Cay after you returned from the past."

"Then it must be Mina."

"It's possible. I couldn't say definitively. It's not like we've been tethered together for the past hundred years. I've spent much of that time helping my mother run Classified Universal Special Projects, but I've also spent a good deal of time away from CUSP, living my life. I can tell you this much. After you followed Celine Rothman through that portal and back to your own time, Mina found the past a lonely place. She missed you, and I think a part of her wished she had gone with you."

"It was never the plan to leave her back in 1912," Decker said. "I thought she was coming with me right until the portal opened and she refused to leave. She stayed and took the long way around because of you and Thomas Finch."

"And a good thing she did, considering that I stopped aging shortly thereafter. If she had not been there to explain what was happening, I shudder to think what might have become of me. As it was, I struggled to deal with the truth of my situation for many years. Finding out that the woman you think of as your mother is no such thing, and that your real mother is a practically immortal and indestructible half vampire who inherited her longevity from one of the most feared serial killers in the world is bad enough. Discovering that blood also runs in your own veins, and that you share many of the same traits, is worse." Daisy caught her breath. "But that is all beside the point. If Mina showed up at the scene of your mother's death, then it was because of her strong bond with you, the man who first showed her that there was life outside of a small fishing town in Alaska, rather than any intention to interfere with your timeline. She thought of you as a surrogate for the father she never knew, missed you dreadfully for so long after you were separated by time. She talked about you frequently over the years and couldn't help but watch you from afar when she was finally able to do so. But even that was a mixed blessing, because for the first several decades of your life you had no idea who Mina was, which meant that she had to stay in the shadows."

"I never thought of it like that," Decker said. And it was true. He had assumed that in the many long years it took for her to catch up with the present, Mina had been preoccupied with the Order of St. George, and later, CUSP. That she had thrown herself into work and found satisfaction there, becoming a different person in the process. But now he realized that her choice to remain in 1912 was bittersweet. One way or the other, she would lose someone she loved. That she chose to stay and watch Daisy grow up in no way diminished the anguish she felt at being separated from everyone and everything that she loved in her own time, including himself. "When I saw that photograph, I assumed the worst. That her presence in Wolf Haven back when my mother died was a self-serving attempt to make sure the timeline progressed in the right way to ensure events unfolded how she needed them to."

"It wasn't," Daisy said quietly. "She knew the timeline would unfold correctly because it already had. If something changed, then that version of Mina would not have existed anymore. She simply wanted to be close to you in both the good times and the bad." Daisy smiled. "I remember my mother insisting that we take a weekend trip to New York many years ago. I had other plans and said we should do it another time, but she was adamant that it had to be that exact weekend. Wouldn't take no for an answer. Turned out that she wanted to attend a college graduation."

"My graduation," Decker said, a lump forming in his throat.

"Yes. We sat near the back of the auditorium and kept to ourselves, but we were there. She said it was important that you have someone to support you, even if you hadn't met either of us yet, because you had no other family. She enjoyed that weekend so much, even though she couldn't congratulate you in person. Spent a week talking about it afterwards. She still has a photo of you accepting your diploma on the wall in her private quarters back in Maine."

"Why didn't she tell me any of this herself?" Decker asked as they pulled up in front of the guesthouse.

"That's something you'll have to ask her yourself." Daisy opened the passenger side door. "In the meantime, I suggest you go get some shut eye since we've been up half the night. We'll reconnect later and make sure everyone is on the same page about how to deal with Ben. Then, hopefully, we can get the hell out of this place before we have to spend another night here. The mosquitoes are brutal, and I really don't like alligators."

Decker nodded. "Call me when you wake up."

"Sure." Daisy closed the car door and headed into the guesthouse.

Decker sat there for a moment longer, thinking about Ben, and the likelihood that he was going to end up locked away without a trial for his crimes. Then he pushed the maudlin thoughts aside and pointed the car toward his house, and some well-deserved hours of sleep.

TWENTY-SEVEN

IT WAS six-thirty in the evening. Shirley Davenport, head lawyer for L&M Construction, Inc., the company building the road to Wolf Haven from the interstate, had spent the entire day sitting in hot offices, and she had reached her limit. After catching an early flight from the East Coast, then driving all the way from New Orleans in a rental car that smelled vaguely of old socks, she had spent the latter part of the morning and most of the afternoon in a stifling hot portable building out at the worksite talking to the site supervisor and trying to figure out exactly how three teenagers had broken into the construction area after dark, wandered around at will, and then gotten themselves killed by a wild animal.

The situation was a liability nightmare. The job site boasted a complete lack of security—no cameras, razor wire, or even a rent-a-cop guard to wander the perimeter overnight—which was likely to be a big deal if any of the grieving parents sued. On top of that, there was a tear in the fence big enough to drive a truck through. Not that anyone could do anything about a wild animal, of course. It was just as likely that something could have attacked those teenagers on the road before they ever reached the construction site. It was pure misfortune that they had ended up dead on company land. In different circumstances, they would have been in trouble for trespassing. But none of that mattered. The wolf, or coyote, or whatever the hell had torn into them, did so on a piece of dirt that was currently occupied by L&M, which made the company liable, or at least susceptible to a lawsuit that could drag on for months, or even years, with no guarantee that they would prevail. Which was why Shirley had come to town. To see for herself, gather the facts, and make a recommendation to the boardroom suits on how to proceed once she had weighed all the options.

That opinion wouldn't come for at least another week because Shirley didn't want her bosses to think that she had given the situation short thrift, but she already knew where this was going. The same place these things always went. A preemptive settlement offer framed as a gesture of goodwill by the company and accompanied by an ironclad agreement that slammed the door on any future legal action.

Now, as she drove out-of-town wishing that the spur road was already built, and she could just hop on the interstate instead of taking such a long route back to the airport, Shirley relished the thought of getting home, shucking off her heels, and sinking into a hot foamy soaking tub with a glass of wine. Which was why she wasn't too pleased at the alert that dinged on her phone, and also flashed up on her watch, even though it vanished a little too quickly for her to read the message in its entirety. But she saw enough to know that it was from the airline, and that there probably wasn't a soaking tub in her immediate future.

Shirley grimaced and pulled over in front of a dilapidated tavern on Wolf Haven's Main Street, ignoring the loading zone sign on a pole at the curb. Then she pulled her phone out and checked her email. As expected, it wasn't good news. There were five emails from the airline, cataloging a litany of delays to her flight and one last email that capped it all off. Flight canceled— Please call *1-800-you're-not-going-anywhere-tonight* to reschedule.

Crap. Shirley stared at the message. Of all the places to get stuck overnight. She closed the email and was about to dial the number for her personal assistant, Chloe, back in New York, when the young woman beat her to it.

"Tell me you found a seat on another airline," Shirley said, answering the phone and diving in without waiting for her assistant to utter a word.

"Sorry. I tried. Jumped on it as soon as I saw the email. Everything is booked solid." Chloe didn't sound very apologetic. "There was some sort of event in New Orleans. College bowl game or something. All the flights out are full the next two days and there's barely a hotel room to be had."

"And the flight I was supposed to be on?" Shirley gritted her teeth, barely contained her frustration.

"Canceled because of weather at JFK. Thunderstorm. The airline rebooked you on the same flight tomorrow evening."

"Which means I'm stuck here for another twenty-four hours." Shirley cursed under her breath. "Please tell me you have a place for me to stay."

"That much I can do. Although, like I said, it won't be in New Orleans. To be honest, you're lucky I found you anywhere at all. There's barely anywhere to stay in Wolf Haven. I guess their hospitality industry hasn't caught up with the road they're building to bring in tourists." Chloe stifled a chuckle. "I tried the local guesthouse, but it was full, which isn't hard since it only has four rooms."

"What does that mean? I'm sleeping in the rental car?"

"No. I found another place a few miles outside of town. Bayou Brook Campground."

There was a moment of silence as Shirley contemplated this, then she shook her head. "Thanks, but no thanks. I'm *not* sleeping in a tent."

"Relax. You're not sleeping in a tent," Chloe said quickly. "You really think I'd do that to you?"

"No." A wave of relief engulfed Shirley.

"You'll love this. They have cabins. The man I spoke to when I made the booking said that they're very nice. They even have internet and cable TV."

"A cabin?"

"It has a king bed."

"Let me get this straight. You want me to spend the night *in a cabin*?"

"Well, yes." Chloe's voice had fallen almost to a whisper, perhaps because she was thinking about what would happen when her boss finally made it back to the office.

"*A cabin in the woods.*"

"It might be interesting."

"And it might be the start of a horror movie. Do you have any other options? Anything at all?"

"No. Sorry. Not unless you fancy driving all the way to Baton Rouge."

"Which is at least an hour in the wrong direction." There was no way Shirley was adding another sixty minutes or more to her trip the next day. And that wasn't even accounting for traffic. "It's fine. I can use the extra time to make some more inquiries out at the construction site tomorrow morning. I guess it never hurts to be better prepared. Send me the address. I'll go there now."

"Already done. The reservation is in your inbox."

Shirley thought she detected a note of relief in Chloe's voice. Just to make sure her assistant didn't start to feel too comfortable, she said, "We'll talk about this when I get back."

Then she hung up without giving Chloe a chance to respond and checked her email again. Five minutes later, she was heading out of town—in the opposite direction this time—toward the Bayou Brook Campground and what she suspected was going to be an unpleasant night.

TWENTY-EIGHT

IT WAS LATE when Decker woke up. Already evening. He had slept for almost nine hours. Rising, he made a pot of coffee, then put together a quick meal that would have been breakfast if it wasn't so late. After that, he called Daisy and told her to meet him at the sheriff's office. Then he called Chad and Carol and made the same request of them. Regardless of his eagerness to get out of the town where he grew up and return to Maine, and Nancy, there was still one loose end to tie up.

Ben Donelson.

Despite sleeping on it, Decker still hadn't reconciled the need to punish him for his actions with the knowledge that he could never go to trial. If Ben had been a real supernatural creature, instead of a boy playing around with a spell book, it would have been easier. But without the incantation that turned him into a wolf, Ben really was nothing but a misguided teenager who messed with something he shouldn't have.

How much of the bloodlust was always inside of him, just waiting for an outlet, and how much of it was the loup-garou's influence? The answer to that question, in Decker's mind, would determine his punishment, and whether he deserved to end up somewhere like the Zoo. The problem was that it was impossible to know. Ben wouldn't even admit that he had done anything wrong, and he certainly wasn't owning up to multiple murders.

By the time Decker arrived at the sheriff's office, he was convinced there was no right answer. Daisy was there waiting for him, lingering out on the sidewalk, leaning against a lamppost with her hands pushed into her pockets, and the look on her face told him she was battling her own inner turmoil.

"Maybe we should leave town right now," she said as Decker climbed out of the rental car. "Head straight to the airport, board our private jet, and let Sheriff Hardwick figure out how to handle his girlfriend's son. After what he did to you the last time a loup-garou was running around, it would be poetic justice."

"It's tempting, but no." Decker couldn't recall another case that had led him into such a gray area. Most monsters were either born that way or became irredeemable by choice. Ben might have dabbled with witchcraft—broke into the Sheriff's office and stole that spell book—but unlike Annie Doucet, he didn't intend to commit murder. At least, so far as they knew. But turning his back on the situation, letting his erstwhile deputy shoulder the burden of deciding Ben's fate alone, still felt wrong. Decker had come here to do a job, and he intended to finish it, even if that meant making a tough choice. He stepped toward the door to the sheriff's office, opened it. "Might as well get this over with."

Daisy hesitated a moment, then stepped silently across the threshold past Decker.

Carol looked up as they entered, but there was no smile. None of her usual cheery greetings. Instead, she glanced over her shoulder, then spoke in a low voice. "Fair warning. Chad is *not* in a good mood."

"And with good reason," came a voice from somewhere near the back of the room. A moment later, Chad appeared from the direction of the holding cells, a scowl creasing his face. "A few days ago, this town was peaceful. It was safe. Now I've got a bunch of dead bodies in the morgue and an impossible suspect."

"Been there and done that," Decker said, resisting the urge to make a quip about karma.

"Yeah, but you weren't dating the killer's mother." The scowl deepened. "Of all the people, did it have to be Ben? Everything was going so well. For once, I was happy in my personal life. Now I'll be lucky if Kiera will pass me on the other side of the street, let alone let me share her bed."

"Still not talking to you, huh?" Decker asked.

"That's an understatement. When she said we were through if I arrested Ben, she wasn't joking. I went around there earlier today hoping we could talk. That she would see sense. It was a no go. Wouldn't even answer the door to me. Even worse, she gathered up everything I'd left at her house over the past few months and put it out on the sidewalk. It was just sitting there baking in the sun." Chad rubbed his temple where a vein throbbed. "I don't suppose you've come up with a better solution to this situation than the one you presented to me earlier?"

Daisy shook her head. "No. I already spoke to my superiors and they're putting the wheels in motion."

Chad's shoulders slumped. "I was afraid you'd say that."

"Where is Ben now?" Decker asked.

"Where do you think?" Chad said. "He's at home. Keira left with him not long after you went to get some sleep."

"You let him go?"

Carol spoke up for the first time since they'd entered the building. "We had no choice."

"You could have held him for forty-eight hours without filing charges," Decker said.

"Maybe," Chad said, sounding defeated. "But he's a juvenile and his mother wasn't about to let me put him in a holding cell. She said that if I did that, she was getting a lawyer for him. You can imagine how that would've gone under the circumstances. He wasn't even technically under arrest. I hadn't read him his rights because that would mean making it official, and I could hardly write out a charge sheet claiming that we suspected him of being a werewolf."

"It doesn't matter," said Daisy. "We'll have a team here by morning to extract him."

"You mean take him to this facility of yours where he'll sit in prison without trial," Chad said.

"Yes."

"What kind of team?"

"One that's trained for situations like this. Dealing with supernatural creatures. We call them the Ghost Team."

"Almost sounds like a military unit," Chad said in a flat voice. "All for one scared teenager."

"Don't worry. We'll stick around until morning to make sure everything goes smoothly. That he isn't mistreated," Daisy said. "Then we'll be out of your hair."

"And Ben? How long do you intend to keep him?"

"At least until we can determine that he's not a danger to those around him."

"He's not." Chad shook his head. "It was the creature that committed those crimes, not Ben."

"That's the problem. They're one and the same. We don't know how much of the killing was Ben, and how much of it was the loup-garou. After all, Annie Doucet used the beast to exact revenge, but the bloodlust was all hers. Why would Ben be any different?"

"Because he says it wasn't him. You heard what he said in that interview room. He remembers being the beast, but he has no recollection of killing anyone."

"We only have his word for that, and given the source, it's hardly trustworthy. Besides, not remembering it and not doing it aren't the same thing."

"Please don't do this." Chad looked miserable.

"My hands are tied," Daisy said. "If there was any other way…"

"There is. Leave him here and let me take responsibility for him. I'll make sure he doesn't cause any more trouble."

"That isn't an option." Daisy sighed. "Maybe once we've had a chance to assess him, figure out the risk he poses to those around him…"

"And how are you going to explain this to his mother? Everyone else in town. People are going to ask where he went. You can't just abduct someone, especially a kid, and expect it to go unnoticed. Even if you silence me, you won't be able to keep the State Police from looking for him. The FBI."

"We're not abducting Ben. Arrangements will be made. The authorities won't get involved. Trust me, we're very good at making sure people don't ask questions."

"That doesn't sound ominous at all." Chad clenched his jaw.

"This isn't up for discussion," Daisy said. "I'm doing the best that I can. If Ben didn't want to face the consequences of his actions, he shouldn't have stolen that spell book and murdered those people."

"You're the one that asked us to come here," Decker reminded him.

"You." Chad jabbed a finger toward Decker. "I asked *you* to come here because you've dealt with this before. Not her. I wasn't expecting some black ops outfit to show up and steamroll everyone."

"Come on, Chad. Calm down. She doesn't work for a *black ops outfit*, and no one is getting steamrolled," Decker said. He understood Chad's anger, still couldn't shake the feeling that there was no good answer. But Daisy was right. Ben was a killer, and since they couldn't put him on trial, this was the next best way to keep everyone safe going forward. Because like it or not, they couldn't guarantee that he wouldn't kill again, as the wolf or otherwise. Hell, for all they knew, he'd made multiple copies of that incantation. Hidden them where only he could find them. In the end, it came down to one simple fact. When emotion was stripped away, Ben was simply too dangerous to remain free.

TWENTY-NINE

SHIRLEY DAVENPORT STOOD in the open doorway and stared at her accommodation in disbelief. It was a cabin all right, constructed of rough-hewn logs and sitting in a small clearing among the pines, just like the other six cabins she had passed on the winding woodland trail that led from the Bayou Brook Campground's registration office. A building that appeared to be nothing more than a converted shed sitting on a support of wood pilings designed to stop floodwater from getting in during heavy rains.

But the cabin was hardly idyllic.

A thin, green carpet of moss covered the exterior. The small porch had a visible sag in the middle of the roof, and one of the exterior lights that flanked the front door didn't work. Even worse, she could see the silky strands of a large web taking up most of the space inside the shade. She also saw the unmistakable shape of an enormous spider with thick, black legs. At least two inches across, and poisonous for all she knew.

Shirley tore her gaze away from the vile arachnid and heaved the bag she had taken with her on the plane across the threshold and into the cabin's gloomy, stale interior, then fumbled for the light switch and flicked it on.

Pale yellow light from a chandelier hanging down through the rafters from the vaulted ceiling above pushed away the darkness. A chandelier that was, she noticed with a shiver of repulsion, made from deer antlers lashed together and hanging from a chain.

The rest of the tiny cabin was no better. There was a burgundy loveseat with a knitted throw folded across the back. An older model flatscreen TV sat on a pinewood stand that was too shabby to be distressed on purpose. Behind the couch, against the far wall, was a king size bed with a tarnished brass headboard. A faded and threadbare rug covered most of the floor. The only other door, apart from the one through which she had entered, led to a bathroom. It was half open and she could see the toilet, which was bright pink, with a seat that had no lid.

Shirley dropped her bag on the couch, ignoring the faint whiff of decay that rose from the aging fabric. She opened it and rummaged inside, pulling out a toothbrush and a travel-sized toothpaste which she took to the bathroom and placed on the sink. She went back to the bag and removed her phone charger. Other than her laptop, a protein bar, and a can of soda she had bought at a gas station on the way to Wolf Haven earlier that day and hadn't gotten around to drinking, the bag was empty. She hadn't intended to stay overnight, and had not packed a change of clothes, which meant she would have to wear the same outfit again the next day. She didn't even have anything to sleep in except for her undies. The only reason she had a toothbrush and toothpaste was because she liked to freshen up and brush her teeth after lunch when she was spending the day at meetings. Especially in Louisiana, where the food had a habit of staying on her breath.

She picked up the remote and turned the TV on, then plugged the internet password into her phone from the card given to her by the guy at reception when she checked in.

Her stomach growled, reminding her she hadn't eaten since lunchtime. She should be in her premium cabin seat right now, a couple of hours from landing in New York, and had intended to pick up Mediterranean food after she left the airport. There was a wonderful hole-in-the-wall restaurant near her house that was open late. Instead, she was stuck here in this abysmal dive of a cabin with nothing to look forward to but a lumpy bed. The protein bar in her carry-on held little interest.

She went back to her phone and did a quick search for somewhere to eat. *Takeout food near me.* There was a restaurant in the center of town—the Main Street Grill—that offered delivery through one of those third-party apps. The menu didn't look very good and the wait for delivery was over ninety minutes.

Cold diner food?

Pass.

That left a Chinese restaurant and a pizza place that closed in an hour, which was ridiculous. Did nobody want to eat after eight o'clock in this town?

Both delivered.

After pondering her options, she chose the pizza, mostly because she figured that if they were closing soon, the food wouldn't take too long to show up.

Ten minutes later, pizza ordered, Shirley settled back on the couch, ignoring the errant spring that pushed into her spine through the loveseat's worn fabric, and waited.

THIRTY

HARLAN VAN CLEVE steered the SUV along a narrow winding road that meandered through the woods eight miles west of Wolf Haven, his full beams cutting a broad swath of visibility into the inky night. There wasn't much time. Tomorrow morning, John Decker and his female companion would board their private jet, currently sitting in a hangar at Louis Armstrong International Airport, and wing their way back to where they had come from, thinking their job was done. Believing they had captured the beast terrorizing the small Louisiana town and put an end to the killing.

They were wrong.

Harlan smiled to himself, his pulse quickening in anticipation of more violence, even as he turned off the road and onto a narrow trail that led to a large three floor brick building and several smaller outbuildings sitting on a swath of land surrounded by chain-link fences and razor wire.

He pulled up to the gates, climbed from the vehicle, and pushed them open. Then he jumped back behind the wheel and rolled forward, ignoring the NO TRESPASSING signs affixed to the fence at intervals. No one had gone anywhere near the abandoned mill for years, possibly even decades. At least, until the organization he worked for came along and surreptitiously procured it for their own use.

Harlan brought the SUV to a halt under the towering front façade of the main building and hurried inside. Most of the sprawling structure, including many of the rooms on the upper floors, were dilapidated and unusable with broken windows, rotten or missing floorboards, and a roof open to the elements. Rats and other rodents scurried through the dank, moldy corridors. But the ground floor remained sound enough to use, especially after a little hurried construction to adapt it for their purposes.

Harlan walked deeper into the building, ignoring the rumble of a commercial generator that provided electrical power, and ran the lights and AC units that made his destination tolerable for human habitation.

Most of the ground level was one vast open space with a towering thirty-foot ceiling that had once been the mill floor, filled with heavy woodworking equipment like commercial band and circular saws, planers, sanders, and mortising machines. Tools designed to cut and process logs into planks of wood that provided the raw materials for a post-war building boom across the southern United States and beyond.

All the machinery was long gone, just like the workers who operated it. Now, the mill floor was nothing but a cavernous empty room waiting for the floors above to crumble eventually and collapse, burying it forever under tons of debris. Except for a new, hastily constructed steel structure sitting in the center of the older building. A structure no one would ever know was there from the outside, even if they ventured beyond the razor wire and no trespassing signs.

It was to this inner building, which would have appeared large enough on its own were it not dwarfed by the vastness of the brick edifice that surrounded it, that Harlan made his way.

He reached the building's only door and pulled it open, then stepped inside. And as he did so, he smiled. Because soon death would stalk the landscape once again, running under the pale white light of the gibbous moon, and John Decker would find out first-hand that everything he thought he knew about the loup-garou was wrong. At least, this time around!

THIRTY-ONE

ALMOST AN HOUR after calling Sammie's Pizza, and much longer than she expected, the phone rang in Shirley Davenport's cabin. But not her cell phone. This was a tan colored hotel-style desk unit sitting on an end table next to the loveseat. It reminded Shirley of the phone her parents had in the eighties, except this one was not a rotary dial. Instead, it had a keypad with chunky buttons that illuminated when it rang.

She picked up the receiver and lifted it to her ear, cutting off the shrill *brring* of the ringer.

"Hello?"

"Mrs. Davenport?" The voice on the other end belonged to the desk clerk who had checked her in over an hour before.

"It's *Miss Davenport*," she said, irritated. Her stomach was growling louder now, and she was getting what her mother would have called *hangry*. "What can I do for you?"

"It's kinda more what I can do for you, honey." The desk clerk coughed, then finished with a phlegmy hack. "You order a pizza?"

"Yes." *And it's about time it got here*, Shirley thought. "You can tell the delivery person to bring it to the cabin and leave it on the front porch. I'll put the tip under the mat."

There was no way she was answering the door to some random stranger in unfamiliar surroundings. Not to mention that she was all alone out in the woods. She didn't even think there was anyone staying in any of the other cabins. At least, not those that she had passed on the way to her own less than stellar accommodation.

"Yeah. Pizza guy has come and gone. They don't deliver to the cabins, only the front office."

"Fine. Then why don't you bring it out to me?"

"What do you think this is? The Hilton?" The desk clerk let out a derisive snort. "Do we look like the kind of place that has room service? You want your pizza, come get it."

"You expect me to walk all the way back through the woods on my own in the dark?"

"I don't expect you to do anything, honey. Don't come get your pizza. No skin off my nose. I'll eat it myself. Once I pick the artichoke off, that is. Gross. I can't abide artichoke. Makes me gag."

"You opened the box?" Shirley could hardly believe what she was hearing.

"Had to make sure they got your order right."

"And how would you know what I ordered?"

"Good point. You want the pizza or not?"

Shirley glanced toward the window, and the dark woodland beyond. "Give me ten minutes."

"Sure thing, hon. Oh, and bring some cash. I took care of the tip. You owe me ten bucks."

"Ten bucks? That's crazy. I only paid fifteen for the pizza, and that included the delivery fee."

"Yeah, well, the tip was only five. You can call the rest a convenience charge. This place don't run on thin air."

Shirley opened her mouth to say something else, tell him what she thought of that convenience charge, then decided against it. She wasn't going to win this one, and she really wanted her pizza. It was either that or the tasteless protein bar, which held about as much appeal as chewing on a cardboard box. Better just to suck it up and put the whole thing down to experience. Someday in the not-too-distant future, when she was sitting in a Manhattan cocktail bar regaling her friends with this story, she might even find it funny. But not tonight. Right now, she just wanted to eat. "I'll be there in ten minutes."

"Uh-huh." The desk clerk coughed up another gob of phlegm.

"And keep your hands off my pizza," Shirley said, not bothering to hide her disgust. Then she slammed the receiver down without waiting for an answer and stood up, then hurried to the cabin door and pulled it open.

A small swarm of mosquitoes and a couple of moths danced under the glow of the single working light fixture next to the door. One of the blood-sucking insects veered off and landed on her arm, burying its tiny proboscis into her flesh. She swatted it away with a squeal and stepped out onto the porch, closing the door behind her.

She could see the narrow path that led back to the registration office weaving off into the darkness between the trees. Given the choice, she would have hopped into her rental car and driven there. But in their wisdom, the people who laid out this place hadn't bothered to build any roads out to the cabins, which meant that her car was inconveniently parked in a gravel lot near the campground's front entrance. With no other choice, she stepped down off the porch and walked briskly past the small barbecue area in front of the cabin and the rusty grill that she doubted anyone had dared to use in years, and onto the path.

The trees pressed in around her, their canopy of branches high above blotting out the light from the almost full moon and plunging the trail into gloomy blackness.

"Would it kill this place to put some freaking lampposts in?" Shirley muttered under her breath as she pulled her phone out and turned on the flashlight, then trained it on the ground ahead of her.

She walked quickly, trying to ignore the sounds of the forest. The hoot of an owl and the rustle of some nocturnal animal in the undergrowth. Sounds that were as alien to her New York City ears as the constant grind of traffic and round-the-clock bleating of car horns would be to the citizens of Wolf Haven.

She quickened her step and hurried along the path, keeping her gaze firmly forward and trying not to think about what might be watching her from the darkness on either side. When the path opened up into the parking lot, and she saw the registration office, Shirley almost cried with relief. All she had to do now was grab the pizza and make her way back to the cabin. Then she could close the door, lock it, and not step foot outside again until morning.

The desk clerk looked up when she entered. "Here she is. The princess of the forest comes to claim her prize."

Shirley ignored the jibe and slapped a ten-dollar bill down on the counter. "My pizza?"

The desk clerk reached under the counter with a grunt and produced a pizza box, the bottom of which was already turning brown with grease. There was a single napkin with the restaurant logo printed on it and a small tub of garlic sauce sitting on the lid.

"There you go, honey. One medium pizza, safe and sound."

Shirley picked up the pizza box and glared at the desk clerk. "Don't call me honey!"

Then she turned and stomped from the office, letting the door bang closed behind her. When she got home, this place was getting a one-star review on Yelp, but only because zero stars wasn't an option. In fact, she was tempted to give the whole damned town a one-star rating if the website would let her.

THIRTY-TWO

JOHN DECKER SAT at the kitchen table picking at a frozen pizza he had purchased at the grocery store the first day he was in town and had thrown into the oven after getting home from the sheriff's office. It wouldn't have been his first choice for an evening meal—it was hardly nutritious—but his options were limited. It was either the pizza, or a can of soup, which somehow felt more like lunch food. And it was a good thing he hadn't stocked up on more groceries, because now that they had put an end to the loup-garou's deadly rampage, he could return to Maine, and the life he had built there. By tomorrow lunchtime, Ben Donelson would be on his way to a secure facility operated by CUSP. Maybe not The Zoo, which mostly housed true supernatural creatures, but somewhere equally as secure. Decker would be winging his way back to Nancy. Mission accomplished. And he had avoided dying at the jaws of the loup-garou, too. A vision the last of three ghosts had shown him in that mysterious mist-shrouded house that had appeared on Boston Common.

But even if he had changed his destiny, there was one thing he couldn't change. His lifelong connection to the beast.

The loup-garou had been a part of Decker's existence since

131

he was a kid. No. Scrap that. It had been there since before Decker was even born. That was something else he had learned in that house. How his past was inextricably linked to Annie Doucet and the creature she became through witchcraft. It went all the way back to his own father's teenage years, and a fateful meeting between Robbie Decker and a young Annie. She fell for him. He spurned her. Angry and embarrassed, she became the wolf for the first time and reaped her vengeance, killing his friends at what had later become known as the Kickoff Kegger Massacre.

Of course, the sheriff at the time blamed a wild animal, in much the same way as his mother's death many years later. But now Decker knew the truth. Annie and the loup-garou loomed large over every sad event in his life. And in an even more extreme twist of fate, Decker might not even have been born if it wasn't for Annie. She had given his mother, who was struggling to conceive, a fertility potion. And it had worked… at least on the face of it. Nine months later, Lily Decker gave birth to a son. A boy who grew up to be town sheriff, and finally ended the bloody reign of the loup-garou by killing Annie Doucet. From John Decker's cradle to Annie Doucet's last breath, they had been connected by a violent and supernatural bond that brought them together time and again.

Decker pushed the maudlin thoughts to the back of his mind. He looked down at the pizza, which was even less appealing now that it had gone cold. There were still four slices left but he had no appetite for them. Instead, he picked up the plate and dumped the food into the trash. Then he made his way into the living room, sat down on the couch, and turned on the TV, looking for a less depressing distraction.

THIRTY-THREE

AT ABOUT THE same time that Shirley Davenport was ordering her pizza, Jeremy Brenner—who until recently was a happily married tax accountant in the town of Slidell across the lake from New Orleans—was having a bad day of his own.

A week ago, he had been out in the French Quarter, celebrating a friend's birthday. As usual, there was no parking anywhere near the city's infamous party district, or the restaurant on Royal Street where they had eaten and drank the evening away. Which was how he came to be stumbling past the French Market back to his vehicle, which he had left on the outskirts of the hipster-heavy residential area known as the Bywater.

He was alone. The rest of his group had headed over to Bourbon in search of a late-night drinking establishment—of which there were many—to keep the festivities going. Brenner had an early meeting the next day and took his leave.

That was his big mistake.

He had just crossed Barracks Street and was passing by the old New Orleans Mint, which hadn't struck a single coin since 1909, when a black panel van screeched to a halt at the curb next to him. The side door slid open. Two men in ski masks jumped out and grabbed him, bundled him into the back before he could even comprehend what was happening. The next thing he knew, there was a needle plunging into his arm.

Soon after, everything went black.

He woke up with a pounding headache to find himself in the cramped cell that he now occupied. A cell that contained only a thin mattress thrown on the floor, a cheap polyester pillow, and a scratchy gray blanket. The sole other item in the room was a plastic bucket in the corner which turned out to be the bathroom.

At first, he was unsure what was happening, why he had been abducted. But it soon became obvious, because to tell the truth, his troubles had started months before he was snatched off the Crescent City's dark streets, on a similar boozy trip to the Quarter.

That time, he wasn't alone. He was with a colleague from work. A man named Chuck Logan. They had spent the evening in a strip club with a prospective out-of-state client, trying to convince him that his company's taxes were in safe hands at the venerable century-old firm of Goldman, Blackett, and Fitch. After three hours, a couple of lap dances, and six double whiskeys, the deal was done. The client, a little the worse for wear but grinning from ear to ear, climbed into a taxi and was soon on his way back to his five-star hotel.

Brenner and his co-worker enjoyed no such luxury. The company might be footing the strip club bill, but they had no intention of paying for hotel rooms. Which was why he and his associate were hoofing it across the Quarter to their cars under the light of the full moon.

And even then, it would have been fine, except that they decided to take a shortcut down a narrow, dark alley. Something they should have known was asking for trouble. It wasn't uncommon for locals and tourists alike to lose their wallets and sometimes even their lives, in such out-of-the-way locales. The city had a crime problem. Muggings, armed robberies, and assaults were at an all-time high. But in this case, it wasn't some low life scumbag with a knife and a drug problem that changed Brenner's life forever.

It was something much worse.

They were halfway down the alley, walking at a brisk pace, when they heard it. A loud metallic crash. They turned, startled, to see a trashcan overturned in the middle of the alley, its contents spewed out across the cobblestones. But it was the shape crouched behind the trashcan that made the blood in their veins run cold. It was like nothing they had ever seen. At least, not anywhere but in a horror movie.

The beast was enormous, with wide shoulders and a long snout filled with sharp, dagger-like teeth. It was covered in coarse black hair and observed them with burning red eyes that glowed with an unnatural fire. When it reared up on its hind legs, Brenner could see the muscles that rippled beneath the skin of its forearms and the curved, wicked-looking claws he knew could slice him open in a fraction of a second.

He stared in disbelief. Crazy as it was, he recognized the impossible creature that stood before them.

A werewolf.

"Run." Logan was turning to flee, even as he uttered the obvious advice.

Brenner would have loved nothing more than to run, but the signal that would have made his legs work had gotten lost on the journey down from his brain. He was rooted to the spot with fear.

Not that it mattered. Logan had barely taken two steps when the creature was upon him, slashing and ripping and biting. He didn't even have an opportunity to scream before the beast removed his throat.

Then it turned its attention to Brenner.

He woke up four days later in the hospital with severe lacerations, a hairline fracture to his skull, and two broken ribs. They released him a week later. Eight days after that, with the next full moon hanging low in the sky, Brenner turned into the beast. Thankfully, his wife was not home, having gone on a girls' night out to one of those wine and painting places that had become so popular. He ran through the woods behind his house and woke up naked the next morning, covered in scratches and mosquito bites. He snuck back into the house and grabbed some clothes from the laundry room and told his wife that he had stayed over at a friend's house after a card game that had run long. After that, he was careful. On the next five full moons, he hid his secret, making excuses for his absence and chaining himself to a tree deep in the piney woods so that he wouldn't do to anyone else what the creature in that alley had done to him.

Then came the night of his abduction.

He woke up dazed and disoriented. Unclothed. The back of his neck hurt like crazy, and when he touched it, he found a fresh incision held together with stitches, and what felt like an oblong metallic object beneath his skin.

But Brenner cared less about that than finding out where he was and why he had been abducted. He spent the next four hours banging on the cell door, demanding to know what was going on. But no one responded to him. He remained a prisoner there for the next two days, his only human contact coming when a bottle of water and food on a paper plate were pushed through a small flap at the bottom of the door.

And then came the night that he killed those teenagers. He could still see the looks on their faces when he tore them to shreds. Their terrified screams still rang in his ears. But he had been powerless to stop himself. Because his abductors had done something to him. They had figured out how to force him to become the beast, even when it wasn't a full moon. It had something to do with the strange light fixture affixed to the ceiling in his cell. A fixture that appeared to replicate the glow of the moon. And that wasn't the worst of it. The device implanted in his neck was some kind of controller, forcing him to do what his abductors wanted. Making sure that he remained under their control.

And now, the light was on again.

Soon, he would run through the woods, unable to help himself as he killed another innocent victim.

"No, not now," he wailed, even as the light increased in brightness and the first pulses of change came upon him. "Please don't do this to me again."

But there was no one to hear. At least, nobody who cared.

Jeremy looked up toward the cycloptic lens of a camera mounted high on the cell wall and waited for what he knew was about to happen.

THIRTY-FOUR

SHIRLEY DAVENPORT LET the registration office door slam behind her and stomped back across the parking lot with the now almost cold pizza cradled in her arms. As she passed her rental car, one of only a few vehicles parked at the campground, she looked at it wistfully. She was tempted to throw the pizza on the backseat, climb in, and drive away from this dreadful place. Except that she had nowhere else to go, and the keys were back in the cabin. It's only one night, she told herself, as she hurried toward the woodland path that snaked back to her accommodation.

Only one night.

Ten hours and she could leave this place behind. Put it in her rearview mirror and never return. That went for the town of Wolf Haven, too. If she never set foot in this backwater outpost of redneck insanity again, it would be too soon.

She stepped onto the path.

The trees closed in around her, the space between them mired in impenetrable blackness. A shiver ran up her spine. Who knew what might be lurking out there in the gloom? All sorts of scenarios ran through her mind. A coyote springing out at her from the undergrowth, slathering jaws wide open. A bear, ready to rake her with its claws. And what about a wolf? Did they even have wolves in Louisiana? She didn't think so, but then again, it was in the town's name. There must be a reason for that.

Get a grip, she scolded herself. *There's nothing out here that can hurt you.*

If there was, she reasoned, the campground would have been out of business long ago. Wild animal attacks would hardly be good for business. Feeling a little better now that she had reasoned away her fears, Shirley pressed on, but she quickened her step, anyway.

The first cabin came into sight, sitting in a small clearing. Its windows were dark and there was no sign of life from within. The other four cabins between here and her own accommodation would all be the same. The Bayou Brook Campground might still be in business, but it was hardly in demand. Which made her wonder why that desk clerk—who for all she knew was the owner of the place—had put her in cabin six when all the other buildings were empty. It didn't make sense. Unless he just thought it was funny to make the big city girl walk all that way through the woods in the dark on her own. Or maybe so few people checked in these days that the other cabins were no longer habitable. Either way, it amounted to the same thing. Shirley was traipsing through the woods in the middle of the night carrying a cold pizza that she was sure would be barely edible. At least there was a microwave in her accommodation to reheat it, which was something.

Shirley tore her gaze away from the lonely cabin and kept moving. When she glanced back over her shoulder, the parking lot was no longer in view. A sudden sense of uneasy solitude overcame her. Then she noticed something else. The owl, which had been so vocal only minutes before when she was heading in the other direction, was no longer hooting, and whatever creatures were ferreting about in the undergrowth had ceased their nocturnal activities.

The woods had fallen still and silent, as if someone had flipped a switch.

Was that normal? Shirley was hardly the outdoorsy type, having grown up in a suburb of Boston before spending most of her adult life in New York City, where she had moved for work, but she didn't think so.

The fear lurched back, stronger than ever.

She stopped, came to a halt on the path, torn by indecision. There were four more cabins dotted along the trail before she reached hers. What had seemed like a short walk now felt like it stretched on forever. The parking lot and the safety of the registration office were much closer. She could turn around and be back there in under two minutes. But then what would she say? That the woods weren't noisy enough, and it scared her? She could imagine what the desk would make of that. And he was hardly going to let her sleep in the office all night. Assuming there was even anywhere to lie down, which she doubted. And even if there was, did she really want to spend time in the company of such an uncouth individual? For all she knew, he might be more dangerous than anything prowling around the woods. He hadn't exactly endeared himself to her so far. Who knew what was running through his mind?

Better to suck it up and keep going.

Which is what she did… at least for a few more steps.

And then she heard it. A low growl coming from somewhere off to her right.

The breath caught in Shirley's throat. She came to a stumbling halt and looked around.

The growl came again, guttural and menacing. Closer this time.

That was all it took. Shirley turned around and ran, her feet pounding on the hard-packed earth of the trail as she fled back toward the registration office. No matter how unsavory the desk clerk was, he couldn't be as bad as whatever was out here with her. And he might even have a gun. This was Louisiana, after all. Didn't everyone have a gun?

Another growl, somewhere in the woods right next to her.

Shirley squealed. In her panic, she dropped the pizza box. Triangles of cheese and artichoke topped dough spilled out, but she didn't care. All she could think about was getting back to the office, slamming the door, and hiding there until the first rays of morning sun swept away the darkness.

And she was going to make it, too. The parking lot was up ahead, framed between the silhouetted trunks of the towering pine trees that bordered the trail. Just a few minutes more, and she would be safe.

She would have sighed with relief, except for the flicker of movement between the trees to her right that drew her gaze. A dark shape that moved against the denser blackness beyond, racing along beside her, keeping pace.

At first, she couldn't tell what she was looking at, but then it exploded through the underbrush, snapping branches and sending twigs flying. It landed a few feet behind her on the trail, snarling and angry.

Shirley risked a quick glance over her shoulder, and what she saw made the blood run cold in her veins. There were wolves in these woods. But not the sort of wolves she had seen in documentaries and nature shows. This was bigger. Meaner. It was more like—it sounded crazy even when she was looking right at it—some slathering monster from a horror movie. It was three times the size of any normal wolf and covered in thick black hair, with rippling muscles, and demonic red eyes that glinted with evil intent. Then, impossibly, it raised itself up on its hind legs and started toward her.

Shirley screamed and stumbled forward, bursting out from between the trees and into the parking lot. Just a few more steps, and she would be safe.

But the creature was too fast.

It gained on her in an instant, swept her up in its powerful arms. Lifted her off the ground. Sharp claws, almost like daggers, sank into her soft flesh, slicing through it like butter.

Shirley would have screamed again, but she never got the chance. Powerful jaws snapped closed around her neck, biting and tearing. Then, as if satisfied with its handiwork, the beast raised her high and threw her with all its might.

The last thing she saw before the welcome embrace of death was the office window shattering as she flew through it, and the startled expression, which soon turned to horror, on the desk clerk's face.

THIRTY-FIVE

DECKER WAS SITTING on his couch talking to Nancy when the phone call came in, interrupting his conversation. He put Nancy on hold and switched to the other call.

It was Chad.

"There's been another attack," he said in a grim voice. "Out at the Bayou Brook Campground. I'm on my way there now."

"Are you sure it's the loup-garou?" It appeared Decker's suspicion was correct. Ben Donelson must have made multiple copies of the incantation and had turned into the wolf again. They should never have released him into his mother's care.

"Sure as I can be." Chad fell silent for a moment, as if weighing the impact of what he was going to say next. "Thing is, it wasn't Ben. I checked with his mother. He hasn't left the house since we let him go. In fact, he's there right now with a couple of friends from school, playing video games."

"That's impossible. It must be him. What are the odds of two loup-garou's showing up at the same time?"

"Well, unless his mother's lying, which we can easily verify by asking the friends of their whereabouts, I'd put those odds are about a hundred percent right now."

"Hang on a moment." Decker switched back to Nancy and

told her what was going on, then ended the call after promising to phone her again later. He returned to Chad. "What do you know so far?"

"Not as much as when I get to the campground," Chad replied. "We have one victim. Female. Name of Shirley Davenport. Thirty-six years old. She's some sort of fancy lawyer from New York. Ironically, she works for the construction company building the spur road. She was in town to do damage control and make sure the parents of those kids that were killed at Annie Doucet's old shack don't sue."

"Then what was she doing out at Bayou Brook? The place was a dump when I was a kid. I can't imagine it's gotten any better."

"Oh, it hasn't. If anything, it's gotten worse. I wouldn't wish that place on my worst enemy. Even the cockroaches don't want to stay there," Chad said. "She had a flight out of New Orleans this evening, but it got canceled. The earliest flight she could rebook was for tomorrow afternoon."

"So why didn't she just drive back to New Orleans and find a hotel there?" Decker asked, even as he scooped up his car keys and headed toward the door.

"In a word, football. It's college bowl season. Big game. There isn't a hotel room to be had anywhere in the city. I spoke to her personal assistant right before I called you and got some background information. Rather than go in the opposite direction to Baton Rouge, she decided to stay locally and avoid the extra drive back. Guesthouse was full. This was the only other option."

"Right."

"There's something else. We have another eyewitness. The desk clerk. Guy named Franklin Snade. Creature had no interest in him. It killed Shirley Davenport, then chucked her through the front window of the registration office, if you can believe that. Then it stood there for a while before turning and running back into the woods."

"Almost as if it was trying to be seen, just like with the other victims."

"Which means the killings have to be connected." Chad's signal was breaking up as he drove. "I know you wanted to get the hell out of Dodge, but this thing ain't over."

"Apparently not. Have you spoken to Daisy yet? Told her what's going on?"

"Figured I'd leave that to you." There was a hard edge to Chad's voice.

"You know, she really isn't so bad."

"Yeah. When she's not going around locking up helpless kids with no due process."

Decker sighed. "She's doing the best she can, just like the rest of us. Would you rather explain what we saw out at that shack in the bayou to a jury?"

There was a moment of silence. Chad cleared his throat. "I'd rather none of this had happened in the first place. It would sure make my life simpler."

Decker wanted to remind him that the spell book had been stolen from under Chad's nose, and that if he hadn't been careless with his keys, leaving them around when he visited his girlfriend, Ben would not have been able to get into the evidence room. But he didn't. Instead, he just said, "How about we focus on the problem at hand and worry about Ben later."

"Suits me."

Decker started the car and pulled out onto the road. "I'll run by the guesthouse and pick up Daisy, then meet you at the campground."

"Or you could leave her where she is and come out on your own."

"Not going to happen. She's part of the team," Decker said. "And she has more experience dealing with this kind of stuff than both of us put together."

"I hardly think so. What is she, like twenty years old?"

"Not even close." Decker had no intention of explaining

145

Daisy's unnatural longevity to Chad. It was none of his business, and the sheriff probably wouldn't believe a word of it, anyway. "I'll see you in a few."

Then he hung up and drove toward the center of town and the Shady Pines Guesthouse. As he drove, Decker called Nancy back and filled her in as best he could, told her they were going to be stuck in Wolf Haven a while longer.

As he turned onto Main, he hung up.

He only hoped they could find this new creature and put a stop to it as easily as they had found and stopped Ben. But somehow, deep down, he suspected it wouldn't be that easy. Something didn't feel right about all of this. He just couldn't put his finger on what.

THIRTY-SIX

WHEN DECKER and Daisy arrived at the crime scene, it was already a hive of activity. With no deputies of his own, Chad had called in the State Police to assist. As Decker turned off the road and into the parking lot for the Bayou Brook Campground, a young officer stopped him with a raised hand, then walked around the car and knocked on the window before telling them that the campground was closed, and they should turn around. Even after Decker explained who he was and why he was there, the officer looked skeptical. At least, until he used his radio to check Decker's story with Chad. After that, he issued a sheepish apology and told them to proceed toward the registration office.

Chad met them at the car as Decker climbed out. "John. Am I glad you haven't left for Maine already. This is a hell of a mess."

"Are you sure this is the work of a loup-garou?" Daisy asked, exiting the vehicle and slamming the passenger side door.

"As sure as we can be." Chad rubbed his chin. "It tore Shirley Davenport up just like all the others. Damned thing ripped her throat out. Desk clerk saw the attack. Said it was the worst thing he's ever seen in his life. Gave a description of the perpetrator and it matches the one given by the young woman who survived the first attack out at Annie Doucet's old place. It also matches the creature captured on video at the grocery store."

"Best guess. Ben shared the incantation with someone else and they used it," Decker said.

"Or maybe he shared it with a whole bunch of people, like all his friends at school, and we're looking at a freaking werewolf epidemic here." Chad grimaced. "And we won't be able to track the perpetrator down as easily this time."

Daisy bit her bottom lip. "Or maybe Ben was telling the truth, and he isn't the killer."

"Which means the real killer was still on the loose even after we thought it was over." Chad shook his head. "I don't know. It's a bit far-fetched. After all, we know Ben turned into the wolf. We saw him change back with our own eyes out at that shack in the swamp. He admits to stealing the spell book and using the incantation. No. The simpler answer is that he gave a copy of that incantation to someone else, who then used it and committed the latest killing."

"That's my point," Daisy said. "If he gave the incantation to one of his friends, they could just as easily have been the killer all along."

Chad shrugged. "It's worth looking into, at least. After I'm done here, I'll stop by and talk to him again. Ask if he let anyone else see the spell book or copy the incantation. If he did, then we've got a real problem on our hands. We won't be able to tell who the actual killer is. What I wouldn't give for a conventional murder and some straightforward DNA evidence."

"That's the spirit," Decker said mirthlessly. He glanced toward the office. "How about you show us the crime scene?"

"Sure." Chad motioned for Decker and Daisy to follow him. He led them through a cordon of police tape and across the parking lot toward the registration office.

As they drew close, Decker noticed a yellow, numbered evidence marker sitting on the gravel near a large red stain that he knew was blood. The spot where the attack had taken place and Shirley Davenport lost her life. Beyond that was the office, and the shattered front window.

"The body is still inside. ME hasn't moved it yet," Chad said, as they ascended the steps leading up to a narrow porch and the registration office's front door. When they entered, he added, "Be careful where you step. There's glass everywhere."

Decker nodded. He was only half listening, because his attention was drawn by the mangled body that lay amid the remains of the registration office's front window. An image of his mother flashed through Decker's mind. Her torn and mutilated body lying on a steel table in the morgue and covered with a bloodstained white sheet. He closed his eyes to clear the unwanted memory and counted to ten, taking long, measured breaths.

"You okay?" Daisy asked, placing a hand on his shoulder.

Decker opened his eyes and nodded. After a moment, he said, "I'm fine."

"You sure?" Chad asked. "You're looking a bit pale there, buddy."

"Really, I'm all right." Decker's gaze shifted briefly back to Shirley Davenport, before he tore it away. "What was she doing here at the registration office so late at night, anyway? She must already have checked in by that point."

"She ordered a pizza from Sammie's," Chad said. "They delivered to the office, and she came to collect it. According to the desk clerk, she left with her food, and then came back about ten minutes later. Looked like she was running for her life. Then he saw the creature chasing her. Watched it kill her."

"And he did nothing to help her?" Daisy asked.

"Said it all took place too quickly." Chad glanced through the open door of the registration office, back toward the woods. "We found the pizza box on the trail leading to her cabin. Figure that's where she first encountered the beast. She tried to run back, probably thought she could make it to the office and barricade herself in. She was wrong. It caught up with her in the parking lot and killed her."

"So close. She almost made it," Decker said. "If only she'd been a little faster."

"Yeah." Chad glanced back over his shoulder toward the entrance. "Not sure it would've made any difference. That door wouldn't present much of an obstacle to a creature like the loup-garou."

"Maybe not, but it would've been better than nothing, and the desk clerk might have been able to help. Fight it off. I'd bet my last dollar that he had a gun stashed under that counter."

Chad nodded. "He did. Pistol. Was too shocked to reach for it in the heat of the moment. By the time he remembered the gun, it was too late. The beast had already run back off into the woods. It probably wouldn't have made much difference, anyway. You know how hard it was to bring Annie Doucet down back at the high school. Took a lot more firepower than a pocket pistol."

"Where is the desk clerk?" Decker looked around.

"In his trailer behind the office. That's where he lives. Figured it was the best place for him. He was pretty wound up when we arrived."

"I'd like to see him if you don't mind. Hear his account firsthand. Now that he's had time to calm down, he might have remembered some detail he missed when you spoke to him."

"Guess it can't hurt." Chad stepped through the door and back out into the humid night air. "Follow me. I'll take you there."

THIRTY-SEVEN

AN HOUR and a half after they arrived at the Bayou Brook Campground, Decker and Daisy were on their way back to Wolf Haven. They rode in silence for the first few minutes, lost in their own thoughts, until Daisy piped up.

"Guess we're stuck in this place a little while longer," she said. "Pity. I was looking forward to my own bed. That guesthouse needs to change their mattresses. I have a hell of a crick in my back. It's like sleeping on rocks."

Decker glanced toward her. "Look on the bright side. At least you aren't staying in a cabin at the campground."

"Yeah. That would be worse." Daisy pulled a face.

"Yes it would," Decker said. "Trust me, I know."

After interviewing the desk clerk and hearing what he had to say—which didn't amount to anything more than they already knew—Chad had thrust flashlights into their hands and led them down the trail leading to the cabins. He showed them where Shirley had first encountered the beast. The pizza box, and the spilled pizza, were still there, next to another yellow evidence marker. After that, he had taken them to her cabin. As Decker suspected, the accommodation at the Bayou Brook Campground had gone downhill in the years since he had last been there. An illicit liaison with Nancy a few months before he left for college. He had scraped together enough money to rent a cabin for the night, thinking it would be a romantic gesture, and soon discovered that their surroundings were hardly conducive to passion. They had made the best of it, anyway. On the way home, he promised never to take her there again. Not that it mattered, because not long afterward, Decker was gone, leaving Nancy behind and ending their budding relationship… At least until his return, decades later.

"John?"

Daisy's voice dragged Decker back from his thoughts of the past, and that uncomfortable night with Nancy at the Bayou Brook Campground. "Sorry. Got distracted there for a moment."

"Were you listening to what I said?"

Decker had to admit that he wasn't. "Sorry. I'll pay attention from now on. Promise."

"Good. As I was saying, I went out to the scene of the first attack. The construction site. I wanted to take a look around and see it for myself."

"On your own? When did you do that?"

"Last night after we ate."

"In the dark?" Decker swung to the side of the road and came to a halt. He turned and glared at her. "What on earth were you thinking? You could have ended up like those teenagers. It wasn't safe. In fact, it was downright foolish."

"Will you relax?" Daisy rolled her eyes. "I was perfectly safe. I was on my own. No witnesses. Whatever agenda that creature has, it isn't attacking solitary targets. It wants to be seen. Besides, it is unlikely the loup-garou would go back to the same place twice."

"You don't know that," Decker said, the frustration rising in him like a black tide. "How did you even get there? It's miles out of town."

"I took a taxi."

"And told the driver to wait for you, no doubt."

"Obviously."

Decker raised his hands in the air. "There you go."

"What?"

"The creature wants a witness, and you provided it with one. The taxi driver."

"Hmm. I guess you're right." A sheepish grin spread across Daisy's face. "It's a good thing the beast didn't show up."

"Ya think?" Decker shook his head. This was exactly the kind of thing Mina would've done. Daisy was just like her mother.

"Still, it was worth the risk. I found something that Chad missed." Daisy reached into her jeans pocket and pulled out a small, white, curved object. "I was going to show this to you. I almost called you last night but figured you'd probably be sleeping. Thought it could wait until morning. But then Ben broke into the sheriff's office, tripped that camera that Carol hid, and… well, you know what happened after that. In all the excitement, it completely slipped my mind."

Decker stared at what Daisy was holding between her fingers and was overcome by a flash of recognition. It was a claw. A big one. He stared at her in disbelief. "And you didn't think to show me when you remembered?"

"Like I said, I forgot. It didn't seem important anymore. I thought we'd caught the killer. Case closed. Then you showed up and dragged me out to the campground. I only just remembered it." Daisy's eyes lit up, as if the claw vindicated her late-night solo trip. "It might give us the answers we need. Tell us if Ben is innocent, like he claims. You wanted a way to figure out if the killings were the work of one creature, or two."

"I don't see how."

"Maybe the medical examiner can compare the wounds on the victims to the claw and tell us."

"That's a long shot. One claw is much the same as another." Decker reached over and plucked the claw from between her fingers. Examined it up close. It reminded him of another claw that he and Chad had found lodged in the bed of a moonshiner's truck. A claw that Annie Doucet had left behind when she attacked and killed them. Except… He handed the claw back to Daisy and swung back out onto the road. "We need to get back to the sheriff's office. Right now."

"We do?" A look of confusion flashed across Daisy's face. "Why?"

"I need to look at something."

"Care to elaborate?" Daisy slipped the claw back into her pocket.

"No. Not yet." He took his phone out and unlocked the screen, then handed it to her. "Call Chad. His cell number is in my contacts. Ask him to meet us there. It's urgent. After that, call Carol and get her to meet us there, too."

"Sure." Daisy looked down at the phone. "What do you want me to say if he asks why?"

"Tell him I have a hunch and if I'm right, then we've been wrong about everything." Then Decker pressed the accelerator to the floor and flew toward town as fast as he dared.

THIRTY-EIGHT

"THIS ISN'T FROM A LOUP-GAROU!" Decker held up the claw that Daisy had found at the construction site. "Which means Ben didn't kill those people."

"What?" Chad stared at Decker as if he were speaking a foreign language. "Now hold on a minute. That claw doesn't prove a damn thing. We saw the loup-garou with our own eyes. Saw it turn back into Ben. If anything, that claw proves Ben was out at Annie Doucet's old cabin, that he killed those people while under the influence of the wolf."

"Actually, it proves the opposite." Decker put the claw down on Chad's desk, next to another claw in a clear evidence bag. When Decker and Daisy had arrived at the sheriff's office, Carol was already there. It had only taken her a few minutes to locate the claw that Chad and Decker had found stuck in the bed of Floyd Benson's truck several years before. As he expected, the claws were not a match. Now, he pointed the differences out to the small group gathered around the desk. "Look at the length and curve of the two claws. They don't match. Now look at the inside edge of each one. The claw we found at the site of the moonshiners' murder, the one we know for certain came from Annie Doucet's loup-garou, has a clean, sharp edge. This new

155

claw has tiny serrations along the inner edge. Not only that, but the base of the new claw is narrower. They aren't from the same creature."

"Or maybe they are," Chad stared at the claw, "and Ben's version of the loup-garou isn't the same as Annie's."

"Kind of a stretch, don't you think?" Daisy said. "That two people using the same spell book, an identical incantation, would transform into different beasts? And then, to stretch coincidence even further, there just happens to be another loup-garou wandering around with no connection to the first one? A beast with an identical bloodlust."

"I never said that it made any sense." Chad pulled a handkerchief from his pocket and wiped beads of sweat from his forehead. "None of this makes sense. Werewolves don't exist. Or at least, they aren't supposed to."

"What makes sense is that the creature that killed Shirley Davenport tonight is the same one that killed those teenagers and the store manager," Decker said.

"Which means that Ben was telling the truth about not killing anyone," Daisy added. "The real coincidence is that he just happened to steal the spell book and start messing around with it at the same time that there was another, more deadly creature on the loose."

"Ok. Fine." Chad didn't sound convinced yet. "Let's assume that you're right. Ben isn't our killer, and there's a different beast prowling the woods and swamps around Wolf Haven. It could still be one of Ben's friends who got hold of the incantation and decided to use it."

"Unlikely." Decker shook his head. "As I just pointed out, the claws don't match, which means it isn't a loup-garou."

"Then answer me this. What is it, and where did it come from?"

"And why is it here?" asked Carol.

Decker rubbed his chin. "Once we answer those questions, we might be able to stop it."

"Hopefully before it kills again," said Daisy. She studied the two claws sitting next to each other on the desk. "It might not be a loup-garou, but that doesn't mean we aren't dealing with a more traditional werewolf."

Worry flashed across Carol's face. "You mean like those werewolves in the movies? Full moons and silver bullets?"

"Exactly like that."

"Wait a minute." Chad tapped the table with his index finger. "You're forgetting about the grocery store surveillance video. The beast looked just like the one we encountered out in the swamp. The one that turned out to be Ben Donelson."

"Did it, though?" Decker asked. "When we watched that video, we all assumed that there was only one creature. We saw what we wanted to see. I bet if we looked again, really looked closely, we would find that they aren't an exact match."

"Except that we're relying on memory to make the comparison," Daisy said. "We all know that memories can't be trusted. That's why eyewitness testimony is so unreliable. The brain alters your recollection every time you think about an event you saw. After a while, the memory that you believe is accurate might not match the reality of what happened at all. They've done experiments to prove this. Even minutes after an encounter, people start to embellish. We can't rely on what we saw in the swamp to differentiate between the loup-garou and the beast on that tape."

"It's a shame no one thought to take their phone out and film the loup-garou," Carol said.

"In hindsight, that would have been useful," Decker replied. "But it's too late now."

"And anyway, we were all too concerned with not being eaten to start making home movies," Chad said. "And I don't know about anyone else, but I wasn't expecting to come face-to-face with a monster."

A faint smile touched Daisy's lips. "You'd be surprised how often that happens."

Chad shook his head. "I'm not sure I want to know."

"Hang on a minute," Carol said, raising an eyebrow. "If we are talking about a real-life traditional werewolf—and believe me, I'm struggling to accept that such creatures really exist even after what happened with Annie Doucet—then why is it running around now? It's not a full moon."

"That's the best question anyone has asked so far," Decker said.

Chad looked around the group. "If the loup-garou can turn at any time with the aid of magic, then maybe there are other types of werewolves that don't need the full moon to change."

Decker turned to Daisy. "I believe that would be your area of expertise."

Daisy nodded. "If we're talking about myth and legend, then yes, there are other lycanthropes that turn without the aid of a full moon. In Norse mythology, becoming a werewolf was as simple as donning skins. They believed that wearing the fur of a wolf would make them stronger in battle. In ancient Livonia, an area that encompasses modern-day Latvia, it was believed that you could become a werewolf by drinking beer and repeating an incantation—"

"Now, there is a legend I can get behind," Chad said. "At least the beer part."

Daisy shot him a look. "Other cultures believed that you could turn into an animal by drinking rainwater from the footprints of the beast, or that becoming a werewolf required a pact with the devil. I could go on. There are werewolf legends all around the world, from Japan to India, ancient Greece, Rome, and even Armenia, where it was believed that women turned into werewolves as punishment for committing sins. But don't confuse myth with reality. All these legends have a basis in fact, but most of them miss the mark when it comes to accuracy. In my experience, and that of the organization I work for, werewolves turn by the light of the full moon."

"Except for the loup-garou," Carol said.

"Yes, with that one exception."

"Which brings us back to the original question," Decker said. "How the hell is this creature out there when it isn't a full moon?"

"That does indeed appear to be the question," Daisy replied. "And one to which I do not have a good answer. Unless we're dealing with a whole new kind of monster that we haven't encountered before."

THIRTY-NINE

"GIVEN WHAT WE NOW KNOW, we can't possibly let anyone take Ben away and lock him up," Carol said.

"It appears that we were wrong," Daisy agreed. "He really was just a dumb kid playing around with stuff he didn't understand. But I no longer believe that he is a murderer."

"Which is what I've been trying to tell you all along," Chad said through clenched teeth. "I can't believe I might've lost the first real relationship I've had in years over this. I only hope that Kiera will forgive me."

"You can hardly blame us for thinking it was Ben, under the circumstances," Decker said. "Especially given the history of this town and the loup-garou."

"Two different werewolves running around at the same time." Carol shook her head. "It doesn't bear thinking about."

"I'll call off the Ghost Team just as soon as I get back to the guesthouse," Daisy said. "They weren't due here until morning, so they probably haven't been dispatched yet."

"Thank you." A look of relief passed across Chad's face.

Daisy acknowledged his thanks with a brief nod of her head. "But I'm going to recommend that we keep Ben under surveillance, at least for now. Killer or not, he was dabbling with black magic, and we need to make sure that he doesn't do so again."

"How are you going to do that?" Chad asked. "Send some of those Ghost Team goons to our town on permanent assignment?"

"Nothing so heavy-handed. But we will be here, watching. At least for a while."

Chad's face dropped. Clearly, the thought of Decker's new employer keeping members of his town under surveillance did not appeal. "There's no need for your organization to become officially involved. I'll vouch for the boy."

Daisy turned to him. "With all due respect, Sheriff Hardwick, it was your inattentiveness that allowed your girlfriend's son to steal the spell book in the first place. Even worse, he took it from *your* evidence locker using copies of *your* keys. I hardly think you're the best person to keep him in line going forward."

"Carol could keep an eye on the boy," Decker said, mostly as a compromise. "She won't let us down. I'd trust her with my life."

Carol beamed at Decker. "Flattery will get you everywhere."

Daisy shook her head. "I don't like it."

Chad looked at Decker with narrowed eyes. "I thought this young woman was your associate."

"She is," Decker replied.

"Well, she's acting more like your boss."

"She's that, too. And don't bother asking for an explanation, because I'm not giving you one. It's complicated."

Chad shook his head. "It always is with you, John."

"Boys, that's enough! Can we get back to the matter at hand?" Carol said. "I really don't mind watching over Ben, and I think it will be less intrusive than an outsider."

Decker looked at Daisy. "She's right. This is the best solution all around. It will be less complicated, and I don't mind being her point of contact. If Ben so much as steps an inch out of line, we'll know about it."

"Very well." Daisy let out a deep sigh. "I suppose it's easier. But I want weekly reports. I want to know that Ben is behaving himself."

Carol nodded. "Not a problem."

"Which only leaves the issue of the real killer," Chad said.

"I'm not sure there's much more we can do tonight." Decker yawned. "It's midnight, and I'd really like to get a good night's sleep after everything that happened over the last few days. We can meet back here in the morning and discuss strategy."

"And if something happens in the meantime?" Carol asked.

"I think we're safe for now. The beast has already struck once tonight. If it sticks to the same pattern as the last two attacks, it won't strike again."

Chad didn't look convinced. "I hope you're right."

"So do I." Decker picked up the claw Daisy had found near Annie Doucet's cabin and handed it to her. "But even if I'm not, there isn't much we can do at this moment. The creature could strike anywhere within a twenty-mile radius, and we have no idea what it wants, or why it's killing people."

"We also have no idea where to start looking for it," Daisy said, slipping the claw into her pocket. "I agree with John. We should all get some sleep. We'll be able to think better when we're not exhausted."

"Suits me," said Carol. "I was about to climb into a nice hot soaking tub with a good book and a glass of wine when you called. Water's probably cold now, but I can still enjoy the wine before I climb into bed."

Chad started toward the front door. He held it open for everyone to leave, then turned off the lights before pulling the door closed and locking it. Five minutes later, they were going their separate ways. Decker drove Daisy back to the guesthouse and made sure that she got inside safely before turning the car in the direction of his own home.

It had started to rain. A light drizzle that settled on the windshield and transformed his surroundings into a dark

Impressionist painting. He turned the wipers on and drove through the center of town, noting how empty it was. At this time of night, the citizens of Wolf Haven were safely tucked up in their beds. That made him happy. Less chance that anyone would encounter the beast, assuming it hadn't returned to wherever the creature laid its head when it wasn't prowling for victims.

When he reached the house, Decker pulled up at the curb and cut the engine. He climbed wearily out of the car and made his way up his front path. There were no lights on in any of the other houses. The only clue that he wasn't totally alone in the world, that the rest of civilization hadn't simply vanished, was a tabby cat that stopped and observed him for a moment with flashing green eyes before slinking away around the side of the neighbor's house.

Decker pulled his keys from his pocket and went to mount the steps leading up to his front door. At that moment, he caught a flicker of movement out of the corner of his eye. He turned to see a silhouetted figure standing at the end of his path. A man with broad shoulders and a muscular physique. The man folded his arms and spoke in a gravelly, deep voice. "Mr. Decker, I've been looking forward to this moment."

"Can I help you?" Alarms rang inside Decker's head. He reached for the gun concealed in a shoulder holster under his jacket. But just as his palm closed over the weapon, there was a stir of air at his rear. Before he could turn his head to look, a firm hand clamped across his mouth and nose. A hand that was holding a folded rag that gave off an odor Decker recognized all too well.

Chloroform.

FORTY

DAISY SAT in a chair in the corner of her room at the Shady Pines Guesthouse with a book on her lap. A novel by Margery Allingham, one of the foremost female crime authors of the 1930's and 40's. Daisy had read every book Allingham had published back when they were new and she still held a soft spot for them, partly because of the author's fascination with the occult, which often found its way into her writing.

Normally, Daisy loved to lose herself in a good book after a long day, but tonight, she was distracted. She couldn't get the image of Shirley Davenport's mutilated body out of her head. The shredded corpse lying on the floor of the Bayou Brook campground's registration office surrounded by the shattered window, shards of splintered glass glinting amid the poor woman's pooling blood. It wasn't that Daisy hadn't seen such violence before. After more than a century working for CUSP and its predecessor, chasing supernatural creatures at her mother's side, she had seen plenty of death.

But this was different.

It felt... pointless. Shirley Davenport wasn't a resident of Wolf Haven. If her flight hadn't been cancelled, she wouldn't even have been at the campground in the first place. Likewise, the grocery store manager. He had been transferred to the new store from out of state and couldn't possibly have had time to make any enemies. Except for Annie Doucet, who surely wouldn't have been pleased with all the new development out near the interstate. But Annie had been dead for years, and even though Daisy believed in ghosts, she didn't think they could manifest as werewolves.

No. Even if you ignored the fact that the beast went out of its way to leave a witness at each crime scene, there was something weird about the way it selected victims, appearing to choose them purely at random.

Which got her thinking. Why would that be?

Then she had an epiphany.

What if the killings were nothing to do with the town, or even the victims, but had everything to do with John Decker. After all, if the loup-garou returned, what was Sheriff Hardwick most likely to do? Pick up his phone and call the one person who could help. A man who had dealt with the monster the first time around. Maybe the attacks, carried out with such brazenness, were intended to draw Decker back to the place where he'd first fought the wolf. Which meant there must be some sort of intelligence behind them. Something more than just a random beast on the hunt.

A mastermind with an agenda.

But what that might be, she had no idea. Still, her theory made sense. And it was a place to start looking. If they could figure out the reason behind the attacks, the reason someone wanted Decker back here, then they could stop them. It was just a shame that Ben Donelson had stolen the spell book and caused them to look in the wrong direction and think the case was solved.

Maybe that was the real reason Shirley Davenport had to die. To draw Decker's attention and show him that Ben wasn't the killer, but just a dumb kid in the wrong place at the wrong time. To keep Decker right where he was, make sure he didn't climb on that jet and leave, until they were ready for whatever they had planned for him.

The more she thought about it, the more Daisy became convinced that she was right. But there was one person who could tell her if she was onto something viable, or just staring down a dead-end alley.

She put the book aside and picked up her cell phone, then called Decker. After four rings, it went to voicemail.

She almost called again, but then thought better of it when she saw the time. 1:20 AM. No wonder he wasn't answering. He was probably tucked up in his bed and snoring already, which was what she should be.

Daisy put the phone down and stood up. Her theory could wait until morning. She went to the bathroom, brushed her teeth, then changed into her PJ's. Five minutes later, she climbed into bed, turned the light out, and settled down to sleep.

FORTY-ONE

AT FIRST, Decker saw nothing but blinding light. He blinked and waited for his eyes to adjust. When they did, he discovered that he was lying on a cot in what looked like a small, oblong cell with smooth metal walls and ceiling, and a concrete floor. A camera mounted in the corner of the room observed him with a dispassionate gaze. A plastic bucket stood in the corner. It didn't take a genius to figure out what that was for.

He lay for a moment waiting for his thoughts to clear. His throat was dry—it felt like sandpaper every time he swallowed—and his head was thumping. There was an unpleasant taste in his mouth. After effects from the drugs his captors had incapacitated him with.

Decker sat up and winced when a new bolt of agony shot through his head.

How long had he been unconscious?

There was no way to tell because the room had no windows. Only a metal door with a small viewing window, no doubt to make sure that whoever occupied the cell was at a safe distance before their captors opened the door, and a longer slit lower to the ground where food could be pushed through. The one thing it lacked was a handle. Any way to open it from the inside.

Other than the construction materials, it reminded Decker of every holding cell he'd ever encountered in his years as a cop.

Except that this time, he was the prisoner.

Decker swung his legs off the bed and sat on the edge. He strained to listen but heard nothing. No conversation. No sounds of movement. Just empty, dead air.

"Hello?" he called out, wincing again when the back of his throat flared like there were a thousand needles stuck down there. "Is anybody out there?"

No answer.

Had he really expected there to be?

He looked down, saw that his jacket was gone. So was his gun and shoulder holster. Likewise, his trouser pockets were empty. No keys, wallet, or anything else. Even his shoes had been removed leaving him in socked feet.

"What the hell is going on?" he muttered under his breath. The last thing Decker remembered was climbing out of his car a little after midnight and making his way toward the front door of his house. Then there was a figure out on the sidewalk. A man who talked to him. Distracted him so that he wouldn't see the man's accomplice sneaking up from behind. A quick whiff of chloroform. After that there was nothing until he woke up here. He tried to remember the man's features but couldn't. Not that it mattered. It wouldn't help his situation because he was sure the man was a stranger.

Decker cursed. He had been so blind. It turned out that werewolves weren't the only dangerous monsters prowling Wolf Haven. There were human ones too. But honestly, how could he ever have anticipated that. The answer was clear. He couldn't.

Decker stood and walked to the door, pressed his ear against it. Still no sounds from beyond the cell.

He raised a hand, balled it into a fist, and pounded on the door, three times in quick succession. Metallic thuds that echoed into the unknown space beyond.

"Let me out of here."

His demand went unanswered.

Decker tried again. Three more thuds. Then he tried a different tack.

"Come on. You didn't snatch me just to keep me locked up and ignore me. Tell me what you want. Let's talk about this."

Decker waited.

As before, there was no response. He was wasting his time.

Decker turned and paced the cell, running scenarios through in his mind. Who would want him out of the way? Who would want to kidnap him? He had made more than a few enemies in his time on the NYPD. There were the people he had put behind bars, some of whom had powerful connections. Mob enforcers. The son of a senator who murdered his girlfriend in a fit of drunken rage. Even the CFO of a large corporation who hired a hitman to kill an accountant who uncovered discrepancies in the company's books. Then there was his ex-partner. A crooked cop who had tried to kill him once already. But this didn't feel like the sort of thing any of those people would do. And most of them were still behind bars. Sure, they might use accomplices on the outside, but he didn't think so. They would just put a bullet in his head, not abduct him and put him in a metal cell.

No, there was something deeper going on. He just couldn't figure out what. But he couldn't help wondering if it had something to do with the werewolf that had been terrorizing Wolf Haven. If not, it would be one hell of a coincidence, especially since the recent killings were so strange, with the beast going out of its way to be seen. To leave witnesses. And Decker didn't believe in coincidence.

He returned to the bed—the only piece of furniture in the room—and sat back down. The camera was still watching him. A red blinking light above the lens told Decker that it was relaying everything he did to whoever was behind this. Were they sitting on the other side of that cell door, mere feet away, or were they somewhere else entirely? They might even be on the other side of the world for all he knew, thanks to the wonders of modern technology.

It didn't take long to get an answer. No sooner had he sat back down, than he heard the sound of deadbolts retracting. Moments later, the door swung open.

A stocky man with a square jaw filled the doorway. He held a pistol with a silencer attached. Decker recognized him as the person who had distracted him moments before he was drugged.

"Mr. Decker," the man said. "I hope you're finding the accommodations to your liking?"

Decker ignored the question. "Who are you, and why am I here?"

"All in good time." The man stepped into the room.

"I'm not very patient. How about you tell me right now."

Another man appeared in the doorway, trailed by a woman carrying a brown leather doctor's bag. "What, and spoil the surprise?"

Decker stared in disbelief because he knew this man all too well. They had crossed paths several times, and it never ended well. He stood up, glared at the newcomer. "Thomas Barringer. I should have known you were behind this."

"I'm flattered, Mr. Decker." Barringer smiled. "You remember me."

"You're a hard man to forget." Decker had first crossed paths with Barringer deep on the ocean floor in a subaquatic habitat filled with scientists who were studying a sunken U-Boat. The man had almost killed them all, then escaped, albeit without the advanced technology he was there for. The next time he ran into Barringer was during an expedition to the Amazon and a mysterious pyramid of unknown design guarded by ferocious beasts from Egyptian and Greek myth. As before, there had been a confrontation and Decker was lucky to escape with his life. Now, he might not be so fortunate. He took a step forward. The goon waved the gun in warning, and he came to a halt. "What's going on here? Why did you abduct me?"

"It's simple Mr. Decker. We need you for what we have planned. In fact, you're the key to everything." Barringer motioned for the woman to enter the room.

She approached Decker, placed the bag on the bed, and opened it. "Please sit back down."

"No." Decker shook his head. He summed up his chances of overpowering her and finding a weapon in the bag before the goon shot him. Of escaping. Decided the odds weren't stacked in his favor. "I don't think so."

"Mr. Decker, don't make this harder than it needs to be. We'll use force if we have to, but I'd rather not."

Decker sat down. He looked up at Barringer. "What did you mean? That I'm the key to everything?"

"Exactly what I said. Now, we understand that you aren't likely to cooperate with us, and we wouldn't expect you to. That's where my friend here comes in. She'll make sure that we get exactly what we want." Barringer smiled and motioned for the woman. "Francesca. Whenever you're ready?"

The woman nodded and reached into her bag, then came out holding a long syringe. She closed the bag and turned to Decker. "Relax. This won't hurt a bit."

FORTY-TWO

DAISY AWOKE AT 6 AM, having gotten less than five hours of sleep. This was not unusual. In fact, for Daisy, it was the equivalent of sleeping in. Ever since she had stopped aging, her body required less of everything. Less sleep. Less food. Even less exercise. She rarely felt fatigued or stressed, at least to the extent of those around her. Her agility and strength, while not in the realm of superhuman, would certainly give even the most well-trained athlete a run for their money. It was like whatever supernatural power coursed through her veins had not only stopped her march toward old age but had also blessed her with unlimited stamina.

She rose and got dressed, then sat in the same chair by the window that she had occupied the previous night. A decent cup of coffee would be nice, but the only place in town to procure such an item was the restaurant she and Decker had eaten at the first night they were in town—the one that used to be Nancy's diner—and it would not be open yet.

She eyed the coffee maker sitting on a desk underneath the TV. Next to it was a basket containing pouches of coffee, single serve milk portions in small plastic containers, and a selection of sugar and sweeteners, along with two paper cups. She almost got up to make herself a cup, but soon rejected that idea. In over a hundred years, she had never tasted a decent hotel room brew, even in the years before most large hotels had a Starbucks or some other fancy coffee chain in the lobby to provide a better, and more expensive alternative. Better to wait and meet Decker at the diner before heading over to the sheriff's office to figure out how they were going to track the beast and bring its reign of terror to an end.

Speaking of which, the theory that had filled her mind the evening before was still front and center. After sleeping on it, she was even more sure that the killings were meant to lure Decker back to Wolf Haven. If the beast hadn't left anyone alive to report on what they saw, if it hadn't been clearly aware of the camera at the grocery store, then she could have put the slaughter down to the creature's animalistic urges. But despite the apparent random nature of the attacks, she was sure there was a method behind the madness.

She glanced at her phone, wondered if it was too early to call Decker. Decided that it was. Unlike her, Decker didn't perform well with only a few hours of sleep. She decided to give it a couple of hours, then ask him to meet her at what used to be Cassidy's Diner. She could run her idea by him then, over a steaming mug of joe.

In the meantime, there was nothing to do. She picked up her novel and opened it to a place halfway through the book, marked by an ornate silver bookmark that she had purchased in a London jewelry store many decades earlier. It was one of Daisy's favorite Margery Allingham novels. Death of a Ghost, an early installment in the Albert Campion series. But she had barely started to read when there was a knock at her bedroom door.

Daisy looked up, surprised. It was so early. Who would be calling on her at this time in the morning? Maybe it was the proprietor of the guesthouse and there was some sort of problem. Then a worse thought occurred to her. That it was either Chad or Decker, and there had been another killing. But if that were the case, why hadn't they just called? Her phone was fully charged and turned on, and she never used the *do not disturb* feature. She looked at the screen and confirmed that she had received no calls. Weird.

The knock came again, sharp and insistent.

Daisy put the book down and rose from the chair. There was only one way to find out who it was. She crossed to the door and went to open it, but then hesitated, overcome by a strange and powerful sense of foreboding.

She stood there for a second, her hand resting on the handle. "Who is it?"

"It's me. John. Let me in."

So much for the frisson of unease that had sent the hairs on the back of her neck standing up. She finally disengaged the bar lock, turned the handle, and let the door swing wide.

Decker was standing in the hallway, his face expressionless. He said nothing.

Daisy took a step back to let him in and waited until he had crossed the threshold and closed the door quietly behind him, before turning and heading back toward the chair, and her book. She placed the silver bookmark back between the pages and closed it, then turned to face Decker. "What are you doing here so early? Has something happ—"

The words caught in her throat when she saw the gun in his hand. A 9mm Glock pistol with a silencer attached. It was pointed directly at her.

The unease rushed back. Her heart was pounding against her rib cage.

Decker still hadn't spoken since stepping into the room.

Now Daisy found her voice again. "What the hell are you doing?"

Decker didn't respond, at least not verbally. Instead, he pulled the trigger several times in quick succession.

Phut. Phut. Phut.

Three tightly grouped chest shots at close range, the sound barely audible thanks to the suppressor screwed to the gun's barrel.

The bullets slammed into Daisy, causing her to stagger backwards. She stared at Decker in disbelief, even as the full realization of what he had done dawned upon her. She looked down, saw the bright crimson stain eating away at the white fabric of her shirt. Saw the three tiny holes in the garment where the bullets had passed through and entered her.

Daisy gasped. Her legs gave way, and she sank to the floor, even as Decker slipped the gun back under his jacket and turned away. The last thing Daisy saw, the final image that seared itself into her brain, was the man her mother trusted more than anyone else in the world open the bedroom door, step out, and close it behind him as if nothing untoward had happened. But not before hanging the DO NOT DISTURB sign on the outside handle so that no one would find her anytime soon.

FORTY-THREE

DECKER WALKED QUICKLY along the corridor and down the guesthouse stairs. The rest of the guests were asleep. No one had heard the three shots, and with the DO NOT DISTURB sign hanging on the door, Daisy's body wouldn't be discovered for many hours, perhaps even a whole day, which was good. It gave him time to do what came next without unnecessary interruption.

Decker pushed open the front door of the guesthouse and stepped out into the crisp early morning air. When he reached the sidewalk, he slipped the gun—with its silencer still attached —from beneath his jacket and tossed it into a nearby bush where it wouldn't easily be found. At least, not until someone was actually looking for it. Then he turned and made his way down Main Street, as if he didn't have a care in the world.

FORTY-FOUR

ED JOHNSON, owner of the County Line Saloon, was up a good two hours before his usual rising time any other day, thanks to his weekly delivery from the Tchoupitoulas Beer Company, which always came at the crack of dawn because he was the first stop on their route. He'd begged their distribution manager to schedule him for later in the morning, or perhaps even the early afternoon, on the grounds that he was rarely in bed before two in the morning since his bar was pretty much a one-man operation. But to no avail. The manager, a man with the ironic name of Edgar Barley, had merely pointed out that the proprietors of every pub and tavern on the delivery route went to bed late. It kind of went with the territory.

Which was how Ed found himself standing on the curb outside his bar at six-thirty in the morning, holding a mug of steaming coffee, and muttering under his breath while he waited for the truck that would replenish his stock for another week.

The delivery was nowhere in sight, but what Ed *did* see was a familiar face walking briskly down the sidewalk toward him from the direction of the Shady Pines Guesthouse. It was John Decker, Wolf Haven's previous sheriff, and probably the only man who could stop the series of vicious attacks that had spooked the entire town with their similarity to the events of a few years before. Events that had left a slew of corpses, including Beau Thornton, the town's mayor, and eventually cost Decker his job.

"Howdy, John," he said, as Decker drew near. "You're up early."

Decker said nothing. He merely stared at the bar owner as he closed the distance between them.

"You been paying a visit to that associate of yours, the cute young woman you came to town with?" A nasty thought entered Ed's head. He could understand why Decker would be walking toward the guesthouse, but it was real early for someone to be *leaving* it, unless—Ed didn't even want to entertain the idea—he'd been there all night. Which meant that he was cheating on Nancy, a woman he'd married less than a week before. At least if what Decker had told him two evenings before when he and Chad were in the bar was true.

Decker drew level. He stopped and observed Ed for a moment before speaking. "Just had some business to discuss."

"Right." Ed wasn't sure how to respond. "Like to do with the attacks?"

"Yes." Decker nodded. "The attacks."

Ed observed Decker with narrowed eyes. He didn't sound like himself. His voice was flat and unemotional, his responses curt. He couldn't think of anything worthwhile to say that would keep the conversation going and wasn't sure that Decker would respond with anything but a terse reply, anyway. In the end, he cleared his throat, and said, "Well, umm, it was good seeing you this morning, John."

Decker stared at him for a moment, then nodded before stepping around the bar owner and moving on.

Ed watched him continue down Main Street for a while longer before he stopped at a car parked at the curb. After Decker climbed in and drove off, Ed went back inside to pour himself another coffee. He couldn't help wondering why the usually affable ex-sheriff was acting so strangely. But he didn't have long to ponder upon it, because no sooner had he refilled his mug than he heard the blare of a horn from out on the road. The delivery truck had arrived. Putting the odd conversation with Decker out of his mind, Ed went back outside to meet the delivery and get his day started.

FORTY-FIVE

DAISY'S EYES SNAPPED OPEN. She sucked in a huge mouthful of air, filling her lungs. Pain blanketed her chest. It felt like she'd walked in front of a speeding train. Another dull ache pulsed up her spine thanks to the hard surface she was lying on. When she turned her head, she discovered she was lying on the floor of the guesthouse bedroom, although how she'd ended up there was a mystery. The last thing she remembered was answering the door to Decker.

She sat up and took stock of her surroundings. A thin sliver of sunlight inched past the mostly closed curtains and splashed across the floor toward her. She was alone in the room. An alarm clock on the nightstand next to the bed told her it was almost one-thirty in the afternoon. She had spent the last seven hours sprawled on the floor in a deathly torpor.

Looking down, she realized her injuries were not the result of a speeding train, but a trio of bullets. She could see the holes where they had punched through her shirt and slammed into her chest. Her clothes were drenched with blood, but when she lifted her hand to the spot where the bullets had entered, unbuttoned the shirt and pulled it aside, she found nothing but smooth unbroken skin, albeit more than a little bruised.

This was another gift she had inherited from her mother and Abraham Turner. Practical invincibility and super-fast healing. When she looked down, Daisy saw the three flattened and distorted slugs lying on the rough wood planks of the guesthouse floor. They hadn't passed all the way through her— that much was obvious by their location—but during the time she was technically dead, her body had rejected them, pushed them back out, before it started repairing the immense damage they had caused to her chest.

Daisy picked up one of the slugs and turned it over in her palm. And at that moment, the memories came rushing back. John Decker standing in the doorway, gun raised. Three quick close-range shots that would have been deadly to any other person. She dropped the slug like it was scalding hot. What the hell? Decker had tried to kill her, a feat that he should have known was all but impossible, given her unusual affliction.

She climbed to her feet, removed the bloodied shirt and threw it on the floor, overcome by a sudden fit of uncharacteristic rage. She had been shot before, stabbed, pushed in front of a fast-moving tram in Edwardian London, and during one particularly ferocious fight with a supernatural creature in Lisbon, she was even impaled not once, but twice by a bayonet. None of these normally deadly attacks had resulted in her demise. And none of them had been delivered via the hands of a trusted friend. Even worse, she could think of no earthly reason that Decker, or anyone else, would want to kill her right here and right now. They were investigating a spate of werewolf attacks, after all. Not the kind of mission that normally got you shot in the chest.

Daisy clenched and unclenched her fists, exhaled and counted to ten several times until the anger had diminished to nothing but a faint background noise. But one thing didn't change. She wanted answers, and she wanted them fast. First, though, she had to clean herself up. She reached for the clasp of her bra, undid it, and dropped the bloodstained underwear onto the floor next to the ruined shirt. Then she finished undressing and ran a shower, which she stood under for a long time, letting the steamy, piping hot water soothe her aches and pains. And she thought of Decker. Let the memory of his attack loop through her mind. But no matter how many times she replayed his betrayal, she could not find a single clue regarding his motive. Eventually, she gave up and stepped out of the shower, dried herself, and put on fresh clothes.

Her phone was still sitting where she left it next to the book she had been reading. She picked it up, almost dialed her mother back at CUSP's headquarters in Maine. But at the last moment, with her finger hovering over the call button, she changed her mind. Despite the evidence to the contrary, she did not believe that Decker would ever try to kill her. This was the man who had rescued her mother from a lifetime of drudgery and manual labor in the fisheries of Shackleton, Alaska. The same man who had followed Mina onto the Titanic and almost lost his life, protecting her from a powerful and ancient vampiric creature on a doomed ocean liner. But the memory Daisy found hardest to reconcile with the murderous and coldhearted man who had put a trio of bullets in her chest was a chess game over a century before, in December 1911. Before she knew he had traveled back in time, before she discovered her own impossible longevity, he had played chess with an innocent teenager who had no idea of the dangerous and strange future that lay in store. He had been kind. Treated her like an equal. In the years and decades that followed, she had listened to her mother talk about Decker like he was the one uncorruptible person left on the planet. A modern-day picture of chivalry. She had raised him up to an almost mythical status. And Daisy trusted her mother's intuition.

No, whatever was going on, she was sure of one thing. John Decker would *never* willingly harm her. Which was why she had no intention of alerting CUSP, or anyone else, to the situation. Not yet. Not until she understood how and why he had been standing at her door with a loaded weapon like some sort of Manchurian candidate. She would figure this out on her own. Rescue him from whatever trouble he was in. But to do that, she needed to find him. The only problem was, she doubted he would make it easy.

FORTY-SIX

THE FIRST PLACE Daisy went to search for Decker was the old family home that he still owned. As she had expected, he wasn't there. Neither was the rental car. The house was locked up and dark. After that, she made her way to the restaurant that had previously been Cassidy's Diner, but again, there was no sign of him. Which made sense. You didn't try to murder someone, then go get yourself a nice bowl of gumbo and wait for the repercussions. There was only one other place she could think of to look, the sheriff's office, although she couldn't imagine that he would be there, for similar reasons.

And she was right.

When Daisy entered, Chad looked up from his desk with a scowl. "Where the hell have you been all day? Did you forget that we have a werewolf to catch?"

"Didn't forget," she replied, lifting the counter hatch and stepping into the back part of the office. She looked around. "Where's Carol?"

"Picking up a couple of calzones from Sammie's for lunch. Personally, I'd just have them deliver, but she likes the exercise." Chad looked past Daisy, toward the open door. "Speaking of which, where's John?"

"Following up on a lead," Daisy lied.

"Well, it had better be a good one since the two of you left me to handle the situation on my own. Which reminds me, you never said where you've been all day until now. Following another lead?"

"Not quite. I got unexpectedly… waylaid. Not a big deal. I'm here now." She glanced back toward the door. How was she going to find Decker now that she had exhausted the only locations she could think of to look for him? And how was she going to keep Sheriff Hardwick in the dark about her efforts? Eventually, he was going to realize that Decker wasn't just off chasing some hunch but was missing. That would lead to some uncomfortable questions, and she was hardly about to tell the sheriff that her partner had tried to murder her. Then an even worse thought occurred to her. What if she wasn't Decker's only intended victim? What if he came after Chad, or even Carol next? What if he tried to kill both of them? It seemed unlikely, but then again, she had no idea what state of mind he was in or what his motives were. She had to find him before he did something there was no going back from.

The question was, how?

And then an idea occurred to her. She glanced toward Chad's desk, saw his keys, including the key to the evidence room, sitting there next to his laptop, before her gaze slipped past the sheriff to a door at the back of the building marked RECORDS STORAGE. Her idea was risky, but it just might work. She would have to distract the sheriff long enough to get into that evidence room if she had any hope of putting her newly minted plan into action.

After a moment's thought, she said, "Sheriff, I don't suppose that you have the original police reports and crime scene photos from the Annie Doucet incident?"

She held her breath. If the Wolf Haven Sheriff's Department kept a digital database of their records, then all was lost. She would need to figure out another way to get into that evidence room. For good measure, she made another request that she thought was less likely to have been digitized. "I'd also like to see the police reports on Lily Decker's death."

"John's mother, why?" Chad narrowed his eyes. "That was so long ago. You think there's a connection to what's going on now?"

"I think there's at least a possibility," Daisy said quickly. She could feel the time ticking away. If Carol returned with those calzones before she managed to distract Chad, it would make things exponentially harder. "I know it might take a while to find them, but I think it's important."

Chad shrugged. "No problem. I'll get Carol on it when she gets back. After we've had lunch, of course."

Damn. She should have expected the sheriff to say that. "I'd rather not waste the time. Every second counts. Lives may depend upon it."

"Really?"

"Really." Daisy nodded vigorously.

Chad didn't look happy. He glanced toward the records storage room. "I suppose I could go take a look. But I'm not missing my lunch. If I can't find what you need before Carol comes back, then it will have to wait. I need to eat regularly, or I can't think straight."

"I appreciate it, sheriff." Daisy breathed a sigh of relief. They clearly hadn't digitized any of their records. Paper all the way. Not surprising given the size of the department. They didn't even have a deputy anymore, which she assumed was down to a lack of budget, so what chance was there that they had shelled out for an expensive database? "It just might be the break we need to stop the beast before it strikes again."

"Yeah. I hope you're right." Chad rose to his feet with a grunt and started toward records storage. "Someone better come get me when Carol gets back. I'm starving."

"I'll make it my priority," Daisy said.

She waited for Chad to disappear into the records room, then hurried to his desk and scooped up his keys. Thankfully, they didn't keep records storage locked, or Chad would have taken the keys with him, and her plan would have been for naught. She had gotten lucky.

Casting a quick glance toward the front door and the street beyond to make sure that Carol was still nowhere in sight, Daisy hurried to the evidence room. She flipped through Chad's keys, searching for one that looked like it would fit the lock. Her first attempt was a failure. The key wouldn't turn. She tried a second key with the same results. On the third attempt, she was successful. The door opened.

She stepped inside and flicked the light on, then made a beeline for the shelf holding the evidence box containing Annie Doucet's spell book. Thankfully, she remembered the location from the last time she was here, after Ben Donelson had snuck back in to return it.

She pulled the box down from the shelf and set it on the floor, then took the lid off and lifted the spell book out. It only took her a few seconds to find the page with the wolf incantation. The one that would turn whoever recited it into the loup-garou. That was the part of the plan she wasn't looking forward to. The only way that she was going to locate Decker quickly was to track him, and the best way to do that was to become the wolf. Its heightened senses would lead her directly to him. It was a crazy plan, but it was all she had. Slipping her phone out, she photographed the page, then closed the spell book and returned it to the box, put the lid back on, and set it back on the shelf.

She checked the photograph to make sure the incantation and the list of ingredients required to make the wolf potion were readable. Then, satisfied, she raced back to the door and peeked out to make sure the coast was clear before slipping into the office again and locking it behind her.

There was only one thing left to do. Return the keys to Chad's desk. Thankfully, he was still in the records room. She could hear him rummaging around and muttering under his breath. He wouldn't be happy when he came out and discovered that she was gone, but there was nothing she could do about that.

Daisy hurried across the office with the keys clutched in her hand. She was about to set them down on the desk when a stern voice spoke to her rear.

"What are you doing with those keys?"

Daisy whirled around, wide eyed. Carol had returned and caught her red-handed.

FORTY-SEVEN

DAISY'S HEART FELL. Had Carol seen her coming out of the evidence room? She froze, caught in a rare moment of uncertainty. Then she said the only thing that came to mind. "Um… the keys fell onto the floor. I was picking them back up."

Carol observed her for a moment with dispassionate eyes, then she nodded. "Thanks. Where's Chad?"

"Records room," Daisy put the keys back on the desk, then glanced toward the back of the building. "He's pulling the Annie Doucet files."

"Really? Why?" Carol stepped past the counter and went to her chair. She placed the two calzones on the counter. "You think there's a connection between those killings and the current ones?"

"I don't know, maybe. We thought it was worth checking out." Daisy made a move toward the front door. Chad might be back at any moment, and she didn't want to end up actually having to look through all the records she had requested. That would take a long time and she desperately wanted to find Decker before he did something that they couldn't walk back. "I'll be back, going to get some lunch. I'm starving."

Carol pulled one of the calzones toward her and unwrapped it. "Word of advice. Don't bother with the Chinese restaurant. It's really not that good."

"Thanks. I'll remember that," Daisy said, hurrying toward the door and stepping outside. The phone was heavy in her pocket, a reminder of her deceit. But it didn't matter. She had what she needed. The incantation. Or at least, she had *part* of what she needed, because there was still the small matter of the potion she would need to drink in order to transform into the wolf, and the ingredients required to make it.

Those would not be so easy to find, and she didn't particularly relish the idea of spending hours trudging through an alligator infested swamp to find the slimy carcasses of toads and a bunch of obscure mushrooms. But she had no choice if she wanted to find Decker quickly. Or did she? Because a thought had occurred to her. Ben Donelson. He must already have gathered the ingredients needed to make the potion, because he had turned into the wolf on more than one occasion. Maybe those ingredients were still hidden somewhere in his bedroom.

It was a longshot, but if she was lucky, there would be no need to go anywhere near the swamp. Getting into the teenager's bedroom and searching for the potion ingredients without getting caught wouldn't be easy. Ben was under the close supervision of his mother, for obvious reasons. Sure, she could walk right up to the front door and try to convince Keira Donelson that Daisy was there on official business and that the sheriff had approved a search of Ben's room, but it would only take one phone call for her story to crumble like chalk. And since Keira and Chad had been an item until the sheriff had arrested her son, the odds of Keira protesting what she was sure to view as another slight against her family was high.

Which left only one option.

Daisy would have to break into the house, possibly with Ben and his mother inside, to conduct her search. It was an even bigger risk than distracting the sheriff and using his keys to gain access to the evidence room, but she saw no alternative. With her mind made up, Daisy pushed her hands into her pockets and set off at a brisk pace toward Ben Donelson's home.

FORTY-EIGHT

DAISY WALKED past Ben Donelson's house at a slow pace, observing it from the corner of her eye. To anyone who observed the young woman walking down the sidewalk, it would appear that she was out for an afternoon stroll, and not surreptitiously surveilling the property to see if anyone was home.

Which they were.

Keira's car was parked in the driveway. Daisy could see the TV—mounted in the living room above the fireplace—through the front window. It was turned on, with what looked like an action movie flickering on the screen.

This was unfortunate. She had hoped that the house would be empty. That Keira and her son might have gone out shopping or left the house on some other errand.

She considered her options. It would be easier to come back later, under the cover of darkness, but time was not on her side. She had already rejected walking straight up to the front door and bluffing her way in. Telling Keira that she was there representing Sheriff Hardwick. Even if she didn't get caught outright in her lie, it would surely get back to the sheriff at some point and she didn't want him asking questions she was unwilling to answer. That left the riskiest option. Finding a way into the house in broad daylight, locating the stash of ingredients that Ben had been using to transform himself into the wolf—assuming any of them remained—and exiting again. All without being seen.

Daisy thought back to the last time she had visited this house, when they had been looking for Ben. He hadn't been there, having climbed out of his bedroom window to evade them, but the brief visit had provided her with valuable information. Ben's bedroom was on the ground floor on the left-hand side of the house at the back. The living room, where the action movie was playing, was at the front on the right. If she was lucky, Ben was watching that movie. And she suspected he was, because it looked exactly like the sort of flick that a bored teenage boy who wasn't allowed to leave the house would put on. If luck was really on her side, Keira would be watching it right alongside him, but Daisy couldn't count on that.

Daisy continued down the street until she reached an intersection, then turned and strolled casually up the road. Approaching the house from the front would leave her too exposed. All it would take was a neighbor to look through their window or step outside and she would be seen immediately. And worse, Keira had one of those video doorbells that would activate and start recording the moment it sensed motion. She would have to find a less obvious way onto the property.

And she found it a little way down the side street.

There was a two-story condo building up ahead on her right with parking at the rear. And behind that was a patch of undeveloped woodland that backed up directly to the houses on Keira's street.

It was perfect.

Daisy stepped off the sidewalk and hurried past the condos and through the parking lot. The woodland was dense and overgrown. It was also full of trash, mostly crushed beer cans that had probably been left there by local teens looking for a place to drink. She wondered if Ben had been back here, hanging with his buddies and getting drunk. Maybe that was where the idea to steal the spell book had come from. She could imagine Ben's friends goading him into taking Chad's keys when the sheriff spent the night with Keira. Urging him to break into the sheriff's office and the evidence room. Maybe Ben wasn't even looking for Annie Doucet's old spell book, because there would surely be other, more obvious items in that evidence room. Like illegal moonshine and pot. The kind of things that would really get the party started. Had he stumbled across the spell book by accident?

It didn't matter.

Daisy pushed the wandering thoughts to the back of her mind and focused on the task at hand. She was on the other side of the woods now, facing a six-foot wooden fence. If her calculations were correct, then Ben's house was on the other side. She glanced around to make sure she wasn't being observed, even though it was unlikely there would be anyone out in this small plot of overgrown woods right now other than her, then reached up and gripped the fence, heaving herself up and over the top.

She dropped down on the other side with catlike stealth and hurried across the small backyard, which had probably been grass years ago but was now nothing but weeds and dirt. A child's bicycle that had lost most of its paint lay near the house, chain rusty and tires deflated. A sad end to what must once have been a cherished childhood toy.

Daisy let her gaze stray to the bicycle for a moment, then she moved on past it to the side of the building, and the window that she surmised must be Ben's bedroom. It was closed. She flattened herself against the wall and peeked around the window frame. It was Ben's room, all right. She recognized it from her previous visit. The curtains were open. There was no light on inside the room. The door stood ajar. It appeared to be empty.

So far, so good. Now to find out if luck was really on her side.

Daisy stepped away from the wall and pushed her fingers under the sash. When she lifted, the lower windowpane slid up.

Success.

Daisy pushed it all the way up and climbed through the gap, then lowered herself down into the room. She was in. Now all that remained was to find Ben's stash of the ingredients he'd used to make the potion that had turned him into the loup-garou and get the hell back out of there before she got caught.

FORTY-NINE

DAISY TOOK a moment to study her surroundings. Ben's bed was unmade, the sheets pushed back and crumpled, and the pillow crushed into the shape of a head. His nightstand was littered with the kind of objects a teenage boy coveted. A handheld portable game system, a comic book with creased pages, and a half-eaten chocolate bar. A shelf above the bed was crowned with action figures from popular superhero and sci-fi movies.

Daisy smiled despite herself.

Ben was a nerd.

She tore her gaze away from the shelf and examined the rest of the room. There were only a few places where he could hide a stash of spell book potion ingredients. She got down on her knees and checked quickly under the bed, but there was nothing but a couple of odd socks and a pair of dirty sneakers. She turned to the dresser, opened each drawer one by one and rummaged through the contents. Nothing but tee shirts, shorts, and underwear. That left only one place to look. The closet.

Daisy crossed to the other side of the room and slid the doors open. She was greeted by shirts and polos on hangers. On the floor beneath the hanging garments were several sneaker boxes, a basketball, and a pile of shoes. She pushed the clothes aside, then kneeled down and went through each of the shoeboxes in turn. As before, she found nothing except the usual junk that a teenage boy might keep around. Frustrated, Daisy put the boxes back as they were and stood up. This had been a waste of time. Either Ben had hidden the ingredients required to make the potion somewhere else, or he had gotten rid of them after being hauled down to the Sheriff's office and questioned. Either way, it amounted to the same thing. Daisy wasn't going to find what she needed here, and with no idea where else Ben might have stashed the ingredients, she would have to venture out into the swamp and collect them all over again. Something that would waste valuable time if she wanted to track Decker and figure out what was going on before he tried to kill someone else and ended up with both the police and CUSP looking for him.

Deflated, she went to close the closet doors, intending to sneak back out the same way that she had gotten in. But then, from the corridor outside the bedroom, she heard voices. And they were close.

Ben and his mother were on their way to the bedroom.

Daisy glanced at the door, weighing her options. She only had a couple of seconds to make up her mind before that door swung open and she was caught. She could make it to the window, but could she climb out in time? Questionable. And to be caught breaking into Ben's room when she hadn't even gotten anything out of it? That was too much. There was only one other option.

The closet.

Now that she had made her mind up, Daisy swung into action, pulling the closet doors open again. Kicking the pile of shoes to one side, she stepped inside and closed the doors. Just in the nick of time.

The bedroom door opened, and Ben walked in with his mother behind him.

Daisy shrank back in the closet, letting the clothes on their hangers embrace her. She watched through the slats of the closet door as Ben argued with his mother about dirty laundry, his voice full of anger at being pulled away from the movie he was watching, although Daisy suspected that his real ire was in being confined to the house.

He stomped across the room, coming dangerously close to the closet. Daisy pressed herself even further back, expecting him to fling the closet doors wide open at any moment and see her. Instead, he walked past the closet and stooped to pick up a pile of discarded clothes lying on the floor in a heap near the dresser.

With the clothes in his arms, he turned to his mother. "There! You satisfied now?"

Apparently Kiera Donelson was satisfied, because she merely nodded and said, "Laundry room. Now!"

Ben stomped past her back into the corridor, ignoring a single sock that fell from his arms and onto the floor.

Kiera watched him go, then stepped back out of the room, pulling the door closed behind her.

Daisy let out a long sigh of relief. That was too close. She pushed the clothes aside, happy to catch a breath of air that didn't smell like teenage sweat, and went to slide the closet doors back open to make her escape. But as she did so, the heel of her foot banged into the wall at the back of the closet.

And to her surprise, an entire section moved and fell to the side.

Daisy looked down. Where she had previously seen only smooth, white painted drywall, there was now a dark, square opening. And next to it, leaning against the shoeboxes, was a piece of the wall, its edges neatly cut.

She stepped out of the closet and dropped to her knees, peered at the opening. And then she realized what it was.

A hidden compartment between the wall joists.

Ben must have made it to hide items he didn't want his mother to find. Sneaky kid.

Daisy paused a moment and listened. She could hear Ben and his mother talking, their tone still argumentative. They didn't sound far away. If she lingered too much longer, they might return.

She took out her phone and turned on the flashlight, shining it into the compartment. She saw a couple of joints and a lighter. A bottle of beer. A couple of pornographic magazines. And something else. A Tupperware container wedged sideways in the small space. Daisy reached into the closet and pulled it out, then took the lid off. Inside was a collection of herbs and leaves, some dried mushrooms, and the desiccated skin of a dead frog. There were other items, too. Items that she recognized from the ingredient list required to make the potion.

This was what she had come for.

Daisy put the lid back on the container and quickly repositioned the piece of drywall so that it covered the hidden compartment again. Then she rearranged the clothes, pulling them across so that Ben wouldn't notice that anyone had been there, and closed the closet door. That done, Daisy scooped up the container and sprinted for the window. A couple of minutes later, she was walking back through the woods. Now all she needed was somewhere private to make the potion and transform herself into the loup-garou.

FIFTY

THERE WAS ONLY one place Daisy could think of to go. Decker's house. She'd already checked earlier that day and he wasn't there, which meant that she could perform the ritual to turn into the loup-garou in private. There was another reason, too. The wolf would need Decker's scent in order to track him, which meant she would need an article of his clothing or some other item that he had recently interacted with.

It was getting dark. The western sky was ablaze with fiery tinges of red and yellow. Decker had a good ten-hour head start, and with the hire car, he could be hundreds of miles away by now. If that was the case, not even the wolf would be able to catch him. Daisy would have no choice but to place a call to her mother and Adam Hunt. Tell them what Decker had done and let CUSP handle it from there. She only hoped that he hadn't committed any other crimes in the meantime. A rare moment of self-doubt overcame Daisy. Maybe she had made a mistake by trying to handle the situation herself. Catch up with Decker and find out what was going on. Save him from himself. But it was too late to second-guess her choices now. She could only hope that he was still close by.

Daisy exited the woods behind Ben Donelson's house and

made her way toward Decker's house. She avoided Main Street, taking a longer route on back streets that she was not familiar with because she didn't want to run into Carol or the sheriff, who surely ask awkward questions that she wasn't prepared to answer. Thankfully, the GPS on her phone managed to lead her there in short order.

When she reached the house, Daisy ignored the front porch and hurried down the side of the building to the back. If the houses belonged to anyone else, Daisy would have searched for a spare key hidden under the front doormat or beneath a plant pot. But she knew that Decker would not do such a thing. He was too security conscious. Before a few days ago, he hadn't been back to the house in a couple of years and wouldn't leave a key lying around that long to be discovered by a person with nefarious intent. In all likelihood, he paid someone in town, maybe even Carol, to keep an eye on the place. But if so, he hadn't mentioned anything about it.

Which meant that Daisy would have to break in—an activity she was becoming too comfortable with—if she wanted an article of clothing to give the loup-garou his scent.

The backyard was not fenced, which would make Daisy's task harder, but at least there weren't any houses that directly overlooked it. She hurried up onto the back deck and tried the rear door, but it was locked, just as she expected. That left her with only one option. Daisy slipped her jacket off and wrapped it around her arm, then drew her elbow back and rammed it into one of the door's glass panels. The panel cracked but did not shatter. A second blow finished the job, and she could reach inside and disengage the deadbolt. Moments later, Daisy was inside.

She went straight to the bedroom and found a wrinkled polo shirt draped over a chair near the bed. She recognized it as the one he had been wearing the day they flew down from Maine. He clearly hadn't washed it yet, which meant that his scent would be embedded in the fibers. She snatched it up and hurried back through the house to the kitchen, then set about making the potion using the ingredients she had found in Ben Donelson's bedroom and the instructions from the spell book page she had photographed with her phone.

Forty-five minutes later, after boiling the concoction in a pot on the stove, Daisy was ready for the last step of the process. Transforming into the wolf.

Butterflies swarmed in her stomach. She had never done anything like this before. Daisy stood for a while, staring at the still warm potion and wondering if she really wanted to do this. After all, she had no idea if the loup-garou would retain enough of her personality and memories to carry out the task she needed it to. For all Daisy knew, she would turn into a slathering, bloodthirsty beast without the self-control to stay focused on finding Decker. But Annie had followed her agenda, murderous as it was, back when she had transformed into the wolf, and Ben had run free in the woods as the beast without killing anyone. At least, according to the latest evidence.

It's going to be alright, she told herself. *Nothing to worry about.* But even so, Daisy's heart pounded in her chest as she transferred the potion to a drinking glass. It smelled awful, and she resisted the urge to gag. It could only taste worse. But Daisy had come this far and had no intention of backing out now.

She picked up the glass, Decker's shirt, and her phone, then stepped back out onto the deck. She dropped the shirt, then placed the glass and phone on an outdoor table. Now came the bit Daisy was least looking forward to. Becoming the wolf. With a deep, calming breath, she started to undress, because unlike in the movies, her clothes would not magically transform along with her. A few moments later, she was standing naked and exposed to the cool evening breeze. She picked up the glass, and the concoction contained within, hesitated a moment, then tipped her head back and drank it as quickly as she could.

Her suspicion was correct. The potion tasted even worse than it smelled. It was all she could do not to vomit the disgusting, slimy liquid back up. Her stomach roiled. Daisy leaned over, pressed her lips closed, and waited.

When the worst of the nausea had passed and she trusted herself, Daisy turned her attention to her phone and recited the incantation.

For a moment, nothing happened. The breeze whipped around her, raising goosebumps on Daisy's pale flesh. She wondered if she had done something wrong, maybe missed an ingredient when she was preparing the potion, or even skipped a word when she was saying the incantation. But then, even as she was considering going back into the kitchen and brewing another batch of the awful liquid, a faint tingling, not unlike pins and needles, pulsed deep within her.

At first, Daisy wondered if it was just her body reacting to the vile potion, but soon the sensation flared into a burning agony that enveloped her whole body. She cried out, dropped to her knees.

Her limbs twisted back upon themselves. Bones cracked.

Daisy screamed. It was like nothing she had ever experienced before.

A brief thought flickered through her mind. Why would Ben have wanted to put himself through this? It was torture. Then the thought faded, along with the pain, and the animal took over.

Daisy, or rather the creature she had become, lifted itself up and padded over to Decker's polo shirt, sniffed it for a long moment, then turned and raced off into the growing darkness.

FIFTY-ONE

THE LOUP-GAROU BOUNDED through the night. At
first, Decker's scent had been strong, but had soon faded to
barely perceptible snatches that would have been imperceptible
to most other animals. But not to this creature. Its sense of smell
was preternaturally heightened, as were its other senses. If any
creature could find John Decker, it was the loup-garou. And
right now, it was close.

It had followed the scent for several miles, first through the
center of town—which required it to exercise extra caution to
avoid being seen—and then out into the wilderness beyond.
Now it was approaching a remote property surrounded by
chain-link fence and barbed wire. The beast leaped the fence
easily, clearing the razor-sharp coils of wire running along the
top with a foot to spare, then dropped on the other side and
approached a large, dilapidated building.

"Stop right there." A voice echoed in the darkness.

Moments later, a man wearing camo and carrying a rifle
appeared from inside the building.

The beast didn't stop. It surged forward out of the darkness,
heading directly for the lone figure.

The man stared in horror, took a step back as he caught his

first clear glimpse of the intruder. Then, shaking off his terror, he raised the gun and fired.

The loup-garou weaved to avoid the shot, and it whistled harmlessly into the night.

The man fired again, his second shot going just as wide as the first.

From somewhere inside the building, shouts went up. More men responding to the gunfire. But the guard wasn't waiting around for reinforcements. He had seen enough. He turned, tried to run.

But the beast was too close now. It leaped and slammed into his back, throwing him to the ground. Then its jaws found his throat and snapped closed, silencing his scream before it even began.

FIFTY-TWO

DECKER PACED HIS CELL. He had seen no one since the mysterious woman had inserted a syringe into the base of his neck at Barringer's instruction and withdrew a clear liquid that she called cerebrospinal fluid, which she deposited into a small vial. His only human contact since then was a brief visit by someone who had pushed a tray of food through the slot at the bottom of his cell door several hours before. When he had called out to them, asked them what was going on, he received no answer.

Now, his mind was on Barringer. The man hadn't been forthcoming regarding his plans, except to say that Decker was instrumental in whatever he was plotting. Which meant that he knew Decker would be in Wolf Haven, otherwise he wouldn't have had operatives already in place to abduct him. That raised two possibilities. Either there was a mole in CUSP who had informed Barringer of Decker's movements, or Barringer had lured Decker there.

The mole theory, while plausible, felt wrong. For a start, Decker had quit CUSP after returning from 1912. He had only gone back because of the visions shown to him by the ghosts in the house on Boston Common. Within twenty-four hours of rejoining the organization, he was on a jet heading to Louisiana. It was unlikely that any traitor within the organization could have even found out about Decker's change of heart so quickly, since the only people who knew were Adam Hunt, Mina, and Daisy. He was sure that none of them had betrayed him. That left only one other possibility, and it made a whole lot more sense.

The werewolf.

There was one aspect of the creature's behavior that Decker still could not understand. It had killed three of the teenagers out at Annie Doucet's cabin but left the forth alive as an eyewitness. It also made sure to be recorded on camera when it killed the grocery store manager. If the reason for the attacks was to convince Chad that the loup-garou had returned, and prompt him to call Decker for help, then the beast's obsession with being seen suddenly made sense.

It also explained the attack at the Bayou Brook Campground, because they had mistakenly focused their attention on Ben Donelson and assumed him to be the killer. Sure, he had stolen the spell book and started messing around with it, transformed himself into the loup-garou for kicks, but he wasn't responsible for those attacks. It was merely coincidence. Which meant that Barringer had to orchestrate a third attack, and divert attention back away from Ben, to make sure Decker didn't leave town before he could put his plan into action. Of course, that still left one lingering question. Where the hell did Barringer find a real-life werewolf to carry out his bidding, and how was he controlling it? Decker wasn't going to get the answer to that, or discover Barringer's intent, sitting in this cell.

The problem was, he saw no way to escape.

Decker crossed to the bed and sat down. The tray, food still untouched, was sitting on the floor near the slot in the door. He had figured someone would come back to collect it at some point, providing another opportunity to get more information, but no one had. He wondered how much time had passed since Barringer left him alone. It felt like an eternity, but might only be hours. He leaned back on the bed, pulled his legs up, and closed his eyes.

It was at that moment that he heard the first scream, shrill and panicked, followed by three rapid-fire gunshots.

Decker swung his legs back off the bed and stood up, the hairs on the back of his neck prickling.

Two more gunshots and another scream. This one swiftly cut off.

There was a moment of silence before a third terrified wail, closer this time, reverberated through the walls of his cell.

What the hell was happening out there? It sounded like a massacre.

Decker took a step toward the door, intending to kneel down and peer through the narrow slot at the bottom. But then he stopped, overcome by a sudden, inexplicable sense of foreboding.

The screams had stopped now. A deathly quiet had descended.

Decker didn't move, hardly dared to breathe. He didn't know why, but he had the strangest feeling that someone, or something, was standing on the other side of the cell door, listening for any sound, just like he was.

Decker pressed his lips together, swallowed. His mouth was dry. Butterflies swarmed in his stomach.

Then he heard it. A faint sound, like fingernails dragging down the other side of the metal door. No, not fingernails. Claws!

Decker took an instinctive step backward, just as something slammed into the door, shaking it in its frame.

The door rattled again, harder this time, and buckled inward.

Something was trying to get into the cell.

Decker looked around for a weapon, even though he knew it was pointless. The bed was screwed to the floor, which left only the plastic toilet bucket. If men with guns hadn't been able to stop whatever was on the other side of his cell door, a plastic bucket wasn't going to do much except annoy it.

The door shook again, giving out a metallic groan under the unrelenting assault. The doorframe buckled with a loud crack.

Decker took another step back.

Another shuddering blow.

This time, the door couldn't hold on. It flew out of its frame and into the cell, barely missing Decker before hitting the back wall and toppling to the ground.

And standing there, filling the open space it had left behind, was the loup-garou.

The breath caught in Decker's throat.

The beast locked eyes with him.

Then it leaped forward, slamming Decker in the chest and sending him tumbling to the ground. Then it dropped its head and went for the kill.

FIFTY-THREE

THE CREATURE SAT ASTRIDE DECKER, front paws crushing his rib cage and making it hard to breathe. He twisted sideways, fighting against the beast's weight bearing down on his chest, and narrowly avoided its snapping jaws.

He raised his arms and batted away a second assault. Sharp teeth grazed his skin, drawing blood. He couldn't keep this up for much longer. He had been lucky so far, but he was also losing strength. A flash of the vision shown to him by the last of the three ghosts in the house on Boston Common flitted through his mind. The one where the loup-garou ripped his throat out and killed him. With a shudder of horror, he realized it was actually happening. Any moment now, the beast would finish him with one last, vicious bite to the neck. It was inevitable, because he had failed to change the things he did wrong and alter his destiny. He had been on a collision course with this moment in time ever since he stepped into that house on Boston Common.

He was going to die, leaving Nancy a widow, and there wasn't a damn thing he could do about it.

Or was there?

Because a dainty silver chain hung around the creature's sinewy, thick neck. A chain upon which hung a small pendant that Decker recognized. A snake coiled around a pyramid. The symbol of CUSP. And in that moment, he knew.

"Daisy?"

The beast hesitated, stared down at him.

"Daisy. It's me, John. You don't want to do this."

For a moment, the beast didn't move, then it slowly retreated, releasing him, and reared up on its hind-legs, breathing heavily.

No longer pinned by the creature's weight, Decker scrambled backwards and climbed slowly to his feet. His lungs were burning, and his chest ached, but he was alive. At least, for now.

"Please, Daisy. I'm not your enemy." Decker summed up his chances of dodging the creature and getting to the door, but decided he'd never make it. And even if he did, the creature would chase him down before he'd gone even ten feet. Instead, he took a step forward, hands in the air. "You don't want to kill me. We're friends."

The creature lowered its head and watched him with burning yellow eyes.

Decker couldn't tell if his words were having the desired effect, but there was one more thing he could try. "The Christmas party in 1911. Remember how we played chess? How you delighted in beating me over and over. You were kind. Gentle. Full of joy. That's the person you are, not this murderous beast. I know you're in there somewhere, Daisy. Think back and remember."

The loup-garou didn't move. It just stood there, observing him. A minute passed, then another. Decker wasn't sure what was going on. He braced for the worst. For the creature to lunge at him a second time and finish the job. But it didn't. Instead, the loup-garou dropped onto all fours, turned, and padded out of the cell.

Decker didn't dare to move. For all he knew, the creature was out there, waiting for him. But he needn't have worried. After a couple of minutes, a familiar figure stepped back into the room, wearing a set of camos too big for her slight frame.

It was Daisy.

"You shot me," she said, glaring at him. "Three times in the chest. It hurt like hell."

"That wasn't me." Decker shook his head. "I've been locked up in this cell since I dropped you off at the guesthouse. They were waiting when I went home. Drugged and abducted me. Then I woke up here."

"No, you're lying. I know what I saw. You came to my door early this morning. You had a gun with a silencer attached, and you tried to kill me."

"I swear, that *was not* me." Decker wasn't sure what was going on. How could he have tried to kill Daisy—an almost impossible feat given her abilities—when he'd been locked up alone in a cell since his abduction? Unless… "Thomas Barringer is behind this. He's the one responsible for the recent killings in Wolf Haven. He must have a pet werewolf that he was using to lure me here. Not long after I woke up, he came to the cell. There was a woman with him. She drew fluid from the back of my neck, my spine, with a syringe. Then they left, and I've been locked in here ever since."

"Barringer?" Daisy looked shocked. "I was hoping we'd never see him again."

"Fat chance of that. There's a lot of anger inside that man, and the brunt of it appears to be aimed at CUSP. You wouldn't know anything about that, would you?"

"I can guess," Daisy said. "But now isn't the time to get into it. There are more important issues. You said he was with a woman who withdrew fluid from your spine?"

"Yes." Decker nodded. "Does it mean something to you?"

"It does, and if I'm right, it explains how you could come to my room at the guesthouse and shoot me even though you were still locked in this cell."

"Well?"

Daisy took a deep breath. "I think we're dealing with a shapeshifter."

FIFTY-FOUR

"YOU CAN'T BE SERIOUS." Decker stared at Daisy. "A shapeshifter?"

"Sure. Why not?" Daisy shrugged. "You, of all people, shouldn't be surprised by that. And the evidence fits."

"The vial of liquid they took from my neck."

"Precisely. Shapeshifters need DNA to mimic a person. The DNA in cerebrospinal fluid works best. Don't ask me why, because I don't know. Honestly, I'm relieved. It's a better explanation that you turning into a cold-blooded killer for no reason."

"And you?" Decker asked. "You were going to rip my throat out. What was that about?"

"It wasn't intentional. I thought I could control the beast, but I was wrong. The combination of Jack the Ripper's dormant bloodlust, which I inherited from Mina, and that of the loup-garou, combined to create a creature that was more than the sum of its parts. A vicious monster that couldn't stop killing once it got a taste of blood."

"Speaking of which, why the hell did you transform yourself into the loup-garou in the first place?"

213

ANTHONY M. STRONG

"It was the quickest way to find you. The loup-garou's heightened sense of smell led me right here."

"And Chad just handed you the spell book and all the ingredients necessary to make the potion?" Decker couldn't believe that Daisy would take such a risk. It was beyond foolish.

"Not quite. I distracted him, then snuck into the evidence room and photographed the incantation. Then I broke into Ben Donalson's bedroom and found the stash of ingredients he'd been using to make the potion. Speaking of which, my phone and clothes are on your back deck. It was the only safe place I could think of to make the potion and use the incantation. How about we get out of here? I would love to change out of these camos. For a start, the guy who wore them before me bled all over them."

"And whose fault is that?" Decker said, stepping out of the cell and looking down at the mangled corpse outside the door, now dressed only in his underwear.

Daisy followed him out. "Sorry. I got a bit carried away. But they deserved it. I gave them an opportunity to run, but they kept shooting at me."

"Them?"

"There might be a few more of Thomas Barringer's people scattered around this place."

"All in the same condition as this one?"

Daisy shrugged as if that was answer enough. "You want to chitchat or get out of here and find that doppelgänger of yours, because I can't imagine that Barringer went to the trouble of creating his own fake John Decker just to shoot me. He could have used a hired goon for that."

"I agree. He has a larger agenda, and I have a feeling that framing me for your murder is just icing on the cake." Decker looked down at his socked feet, then stooped and relieved one of the dead guards of his boots. They were a few sizes too big for him, but it was better than walking around barefoot. "Of course, he didn't know that you're practically immortal and harder to kill than a cockroach."

"Did you just compare me to a..." Daisy glowered at him. "You know what? Never mind."

"Hey, no insult intended. Just stating a fact. Although *you did* come perilously close to ripping my neck out, so..."

"And you shot me three times in the chest, so we're even."

"Not me. The shapeshifter," Decker reminded her. He looked around. They were standing in a corridor made of the same metal as the cell. There were other doors, most of them closed. An eerie silence lay over the facility, as if they were the only people there. Which was probably true, thanks to Daisy. He started down the corridor toward an open door that looked like the exit. As he went, he opened each door and looked inside.

"What are you doing?" Daisy asked.

"They took my gun and phone. My keys. I'd like them back."

"Good luck with that. Chances are that fake Decker has them. The rental car was gone, so..."

"Crap. You're probably right." Decker opened another door, looked inside. The space beyond was a control room of some sort, with flat-screen monitors affixed to the walls and computer workstations. He assumed that this was where the feed from the camera in his cell went. But there was too much equipment for a simple surveillance camera. It had to serve another purpose, too. There was an oblong window set into one wall, much like those Decker had encountered in police interrogation rooms. Darkness shrouded the space beyond, making it impossible to see what lay within.

"What do you think all of this is for?" Daisy asked, echoing Decker's thoughts.

"Beats me." He turned to her, because a thought had occurred to him. "Question. Do you think the shapeshifter could turn into a werewolf?"

Daisy shook her head. "Not in my experience. I've encountered a few shapeshifters over the decades, and one thing

I know is that they need DNA to transform themselves. They can replicate the werewolf's human form, but not the creature, because the beast is not part encoded into the host's DNA. It's a supernatural ability."

"In other words, the shapeshifter can become Dr. Jekyll, but not Mr. Hyde."

"Exactly. No shapeshifter. Barringer would need a real-life werewolf to mimic the loup-garou. Although I still don't understand how it could turn without a full moon, or how he could control it."

"Maybe this will give us the answer," Decker said, approaching a bank of equipment on a desk directly beneath the observation window. He studied a touchscreen control panel on the desk for a moment, then pressed a button marked MOONLIGHT. The room beyond the window lit up with brilliant white light that pulsed with a strange, ethereal intensity. "I guess that's how they did it. An artificial full moon."

"Crap." Daisy was staring through the glass, her attention focused on a naked figure lying on the ground and curled up on his side in a fetal position. A man with a small, round hole in his forehead, and a larger exit wound at the back of his skull that had sprayed blood and brain matter onto the wall behind him. "I think we've found our werewolf."

FIFTY-FIVE

DECKER RACED out of the room to the adjacent space. The door was unlocked. He threw it open and ran inside, then stopped and studied his surroundings. The cell looked very much like the one he had been kept in. There was no handle on the inside of the door, and a small oblong slit at the bottom for food and water. A camera was mounted in the corner near the ceiling. There was no trace of the observation window on this side of the wall, just a gleaming, unbroken metallic surface. But there was one way in which Decker's cell and this one differed. A second, larger door set into the wall opposite the one he had come through. Decker guessed the door opened to the outside of the building. A way to release the werewolf and send it on its way to complete whatever deadly mission Barringer had assigned to it.

He kneeled next to the prone figure and examined it. The man was dead. That much was obvious. But he hadn't been that way for long. Decker had seen plenty of murder victims during his time as an NYPD homicide detective, and he could often tell how fresh a corpse was with almost the same accuracy as a medical examiner. There were telltale signs he had come to recognize.

"Definitely the werewolf," Daisy said. She was standing on the other side of the room, looking at the blood spatter... and a small, deformed object that had dented the metal wall and become embedded. "This is a bullet, and I'd lay odds that it's made of silver."

"You can really kill a werewolf with a silver bullet?" Decker asked, straightening up. "Huh. I'll have to remember that."

Daisy turned away from the wall and looked down at the corpse. "Poor guy. Bad enough that someone turned him into a werewolf, but to end up like this?"

"They must have killed him when he outlived his usefulness." Decker circled the body, leaned over to examine a spot at the back of his neck. An incision that had not completely healed. When he reached down and touched the wound, he felt a hard, oblong object beneath the skin. "A subdermal implant. I'm guessing this is how Barringer controlled the werewolf."

"Makes sense." Daisy pointed toward the man's hand and one of his fingers, which was encrusted with dried blood. "And he's missing a fingernail."

"The beast left a claw behind at the scene of the first attack," Decker said. "This proves once and for all that it was this creature who committed the killings, not Ben."

"I'm sure the sheriff will be happy to hear that," Daisy said. "Maybe he can repair his relationship with Kiera Donelson, now that he doesn't have to put his girlfriend's son behind bars."

"Maybe." Decker turned toward the door. "Let's get out of here. Barringer is out there somewhere with my double, and whatever they are up to, it isn't going to be good. We need to warn Adam Hunt and your mother. Put CUSP on alert."

"Right." Daisy followed Decker out of the holding cell and back into the corridor.

They made their way toward the exit. Two more men lay dead at the door, sitting in widening pools of blood. A pair of rifles lay at their sides.

Decker glanced at Daisy. "More of your handiwork?"

"Like I said, they were shooting at me." She stepped past them and exited the building. "It really wasn't very polite."

"Whatever happened to that sweet, innocent girl I met in 1911?" Decker asked, following her out.

"About a century of chasing supernatural creatures with only one thing on their minds," Daisy replied. "Killing me. Kind of changes your outlook."

"Right." Decker was only half listening now, as he looked around in surprise.

The building they had just left had been constructed inside of a much larger and older structure that must have once been a factory but was now dilapidated and carried an air of abandonment. Its interior space was immense, with a towering ceiling supported by rusting iron girders and thick pillars at intervals. The newer metal building sat like an island on the concrete factory floor, dwarfed by the one that surrounded it. "What is this place?"

"I have no idea," Daisy answered. "Some sort of abandoned industrial building surrounded by a chain-link fence and barbed wire. It took me a while to get here, even as the loup-garou, so I'm guessing that it's several miles outside of Wolf Haven."

"The old lumber mill," Decker said. "It's the only building outside of town fitting that description." He started toward the set of huge barn doors that led to the outside, ignoring several more corpses. "We'll need to get the Ghost Team out here to do some cleanup before someone discovers this mess and calls Chad out here."

"Agreed," Daisy said. "I'd rather not have to explain this."

"Me either." Decker stepped past the doors and out into the Louisiana night. He looked around, taking in the building's towering façade and the patch of overgrown land surrounding it. "This is definitely the old lumber mill. We have a long walk ahead of us. About seven miles, if I remember correctly."

"Crap. That's time we don't have." Daisy glanced back toward the building. "Maybe we can find a cell phone on one of those dead guys back there and get an Uber. We could call my mother at the same time and warn her."

Decker shook his head. "Already thought of that. Even if any of those men back there are carrying phones, I guarantee that we won't be able to use them. Barringer wouldn't be stupid enough to equip his people with unsecured devices. Even if we could break the screen lock, which will be almost impossible under the circumstances, the handsets will almost certainly be encrypted."

"Guess we're walking, then." Daisy didn't sound happy.

"Looks that way." Decker started toward a gate set into the fence. "Maybe we can flag down a passing car when we get to the road."

"You really think anyone's going to stop for us dressed like this?" Daisy glanced down at herself, then over at Decker. "I'm wearing a set of bloodstained camos, and you're half dressed, with a pair of dead man's boots on your feet. We look like a pair of lunatics."

"Good point." Decker walked past the gates and started down an overgrown trail leading to the road. "But we can always hope."

FIFTY-SIX

IT TOOK them two hours to walk the seven miles back to Wolf Haven. Daisy was right. They saw three vehicles that were going in their direction during that time, but none of them stopped. After being ignored twice, she tried to step in front of the third car and flag it down, only to have the vehicle veer around her and speed off into the night. Even in the middle of nowhere, far from the dangers of the big city, people were hesitant to pick up random hitchhikers at night. Especially ones dressed like they were.

They went to Decker's house first after reaching town. He didn't have his keys to let them in, but it didn't matter. Daisy had already broken a window and unlocked the back door.

She looked at him sheepishly when he saw the damage. "Sorry about that. I had no choice. But I'm sure that CUSP will pay for the damage."

"It's fine," Decker replied, stepping into the kitchen. He pointed Daisy in the direction of the downstairs bathroom to take a shower and change back into her own clothes, while he headed upstairs to do the same thing.

Fifteen minutes later, they regrouped back in the kitchen, looking more like themselves now. Daisy wasted no time in calling Mina. It rang four times before going to voicemail. She hung up and waited a few minutes, then tried again. When it went to voicemail a second time, she left a quick message explaining about Thomas Barringer and what had happened, before trying Adam Hunt's number.

Again, no one answered.

"That's weird," she said to Decker, concern etched on her face. "My mother never ignores her calls, especially from me. And there's no way that both she and Adam would be ignoring their calls."

"Is there another number you can try?" Decker asked.

"Already on it." Daisy browsed through her contacts and placed another call. It rang for almost a minute before she gave up and ended the call. She looked at Decker. "That was the front desk number. There's always someone there, twenty-four hours a day."

Decker held his hand out. "Give me the phone."

Daisy passed it to him and stood with her arms folded, a worried look on her face, while he placed a phone call of his own.

When Nancy answered, his worst fears melted away. "Hey, it's me."

"John. Thank goodness," she sounded just as relieved as he was "You didn't call last night, and you haven't been answering your phone. I was worried."

"I'm fine," he reassured her. "It's a long story. Is everything okay?"

"Why wouldn't it be?" Concern replaced the relief.

"Because things got out of hand here," Decker said. "The situation wasn't what we expected. I don't have time to go into detail, but you might be in danger."

"What?" Nancy's voice rose in pitch. "Why would I be in danger?"

"Because there's someone out there who looks and sounds just like me. A shapeshifter who has assumed my identity, and I don't know what he's up to. Which is why I need you to get out of there. Do it right now. Don't tell me where you're going, and make sure no one follows you. Go to the wall safe in the bedroom. There's a burner phone and cash inside for situations just like this. Leave your phone behind and take the burner, along with enough money to see you through. Do *not* use your credit cards. I'll call when this is over and it's safe to come home."

"John—"

"I mean it. This is serious. And one more thing. He has my phone, so if you receive a call from that number, don't answer. I don't know where the shapeshifter is, but there's a chance he's in Maine, and he might even come to the house, so you need to be vigilant. And next time you hear from me, make sure it's really me."

"Okay. How am I going to do that?"

Decker thought for a moment. While Barringer had probably done enough research into Decker's life to make sure that the double could easily take his place, it was unlikely that he knew every minor detail of Decker's past. "You remember the movie that I took you to on our second date?"

"Sure, it was—"

"Don't say it out loud," Decker cut in quickly. Although he thought it unlikely, he couldn't be sure that Barringer hadn't bugged their house or Nancy's phone. If neither of them said it aloud, he would never find the answer to something like that. "If I call you again—if I contact you in any way—ask me what movie we saw together on our second date back in high school. Then ask me what your mother said when I took you home that night. If I answer either question wrong, then it isn't me. Understand?"

"Yes."

"Good. Now get the hell out of there, fast. Go somewhere that not even I can find you. Stay put until I call and prove that it's really me. Understand?"

"I understand." Nancy's voice had dropped to a whisper.

"Good. I have to go now. Promise me that you'll be careful."

"I will." Nancy hesitated. "I love you, John."

"I love you too," Decker said, then hung up. The abrupt silence on the other end of the line felt like a gaping void in Decker's heart. Regardless of the precautions that she took, he couldn't help worrying that Barringer, and the shapeshifter, would come after Nancy next. He only hoped that she would get away safely before that happened.

"Give me the phone again," Daisy said. "I want to call one more time and see if I can get through to my mother or Adam."

Decker handed the phone over and watched as Daisy made one frantic call after another, all of which went unanswered. Finally, she gave up and pushed the phone into her pocket. "I don't understand it. Someone back at CUSP should have answered by now. I have a bad feeling about this."

"I agree. Something is very wrong." Decker's mind was still on Nancy, but he forced himself to focus. "We need to get back there... and fast."

"How?" Daisy asked. "We don't have any wheels. The hire car is missing, and the jet is a two-hour drive away in a hangar at the airport in New Orleans."

"Leave that to me," Decker said. He held out his hand. "Your phone?"

"What? Why?"

"Because Barringer might be able to trace it, and if he sees it leave Wolf Haven, he'll know you're still alive. He may even figure out that I've escaped. And right now, that's our only advantage."

FIFTY-SEVEN

AFTER HANGING UP WITH DECKER, Nancy went straight to the bedroom and packed a bag, throwing in all the essentials she would need for a week or more away from the house. She opened the safe, placed her cell phone inside, then removed the burner and turned it on, was pleased to see that it was already charged, and took out a thick wad of cash which she stuffed into her bag. Then she went to their home office, took a sheet of paper from the printer, and found a pen. After writing a short note, she went back to the bedroom and placed the sheet in the safe, before closing and locking it. Then she turned her attention back to getting out of there.

It felt weird to be running from an unknown danger without her husband at her side. They had faced so many awful situations together and emerged victorious. Like the loup-garou that had tried to kill her daughter, Taylor, while they sheltered in Wolf Haven's high school during a raging hurricane. Or the beast—a genetically engineered prehistoric alligator—that had almost killed both of them in Florida. She couldn't help feeling like she did when Decker vanished into the past after their wedding was interrupted on Singer Cay. She had been terrified and facing the unknown all alone.

Ignoring the sense of isolation that threatened to consume her, Nancy picked up the bag and swung it over her shoulder, then made her way back into the living room. She crossed to a key rack next to the front door, and was about to take her car keys, when she changed her mind. If there really was someone out there looking to do her harm, they might know what she drove. Worse, they might have put a tracker on it, which meant they could follow her wherever she went.

But she still needed a vehicle to put as much distance between herself and the man who wore her husband's face as she could. And it didn't take long to realize where she could find one. Celine Rothman. The young woman, having finally adjusted to life in the twenty-first century, had moved into her own accommodation several months before. She hadn't learned to drive yet—there were still some aspects of modern life she shied away from—and instead relied on a bicycle to get around, and taxis or rideshare services for longer trips. But she did have a car, or rather, Colum had one, which he left parked outside of her apartment. The two had been seeing each other, and he had purchased the vehicle to make it easier for them to go places when he was in town. It was perfect, and no one would be able to trace the vehicle back to her.

Relieved, Nancy went to the closet and put on her coat, then turned back to pick up her bag, which she had left near the front door. She reached for the door handle, was about to open the door and step outside, when something stopped her. A voice in her head that told her to be careful. She withdrew her hand and went to the window, pulled the curtain back and peeked out.

And that was when she saw him.

Her husband was out on the sidewalk, standing in the gloom between two lampposts and looking up at their house. No, not her husband. John Decker was still sixteen hundred miles away in Wolf Haven. This was someone else who just happened to look exactly like him. It was the man that Decker had warned her about.

Nancy froze, caught in a moment of desperate panic. He hadn't seen her, but his very presence meant that she was in mortal danger. There was only one reason why he would have come here. He wouldn't stay out on that sidewalk forever.

The back door. It was her only chance.

She could slip out that way, climb over the back fence, and escape through the yard of the house behind hers. Then, when she reached the road, it was only a short fifteen-minute walk to Celine's apartment. Unless the man pretending to be her husband had an associate watching the back of the house. If so, she was doomed. But there was no other option.

Especially as the man who looked like her husband was now making his way up the path toward their front door. And the way he was walking told her that he didn't intend to ring the bell and wait for her to answer.

Nancy threw the bag back over her shoulder and sprinted toward the back of the house. She barged through the kitchen door, letting it swing closed behind her, even as she heard the jingling of keys and the deadbolt on the front door clicking open.

She reached the back door and pulled it open, raced outside. The frigid night air felt like a slap in the face, but that was the least of Nancy's concerns right now. She paused for a moment, weighing her options. The man that John had warned her about was in the house and right behind her, meaning she only had a few precious seconds. She could run for the fence, try to climb over and make it through the back neighbor's yard, past their house, and out onto the road, but her pursuer was so close behind that she would probably get caught before she got halfway.

But what other options did she have?

Nancy glanced around the yard, to the small shed where they stored the lawnmower and other garden tools. She would be found even quicker if she tried to hide in there—it was too obvious—but the shed stood on blocks, raising it about a foot off the ground. It was a narrow space, and Nancy wasn't even sure that she could fit. Still, it was better than the alternative.

She rushed to the shed, slid the bag from her shoulder and pushed it underneath, then dropped down onto her belly and inched under the small building. Dirt shifted beneath her, and the shed floor scraped against her back. A spider, spooked out of its web, scuttled away into the dark recesses of the cramped space. Nancy clamped her mouth shut and resisted the urge to cry out, even as she wriggled further under the shed. Then, once she was all the way under, she stopped and held her breath, which was fine because there was hardly enough room to breathe anyway.

At the same time, the back door flew open, crashing back on its hinges. A figure emerged, looking so much like her husband that Nancy could hardly believe it wasn't him even though she knew better.

The man stopped and looked around, seemingly perplexed that his quarry was nowhere in sight. "Nancy, honey. What are you running for? It's me, John. Come on back here and let's talk."

The trapped air burned in Nancy's lungs, but she refused to release it.

The man who looked like her husband stepped further into the yard. He turned toward the shed and crossed to it, opening the doors and peering inside. She could see his feet inches from her face but didn't dare to move further back under the building.

Eventually, after satisfying himself that she was not inside the shed, he returned to the middle of the yard and stood with his hands on his hips. "Honey, I've had a really bad day, and I don't have time for this nonsense. Flew all the way back from Wolf Haven and then had to go take care of business on the island. You won't believe what I've been through. Come back inside and we'll open a bottle of wine or two and unwind. Just the two of us. What do you say?"

Not a chance in hell, Nancy thought. *I'm not that dumb. You might have John's voice, but you don't sound anything like my husband.*

"Nancy?" The man stood there for a few seconds longer, as if he really thought that she would return to the house and let him do who knew what to her. Then he shook his head in frustration, went to the back fence, and peered over into the yard beyond. After another long moment, he turned and stomped back through the yard, and into the house.

Still, Nancy didn't dare to move. For all she knew he was lingering just inside the door, waiting for her to reveal herself. But she couldn't stay hidden forever. After what felt like an eternity but was probably only fifteen minutes, she scooted out from beneath the shed and waited to see if her pursuer would come racing out through the door toward her. But he didn't. The man who looked like her husband was gone.

Relieved, Nancy brushed herself off and pulled her bag back out from under the shed, then she went to the back fence, threw the bag into the yard beyond, and clambered over. After dropping down on the other side, she made her way out to the road, and started walking in the direction of Celine's apartment.

FIFTY-EIGHT

A BLEARY-EYED CHAD answered the door wearing a pair of PJ bottoms and a white tee when Decker and Daisy arrived at his house fifteen minutes later. The TV was on in the living room and Decker guessed that he'd fallen asleep watching a show.

"Dammit, John." Chad said. "You vanish all day and no one can get in touch with you, and then you show up here banging on my door in the middle of the night like it's the end of the world?"

"It's not the middle of the night," Decker replied. "Hell, it's not even ten o'clock yet."

"Whatever." Chad turned his attention to Daisy. "And as for you… What was the deal with showing up and demanding that I pull all those files and then disappearing on me? I should have you arrested for wasting police time."

"Not sure it works like that," Daisy said. "And we don't have time for this. Just shut up and listen."

Chad closed his mouth, anger simmering in his eyes.

"She's right, we don't have time," Decker said. "We need a ride to the airport, and we need it fast."

"*The airport*? Like in New Orleans?"

"That's the one."

"So now I'm a taxi?"

"No. You can drive us there or lend us your cruiser and we'll drive ourselves. I don't care either way."

"And how am I going to get my car back if you take it all the way to the city?" Chad asked.

"Look, lives depend on us getting back to Maine right away." Decker felt like grabbing Chad by the collar and shaking him. "Are you going to help us or not?"

"I thought we were trying to stop a werewolf from killing the citizens of my town. Now you want to fly back halfway across the country on a whim?"

"The situation has changed. The werewolf is dead. It won't be causing you any more problems," Daisy said. "And you can tell Ben he's off the hook. It wasn't him."

"Seriously? Just like that?" Chad's eyes lit up.

"Yes." Decker nodded. "Now either go put some clothes on and drive us to New Orleans or give us your car keys."

"All right, already. Give me ten minutes." Chad turned and went back into the house, pushing the door closed behind him and leaving them standing on the stoop. He was soon back wearing his uniform. He grabbed his hat from a hook near the door and stepped outside, then led them around the side of the house to where the only official police vehicle in Wolf Haven was parked.

He unlocked the doors and motioned to them. "Go ahead. Climb in."

Decker took the front passenger seat, and Daisy climbed in the back.

Chad jumped into the driver's seat and started the engine. "If the werewolf is dead, then where is the body?"

"Don't worry about that." Decker fastened his seatbelt. "We've got it taken care of. It will be like the werewolf was never here."

"I don't like the sound of that." Chad pulled away from the house, heading toward Main Street. "First you want to spirit Ben away, lock him up without trial, and now you have some sort of black ops clean up team coming in to sweep what happened here under the carpet."

"That's not what we're doing," Decker said. "Would you rather deal with the body yourself, and all the awkward questions it would raise?"

"I guess not," Chad said moodily. "Just who exactly do the pair of you work for, anyway? And don't give me that *it's classified* crap."

"Okay. We won't." Decker fell silent.

After a moment, Chad shook his head slowly. "But you aren't going to answer my question."

"Trust me, you're better off not knowing."

"You could let me decide that."

Daisy leaned forward and spoke through the grill separating the back seats from the front. "John's right. The less you know about us, the better."

"Could you at least tell me why we're rushing to the airport in the middle of the night?"

Neither Decker nor Daisy answered.

Chad huffed. "Fine. After all, I'm only the chauffeur."

Daisy took her phone out and placed a call, which went unanswered. She tried a further two times before putting the phone away again with a dissatisfied grunt.

Decker turned to look at her. "You calling headquarters again?"

"No. Our pilot. He's not answering."

"Maybe he's sleeping," said Decker.

"It's possible, but he's supposed to be on call twenty-four hours a day in case we need the jet at short notice. I tried the copilot as well. She isn't picking up either. I don't like this."

Decker wasn't sure what to say, so he said nothing. But deep down, he shared Daisy's apprehension. Something was very wrong.

They rode for the next forty-five minutes in silence. Chad

kept his eyes on the road, staring sullenly through the windshield and into the darkness. Daisy was quiet too, lost in her own thoughts and no doubt worried about the lack of response from not only the jet's crew but also Mina, Hunt, or anyone else at their island headquarters in Maine.

Eventually they reached the city, approaching through the cluster of towns that dotted the north shore of Lake Pontchartrain and taking the causeway, a twenty-four-mile-long bridge that spanned the lake. When they arrived at the airport, Decker directed Chad past the parking garages and passenger terminals that served millions of tourists a year, to an access road near the west perimeter, and a smaller terminal that catered only to private and charter jets.

Chad parked next to the terminal in a space reserved for official vehicles, and they made their way inside the building. At half-past eleven, there was practically no one around. A maintenance worker walked back-and-forth, polishing the floor with a buffer. A bored-looking employee in a navy-blue uniform sat behind the desk of a private charter company with a magazine in front of her, no doubt waiting for a late arrival. She didn't look up as they passed. Classical music floated in the air, piped in from speakers set high in the ceiling.

Chad looked around and shuddered. "This is like something out of a horror movie. You know, where everyone disappears for no reason, leaving the heroes on their own to figure out what went wrong."

"You watch too much TV," Decker said, leading them through the terminal to a set of doors at the back that exited onto a stretch of tarmac surrounded by hangers. After Daisy provided her credentials to a TSA agent at a desk near the door, they went outside and crossed to the hangar where CUSP's private jet was parked. Except that when they entered, the hangar was empty.

The jet was gone.

FIFTY-NINE

TWENTY MINUTES after emerging from her hiding place and jumping the back fence, Nancy arrived at Celine's apartment. She had avoided the most obvious way there, taking a slightly longer and less direct route, just in case the man who looked like her husband had anticipated her next move. Thankfully, she saw no sign of him along the way, and he wasn't waiting for her at the three-story brick building that had once been a cannery serving the local fishermen but had now been repurposed and converted into luxury accommodations.

She hurried inside, thankful that she already knew the code for the front entrance and hurried up to the second floor. Celine answered the door with a look of surprise on her face.

"Nancy? What on earth are you doing here so late at night?"

"It's a long story." Nancy glanced around nervously. "Can I come in?"

"Of course." Celine stepped aside, then closed the door and locked it once Nancy was inside the apartment. "Now, what's going on?"

"I need to borrow Colum's car for a few days," Nancy said, then wasted no time telling her about Decker's call, and the man who looked just like her husband who kicked her front door in and almost caught her.

After she finished speaking, Celine remained silent for a short while, processing what she had been told. Then she said, "Of course you can take Colum's car. He's out of the country on an assignment and won't be back for at least a week. But I'm not letting you go on your own. I'm coming with you."

"Absolutely not." Nancy had no intention of putting anyone else in danger, especially her friend. "It's too risky. We have no idea who this guy is or what he'll do to us if we get caught."

"It wasn't a suggestion." Celine folded her arms. "If you want the car, you get me, too. That's the deal."

"Celine—"

"Look, that guy is out there somewhere looking for you, and for all we know, he'll show up here next. Even if I stay, I'm in danger. Now, make up your mind, because we probably don't have much time."

"Fine. You can come." Nancy wasn't in any mood to keep arguing. Celine was right about one thing. Time was of the essence.

"Fantastic. Give me a moment to pack some clothes and then we're out of here."

"Sure." Nancy nodded. "Oh, one more thing. Leave your phone behind. They probably aren't tracking it, but just to be safe—"

"Sure. Can't be too careful." Celine turned and headed toward the back of the apartment. A few minutes later she returned carrying a small suitcase in one hand and Colum's car keys in the other. "All done. Let's go. The car is down the street in a resident parking spot."

They left the apartment and made their way back downstairs.

At the entrance to the building, Nancy stopped, peering outside. "I think the coast is clear, but we should still be careful."

"Agreed." Celine reached into her pocket and pulled out a compact pistol. "Which is why I brought this."

"Since when are you armed?" Nancy stared at the gun.

"Colum gave it to me. Taught me how to use it, too. Said that being the girlfriend of a CUSP operative was dangerous and I should be able to defend myself when he's not around."

"That seems a bit extreme."

"Really? That's what you're going with when we're running from a clone of your husband, who probably wants to kill you?"

"Fair point." Satisfied the doppelgänger wasn't waiting for them, Nancy pulled the door open and stepped out onto the sidewalk. After Celine joined her, she nodded at the gun. "You should probably keep that out of sight, just in case someone sees you and calls the police."

"The police. That's not a bad idea. Why haven't you called them already?"

"And say what? That a man who isn't my husband but looks just like him wants to do me harm? That my real husband, who works for a secret organization that hunts supernatural creatures, is in Louisiana dealing with a werewolf?"

"Okay. When you put it like that…" Celine tucked the gun back into her pocket, then took Nancy's arm and led her along the sidewalk. A few minutes later, they arrived at the car.

Celine gave the keys to Nancy, then went around and climbed into the passenger seat. "Do you have any idea where we're going?"

"Not yet," Nancy admitted, starting the car. "I figure that we'll put some distance between us and Portland, maybe a couple of hours, then find a motel that takes cash and get a room. We can book by the night and move on if necessary."

"Sounds like you have this all figured out." Celine looked impressed.

"I wouldn't go that far," Nancy said, pulling out of the parking spot and starting down the road. "But I'm damned if I'll let some shapeshifting monster end this marriage before it's even begun. I Haven't even had a real honeymoon yet!"

SIXTY

DECKER STARED IN DISBELIEF. "I guess that explains why the pilots weren't answering your calls."

"They would never have willingly left without us," Daisy said. She was already tapping away on her phone. A minute later, she looked up. "I have their flight plan. The jet took off this afternoon at 1:34 PM bound for Portland, Maine. They landed almost two and a half hours later."

"Can you tell how many people were on board and who they were?" Decker asked.

"No." Daisy shook her head. "I used the tail number to pull up the information on a public flight tracking site. I can tell you the plane's average altitude and airspeed, but not how many passengers were on board or their identities."

"Thomas Barringer is behind this, I'm sure of it." Decker stared at the empty hangar. "And I bet the shapeshifter was involved, too."

"That must be how they gained access to the jet," Daisy said, nodding in agreement. "They took your wallet, which means they have your ID, and you are listed as one of the people authorized to use the jet."

"Now hang on there just a minute," Chad said, looking perplexed. "Did you say shapeshifter?"

"Yes. He used John's DNA to look and sound like him," Daisy replied.

"That's how he was able to shoot me this morning," Daisy said, turning her gaze to Decker. "I swear, that man was a carbon copy of you. Maybe if I had spent more time with him, I would have realized that he was a doppelgänger, or maybe not, but he didn't give me the chance. No sooner had I opened the door than he stepped inside and started shooting."

"Wait. Someone shot you?" Chad studied Daisy. "You look fine to me."

"Three times in the chest," Daisy said, apparently giving up on keeping Chad in the dark. He was too deeply enmeshed in the situation now. "Hurt like hell and put me out of action for hours."

"What, so you were wearing a bulletproof vest?"

"Something like that." Decker said quickly, deciding that there was a limit to how much he was willing to share with his old deputy. He turned to Daisy. "If Thomas Barringer and my double are already in Maine, who knows what havoc they've been wreaking?"

"It explains why I haven't been able to get through to anyone." Daisy's face creased with concern. "I fear that something terrible has happened."

"Which means it's more important than ever that we get back there as quickly as possible." Decker had been thinking about the pilots, and why they hadn't answered Daisy's calls. The jet had landed hours ago, which meant there was no reason why they wouldn't pick up. Unless they were dead.

"Who is Thomas Barringer?" Chad asked.

"He's the person behind the werewolf attacks," Decker said. "It was all a ploy to lure me back to Wolf Haven so he could snatch me without the people I work for becoming suspicious."

WOLF HAVEN

"Then he replaced John with a shapeshifter who looked exactly like him."

"A Shapeshifter who used my face to steal the jet." Decker was mad at himself for not seeing the situation more clearly. "And I bet that he used that same face to gain access to CUSP, possibly with Barringer and goodness knows who else at his side. There's no other reason why he would fly back to Maine."

"What is CUSP?" Chad asked. "I've never heard of it."

"Classified Universal Special Projects," Decker replied. "I work for them. We deal with things like that creature that was terrorizing Wolf Haven."

"And this Barringer guy was in my town? He's the reason all those innocent people are dead?"

"Yes."

"And the two of you were keeping me in the dark all this time?"

"Not at first," Daisy said. "We really thought Ben Donelson was the killer until that second werewolf showed up."

"I'm the sheriff, for Pete's sake." Chad glowered. "I have a responsibility to keep the citizens of Wolf Haven safe. You should have told me what was going on the moment you knew about it."

"Maybe," Decker said. "But what's done is done. We have more pressing issues right now. Like finding another way back to Maine. And quickly."

Daisy was still on her phone. "The last commercial flight of the evening going to Portland left at 9 o'clock."

"What about somewhere else, like Bangor or Boston?" Decker asked. "If we can get close enough, we can rent a car and drive."

Daisy shook her head. "No dice. There aren't any more flights out of New Orleans tonight. First flight that would get us anywhere close to Portland leaves at 7.40 AM."

Decker cursed under his breath. "We can't wait that long."

"What about a charter?" Chad asked. "There must be a bunch of companies around here that have small jets."

"Maybe, but they won't be answering their phones at midnight. And even if they did, it would take hours to get a pilot here and fuel up."

"What are you going to do, then?"

"I have an idea," Daisy said. She turned to Chad. "I need to borrow your phone.

He hesitated for a moment, then dug it out of his pocket and unlocked the screen before handing it to her.

"Thank you." She started toward the hangar doors.

"Where are you going?" Decker called after her.

"To make a couple of phone calls, and I need some privacy." Daisy stepped out of the hangar and vanished into the night.

Chad shuffled his feet. "That colleague of yours is a strange one. I can't explain it, but I get a strange feeling whenever I'm around her."

"She's not so bad when you get to know her," Decker said, his gaze dropping to the floor. If the shapeshifter was in Portland, then Nancy was in more danger than he had imagined. And with no way to communicate with anyone on the island, he could only imagine the chaos that Barringer and the doppelgänger were causing. He could only hope that Nancy had taken his advice and gone somewhere that no one would be able to find her.

"You okay there, buddy?" Chad asked. "You look a bit pale."

"I'm fine." Decker looked back up and forced a smile.

"Come on, I've known you for years. I've seen that look before. You're worried about Nancy."

Decker nodded.

Chad put his hand on his shoulder and squeezed. "We might not have had the best relationship these last few years, but I've got your back. If it comes to it, I'll light up my overheads and drive you all the way to Maine with my needle pushing a hundred."

"That's a generous offer, Chad." Decker said, surprised by the sheriff's amenability.

Chad shrugged. "Hey, you're not the only one with a soft spot for Nancy. Dang, I still miss her seafood gumbo at Cassidy's."

"Yeah." Decker glanced around as Daisy walked back into the hangar.

"We have a ride," she said, crossing toward them. "Only problem is, it doesn't leave from here. We have to get across town, and fast."

"Looks like I'll get to use those overheads after all." Chad pulled his car keys out of his pocket. "Where are we going?"

Daisy came to a stop. "The Naval Air Station Joint Reserve. They have a C-130 Hercules fueled up and ready to go, and it's all ours."

SIXTY-ONE

THE C-130 WAS CRUISING at 28,000 feet on its way to Portland, Maine. They had taken off an hour ago, and still had three hours left to go thanks to the huge aircraft's maximum airspeed, which was less than that of a commercial airliner, and much lower than the speed of their private jet. Decker sat in one of the web seats in the front of the plane near the cockpit. Daisy sat next to him but hadn't said much since they boarded. Chad had driven across New Orleans to the military airfield with his bar lights blazing, before leaving them in the capable hands of an Air Force captain. He would probably be almost all the way back to Wolf Haven by now.

The captain, a man by the name of Forster, had met them at the gates in a Jeep, and driven them straight to the airfield, and their ride. The C-130 was making the jaunt to St. John's, Newfoundland, where it would pick up its cargo and refuel before heading to its final destination of Mildenhall in the United Kingdom. Since the aircraft was flying the first leg empty, and Portland was only a slight detour, the base commander had agreed to let Decker and Daisy ride along. Decker wasn't sure how she had achieved that feat, but CUSP had close ties with many military branches both in the United States and abroad. They also had high-level contacts in the Pentagon, not to mention the CIA, Britain's MI-6, and a host of other organizations known mostly by their acronyms. When Daisy asked, people listened.

Now, she was sitting with her hands in her lap and her eyes closed. It didn't take much to figure out that she was worried. Thomas Barringer and the shapeshifter who looked like Decker had gained a considerable head start on them. Who knew what chaos they had instigated during that time? But Decker knew one thing. CUSP's headquarters going silent for so long was dire.

"Daisy?" Decker finally realized that he had no choice but to speak up. He didn't want to disturb her but had to know why Barringer was so obsessed with CUSP. That information might be vital to stopping him once and for all. "Can I ask you something?"

"You want to know about Barringer," Daisy opened her eyes and looked at Decker, "and what he has against CUSP."

"Yes. This is the third time I've run into him, and I'd like to make it the last." Decker still remembered the hitmen Barringer had sent after he and Rory in the Brazilian city of Manaus. They had barely escaped with their lives.

"Very well." Daisy sat up in her seat and glanced around the cavernous cargo hold. "I guess there's nothing else to do while we're stuck here in this flying truck. The first thing you need to know is that his real name is not Thomas Barringer."

"Hunt already told me that much, although he refused to elaborate. Said it was *above my pay grade* even though the guy keeps trying to kill me."

"Or in this case, frame you for whatever he's planning. At least, if that shapeshifter is anything to go by."

"I figured that's why Barringer didn't just dispose of me outright. Once the shapeshifter reverts to his regular form, I'll be on the hook for the chaos he caused." Decker gripped the sides of his seat as the aircraft bounced through a patch of turbulence. "How about we start with Barringer's real name."

Daisy reached down and checked her seatbelt as the plane dropped into another air pocket. When it righted itself, she said, "His real name is Nathan Bailey, and at one time he was Adam Hunt's best friend..."

SIXTY-TWO

EIGHT YEARS EARLIER-SOMEWHERE *in Northern Maine*

The three black quad-cab pickup trucks moved slowly along the icy road in a convoy. Each vehicle was identical, even down to their alloy rims and the row of high-powered spotlights mounted on a bar atop each vehicle's cab. The only thing that differentiated them was the cargo sitting in the bed of the middle truck. A box made of inch-thick steel large enough to contain a person, except that the occupant of this box was anything but human. Which was why the door was secured not only with two large padlocks but also a heavy steel drop bar that prevented it from being opened from the inside.

Adam Hunt, riding in the back seat of the last truck, peered between the front seats and out through the windshield into the swirling blizzard that had descended upon them faster than expected. The two vehicles ahead of them were almost imperceptible in the whiteout conditions, but he knew they were there, along with the deadly cargo they were transporting.

Next to Adam, ignoring the storm, was Kate Bauman, her nose buried in a book as usual. A historical romance with a cover that depicted an impossibly handsome man in a white shirt torn open to reveal his muscular chest, and a similarly gorgeous woman who wrapped her arms around him and swooned at the sight of his body.

Two men occupied the front seats. Sergeant Shane Fisher, a Ghost Team operative, and Nathan Bailey, who had been recruited to CUSP around the same time as Adam. In the years since, they had become fast friends, even as they rose through the ranks.

Bailey glanced into the back, his eyes alighting on Kate's book.

"I don't know why you read that trash," he said, a lopsided grin spreading across his face.

Kate looked up, her eyes glinting. "Because it's better than thinking about how much further we have to go in this storm before that creature in the truck ahead of us is safely in The Zoo where it belongs." She slipped a piece of paper into the book to mark her place before closing it. "Besides, you act tough now, but I've caught you sneaking a read when you think I'm sleeping."

"That is absolutely not true," Bailey said, casting a quick glance toward Hunt. If the two men were best friends, then Kate was something else entirely to Bailey. Although he would never admit it out loud any more than he would admit to sometimes reading her romance novels, she was the love of his life. A work romance that had blossomed into something deeper. They had even discussed leaving CUSP to settle down and pursue less dangerous careers. But they both knew it would never happen. It was hard to give up the thrill of chasing supernatural creatures once you discovered that they existed.

"Hey, I don't care what you read," Hunt said with a smirk. "I wouldn't read them too openly, though, unless you want your new nickname to be Fabio."

"Funny." Bailey flipped Hunt the bird before glancing toward their driver. "Maybe I'll tell Sargeant Fisher here all about your love of—"

At that moment, before Bailey could finish his sentence, the truck in front of them veered suddenly to the left, fishtailing on the slippery road and traveling sideways for a few moments, before impacting a tree.

Fisher slammed hard on the brakes to avoid a collision, throwing Bailey forward until his seatbelt locked, saving him from a trip into the windshield.

Hunt put his hands out to shield himself from hitting the back of the driver's seat. The book Kate had been reading flew off her lap and fell to the floor, vanishing into the darkness between the seats.

"What the hell was that for?" Hunt asked, regaining his composure.

"Sorry, sir," the driver said. "We have a problem. Alpha Unit is out of action."

"And the cargo?" Hunt leaned forward. "Is it secure?"

"Don't know, sir." Fisher turned on the spotlights mounted above the cab, illuminating a patch of snowy road ahead of them, and the stricken truck with its front-end buried in the trunk of a tall pine tree. The lead vehicle was already backing up. The doors opened and four men dressed in the same uniforms as Fisher jumped out, each holding a semi-automatic rifle. "Alpha Escort is responding."

"I have a bad feeling about this," Bailey said, even as a snow flurry blew across the road, obscuring their view of the immobilized truck.

A moment later, gunfire cracked the air. Three short bursts, quickly followed by a terrified scream.

Hunt squinted to see through the blinding snow, but the world beyond their windshield was nothing but a white swirling haze.

More gunfire, followed by a second scream. Then another.

All four occupants of the truck held their breath. No one spoke. They didn't need to, because each of them was thinking the same thing.

The Wendigo had escaped.

SIXTY-THREE

THE C-130 RUMBLED ONWARD through the sky toward its destination.

Decker stared at Daisy as she recounted the story. "They were transporting a Wendigo in a blizzard?"

Daisy nodded. "There had been several grisly deaths in Quebec, around Lake Saint John. They went up there to investigate and came across the Wendigo. To one of those creatures, minus twenty is like a day in the tropics. They love the cold."

"And they were sure the killer was a Wendigo?"

"Beyond a doubt. They identified the individual who had transformed into the creature. An elderly man who had lived alone in a cabin far from civilization for many years. They also observed that the victims had been partially consumed. Wendigos are cannibalistic."

"And extremely violent, not to mention strong, despite their emaciated appearance." Decker had never encountered a Wendigo, but he had dealt with a similar creature out west in a mining town east of Las Vegas. A monster that had been created by a Gold Rush era miner when he and an associate stole the bones from an old Native American burial site. Both creatures shared some of the same mythology. The biggest difference was that the Nevada beast could fly, whereas the Wendigo could not.

"Right. Which is how the creature was able to break through the steel wall of the box it was confined within and kill the driver and passengers of the truck transporting it, causing the vehicle to crash. The lead truck, a security detail carrying four Ghost Team members, stopped to assist, but due to the low visibility—it was dark, and the blizzard was getting worse—they were all killed by the beast before it escaped into the woods."

"Please tell me that Adam Hunt didn't decide to follow it?"

"I think you already know the answer to that. There were four people in the rear truck, including a Ghost Team driver. They decided not to recapture the creature but instead to eliminate it."

"You mean kill it."

"If you like. It wouldn't have been Adam's first choice, but since they no longer had a way to contain the Wendigo, they couldn't risk it harming more people."

"So they followed it into the woods, at night during a storm."

"They were in the middle of nowhere and reinforcements would have taken too long to arrive. The creature would have been long gone. What choice did they have?"

"It was foolhardy."

"Whatever you think it was, Hunt made the decision. They decided to split up. Bailey wanted to team up with Kate, but Hunt put him with Sergeant Fisher instead. He thought that the relationship between the pair would cloud their judgement if they were partnered."

"He took Kate instead," Decker could guess where this was going, and he didn't like it.

"Yes. They entered the woods but couldn't pick up the creature's trail because of the dense tree canopy, and how fast the snow was falling. The creature had left no footprints, at least none that were obvious. Also, the Wendigo is an excellent climber, and may have taken to the trees rather than moving across the ground. They searched the area and found two possible routes the beast could have taken, but neither was conclusive."

"They split up and went in different directions."

"Right." Daisy hesitated, her eyes roaming the empty cargo hold once again, as if she didn't want to meet Decker's gaze. "That turned out to be their downfall."

SIXTY-FOUR

THEY MOVED FORWARD SLOWLY, *scanning the dense woodland around them for danger. Adam Hunt and Kate Bauman. The Wendigo was out there somewhere, and might attack at any moment, even from the branches above their heads.*

They were both armed with assault rifles that Hunt had taken from a lockbox in the bed of their truck. They also carried high-powered flashlights, the beams cutting a hazy, snow filled swath through the blackness. Sergeant Fisher and Nathan Bailey were off to their left and following a different path. The two groups had agreed to search for an hour, then rendezvous back at the truck if they didn't find anything. Right now, Hunt was not hopeful. The Wendigo had a good head start and could move faster than them through the treacherous winter landscape, where it thrived.

"This is crazy. We should turn back and wait for help." Kate scanned the terrain ahead of them, ever vigilant despite her reservations.

"No. We have to try, at least." Hunt shook his head. "If that creature reaches a populated area, it will start killing again. I won't

have that on my conscience. Besides, this is our job. It's what we signed up for."

"I know." Kate stepped up onto a fallen tree trunk. She lingered a moment, using the extra height to get a better view of the surrounding woods, then stepped down on the other side. "I think there are footprints ahead of us in a clearing. They look fresh."

Hunt stepped over the trunk and followed Kate to the spot where she had seen the footprints. The clearing was small, and snow had accumulated there thanks to the lack of tree cover. Crossing through the patch of clear ground was a set of large, three-toed footprints that were slowly filling in with falling snow.

"Another hour and these prints wouldn't be here," Hunt said, kneeling and examining the closest of them.

"You think they belong to the Wendigo?"

Hunt straightened up. "They aren't deer, moose, or bear. In fact, I don't recognize them as any large animal that might be out in these woods, so…"

"We've found the Wendigo."

"Looks that way." Hunt unclipped a two-way radio from his belt and spoke into it, giving the other team their location. He put the radio away again and started forward. "The tracks run across the clearing to a trail on the other side."

"Maybe we should wait for the others." Kate glanced around.

"And lose our advantage?" Hunt knew that any tracks on the trail ahead of them wouldn't last long. "We keep moving."

Kate nodded.

They crossed to the other side of the clearing and moved onto the trail, where the footprints were less distinct. After a few minutes of walking, the tracks petered out, even though the snow ahead of them on the trail was smooth and unbroken.

Hunt came to a stop. "Where did it go?"

"Up into the trees?" Kate glanced skyward. "Although I don't see why it would do so right here of all places after following the trail for so long."

"I was thinking the same thing." Hunt swung his flashlight

around, its beam playing over the tree filled landscape to their left and right. At first, he saw nothing, but then the spear of light picked out a steep rise with a dark, jagged crevasse cut into its side.

"A cave." Kate drew in a sharp breath.

"That's a great place for the creature to hide and rest up," Hunt said. "Get out of the storm."

"Then let's take a look." Kate stepped off the trail and pushed through the underbrush toward the cave.

Hunt rushed to catch up with her. "If it looks like the Wendigo is in there, we wait for the others before doing anything. Come up with a solid plan. A confined space like that… it could be a deathtrap."

"Sounds good to me." Kate pushed past a large bush near the cave opening. She swung her flashlight around. The beam lit up the narrow cavern until it faded into darkness. "I don't see anything. Goes back a long way."

Hunt played his flashlight beam across the ground where it picked out a faint impression in the snow, followed by another. "Look. Could be footprints."

"They could be anything." Kate turned away from the cave entrance. "There only one way we're going to—"

"Look out." Hunt made a swiping grab for Kate as a dark shape barreled toward them from inside the cave.

She turned, raised her gun as the beast erupted from the opening so fast that it was nothing but a blur. A moment later, she was flying backward, the gun falling from her grip.

Hunt aimed and fired, letting off two bursts of gunfire, both of which missed their mark. But he did succeed in drawing the Wendigo's attention. It turned and leaped, hit him full in the chest and sent him tumbling to the ground. He stared up at the creature, at its emaciated, leathery skin, and sunken eye sockets. It looked like a walking corpse with wiry, thin hair attached to its scalp, and impossibly long arms that ended in razor sharp claws.

Hunt tried to scramble away.

Off to his left, Kate was rising slowly to her feet. Her gun lay several feet away in the snow. She took a step toward it.

The beast observed Hunt for a moment longer. Then, as if sensing the danger, turned to face Kate.

Hunt's chest tightened. He pushed himself up. "No! Leave the rifle. Just run. Get out of here."

But Kate didn't run. She made a dash for the gun, scooped it up.

The creature shot forward.

Hunt threw himself at the beast, wrapped his arms around its waist.

The creature swatted him away as if he were a fly buzzing around its head. He fell hard, his head slamming into a rock.

Then the Wendigo was on Kate before she even had time to aim. The last thing Hunt saw before he lost consciousness was the creature opening her neck with a slash of its sharp claws, even as voices rang in the distance, followed by a fresh round of gunfire.

SIXTY-FIVE

DECKER LISTENED to Daisy's tale with a growing sense of dread. "Bailey blamed Hunt for the death of his girlfriend."

"Yes. He reasoned that if Adam had paired him with Kate, then the Wendigo wouldn't have killed her. He and Sergeant Daniels arrived at the cave too late to save her, although they stopped the creature from turning its attention back to Adam and killing him as well."

"And the creature?"

"It got away despite their best efforts. Help arrived a couple of hours later and they were evacuated from the scene. Bailey was inconsolable. The rift between himself and Hunt only got wider in the following months. In the end, he resigned from CUSP as a bitter and broken man. We kept track of him for the first few years, which is customary whenever an operative leaves the organization, but then he vanished. Went to ground. He didn't reemerge until you encountered him on Habitat One, going under the alias of Thomas Barringer."

"The science outpost on the ocean floor that was studying a sunken German U-boat. He infiltrated them as their head of security to steal the alien technology on the submarine."

"Right. By that time, he had aligned himself with a new

organization. At first, we weren't sure who they were or what their objective was. But we knew one thing. The ease with which they sprang Nathan Bailey out of our high-security detention center meant they were well-funded, highly trained, and very organized. It also meant that they probably had at least one operative within CUSP who was helping them."

"I'd lay odds it was more than one," Decker said, remembering Kyle Garrett, a member of the Ghost Team unit who had accompanied Decker on his trip into the Amazon. The man had turned out to be aligned with Bailey, or Barringer, as Decker had known him back then. "Adam Hunt always suspected there were more moles in the organization."

"And he was right. We smoked out two more operatives and eventually got them to talk."

Decker didn't ask how Mina and Hunt had done that. He didn't want to know. But he hoped they hadn't resorted to the same tactics Finch had employed against a man named Daniel Garrett, who had betrayed the Order of St. George back in 1912.

As if reading his mind, Daisy said, "Don't worry, we didn't torture them, or even drug them. We used more humane methods of persuasion."

"I'm glad to hear it."

Daisy smiled for the first time since boarding the aircraft, although it was probably more for show than anything else, because the deep concern flickering in her eyes was unmistakable. "It turns out that Bailey eventually aligned himself with an organization known as The Watchers."

"I've heard that name before," Decker said, trying to think of where and when. Then it came to him. "They abducted Mina back in 1911. They experimented on her for months, hoping to discover a means of wiping out vampires, and eventually tried to transport her to New York on the Titanic."

Daisy nodded. "Yes. Although over the last century their mission has become less clear. They went from trying to eradicate supernatural creatures like Jack the Ripper and his kind, to using the creatures for their own ends when it suited. At this point, they care more about power than principle."

"Which is why they were willing to use a werewolf and a shapeshifter in Wolf Haven."

"Yes. Although I assume that what happened in Wolf Haven, and whatever might be occurring back in Maine, are more to do with Bailey's vendetta against us, and in particular Adam Hunt, than any official agenda of the organization he is now part of."

"Which raises a troubling question," Decker said. "How high in the organization has this man risen?"

"I'm guessing that it's fairly high," Daisy replied. "Especially since they spent so many resources to free him from our detention center. They were even willing to commit murder."

Decker raised an eyebrow. "Hunt never mentioned that."

"That doesn't surprise me." Daisy leaned forward in her seat, resting her elbows on her knees. "They killed a guard. Shot him point blank. It was a nasty business and a failure that Adam took personally, given his previous relationship with Bailey."

"He couldn't have known that his erstwhile friend would align himself with such dangerous people."

"True. But we pride ourselves on calculating risk, both in the missions that we undertake, and in the people that we surround ourselves with. In this instance, we failed spectacularly. Now Nathan Bailey has come back seeking revenge and brought along with him the full force of an organization that might be as powerful as our own, only less principled."

Decker looked at Daisy, studied her haunted eyes for a moment. "Even the best risk assessments can be wrong. It's not an exact science."

"True, but that doesn't make me feel any better." Daisy leaned back in the web seat and wiped a sheen of moisture from her eyes in an uncharacteristic moment of vulnerability. "Nathan Bailey is more dangerous than any of us ever imagined, and after what he's done in Wolf Haven, I can only imagine the devastation he's wreaked in Maine."

"Mina is resourceful. So is Adam. I'm sure they—"

"Don't tell me you're sure they are alright," Daisy said tersely. "You can't know that, and the lack of communication tells me otherwise. Something dreadful has happened on that island. I'm sure of it. And I'm scared."

"I wasn't going to say that they're okay," Decker said. "Because you're right. I have no way of knowing. But I *was* going to say that they wouldn't go down without a fight."

SIXTY-SIX

NANCY DROVE through the darkness in Colum's car. Celine, sitting next to her in the front passenger seat, cradled the gun in her lap as if she expected trouble at any moment. They had been driving for three hours already and had passed through several small towns with roadside motels that catered to the flocks of tourists who descended upon Maine in the summer and fall, looking for the glorious natural landscapes and peacefulness the northernmost state provided. She had considered stopping several times but had changed her mind, figuring that further was better. Now, though, she was finding it hard to keep her eyes open and decided to pull in at the next motel they saw.

That opportunity came ten miles further down the road when the lights of the Moosehead Motor Lodge shone through the darkness like a beacon. At most other times of the year, the parking lot would be packed with cars and RVs sporting out-of-state license plates, just like every other motel within a couple of hundred miles. But now, in the depths of winter, there were only three other vehicles parked there.

As she pulled in, Nancy worried that the lobby would be closed given the remote location and time of night, but thankfully the motel office was lit up and she could see a person sitting behind the desk.

The rooms at the Moosehead Motor Lodge were exactly as Nancy expected. Two queen beds with thin stained comforters and lumpy pillows. The carpet, a garish shade of crimson, was threadbare and sticky in places, as if something had been spilled on it but not cleaned up. The furniture was dinged and outdated. But it was better than continuing on an aimless drive through the darkness. And it was safe.

After locking the door and pulling the curtains, Celine headed toward the back of the room. "That was a long drive. I need the lavatory."

Nancy sat on the edge of the closest bed and kicked her shoes off, exhausted. She pulled the burner phone from her pocket and opened it, her finger hovering over one of the pre-programmed numbers in the device's memory that would connect directly to her husband's work phone. Except that John Decker would not answer. At least, not the real John Decker. If only she'd taken note of the phone number he'd called on—a number she hadn't recognized—before she ditched her real phone. But she hadn't.

She went to put the burner back in her pocket, then changed her mind. There she was, on the run and sitting in a dingy motel room, and apart from almost being killed by an imposter who looked just like her husband, she had no idea what was going on, or why. In the heat of the moment, she hadn't pressed Decker to tell her. She had been too focused on doing as he said and getting out of there. But now she wasn't willing to sit on the sidelines in ignorance and wait for a phone call from her husband. A call that might never come if the shapeshifter was as deadly as he appeared to be. She needed to know just how much trouble her husband was in, and why there was a man with his face chasing her.

There were three more numbers in the phone's directory. Column O'Shea, Adam Hunt, and Mina. Colum was on an assignment and was probably unaware of the situation. But her husband would almost certainly have contacted the other two people on that list. She decided to start with Mina.

Except that when she called, it rang several times and went to voicemail.

She tried again, then gave up and called Adam Hunt.

No answer.

Nancy stared at the phone, feeling suddenly vulnerable and alone. Isolated. If the shapeshifter had come after her, maybe it had also gone after Adam and Mina. A sudden image flashed through her mind. Of Adam Hunt laying on his office floor surrounded by a pool of his own blood. Then the scene changed, and it was her husband laying there, his dead eyes staring up at her.

She closed her eyes and banished the grisly thought. John wasn't dead. As far as she knew, he was still in Louisiana. But a nagging fear remained. What if she stayed here, hiding in this room for days, a week, or even longer, and no one ever called to let her know it was safe to return?

"Hey," Celine stepped out of the bathroom. When she saw Nancy's face, she stopped. "You're pale as a ghost. Everything all right?"

"No." Nancy shook her head. Now she put the phone away. "I don't know what I'm doing here."

"I thought we were hiding from a man who looks like your husband. A man who wants to kill you."

"We are, and that's just it. This isn't me." Nancy stood up. "I don't want to stay here, worrying about my husband. My friends. They need me."

"I don't get it. What you trying to say?"

"I'm saying that I can't stay here and hide. I'm not going to cower in fear. It's not me."

"Then what *are* you going to do?"

"I'm going back," Nancy said, standing up and grabbing the car keys from the nightstand beside the bed. "I'm going to find out exactly what is going on back there, and if it comes to that,

I'm going to fight. The only question is, are you coming with me?"

Celine hesitated for a moment, then she nodded. "Absolutely. Yes, I'm coming. I wasn't looking forward to sleeping in this dreadful place, anyway. They should be ashamed of themselves, renting a room this shabby. Let's go!"

SIXTY-SEVEN

THE SKY WAS STILL DARK when the C-130 transport plane touched down at Portland International Jetport a little after 6 AM. Instead of taxiing to a gate, the heavy military aircraft lumbered to a parking spot at a remote location on the other side of the airfield to drop them off. The pilot had radioed ahead. Decker and Daisy descended the airstairs to find a golf cart waiting that whisked them straight to the terminal building. Soon after, they were leaving the parking lot in a hire car rented on Daisy's credit card and heading toward the waterfront where CUSP's private ferry departed several times a day, shuttling employees to and from the organization's headquarters on a rocky island in Casco Bay.

"I'd like to stop at my place first," Decker said, as they drew close. He could tell that Daisy was concerned about her mother and everyone else on the island, but she merely nodded and changed direction, taking a slight detour to the house that Decker shared with Nancy.

When they arrived, he jumped out of the car and raced up the path. Then he came to a halt and stared in horror. The front door was standing open, and snow had drifted into the house, covering the wood floor of the entryway with a light dusting.

When Daisy came up behind him, he turned to her. "The doppelgänger was here."

"That doesn't mean anything happened to Nancy," Daisy said, stepping past Decker and into the house. "You told her to leave."

"It also doesn't mean that she made it out before he got here." Decker made his way through the house to their bedroom. On the way, he looked for any sign of a struggle but saw nothing. No toppled furniture. Nothing broken. Even better, no blood. In the bedroom, he went to the wall safe and typed in the code. He was relieved to see that the cash and burner phone were gone. Then he saw something else. A folded sheet of paper with his name written on the front in Nancy's unmistakable handwriting. He took the sheet out and unfolded it.

John,

I'm leaving now. Don't worry about me. I'll go somewhere far away and wait for your call. Stay safe. I can't lose you again.

Love Nancy

Decker was overcome with relief. There was no way he could know for sure, but it was more than likely that she had escaped before the doppelgänger had broken into the house.

Daisy came up behind him. "Happy?"

"Happy enough." Decker folded the sheet, then folded it again and slipped it into his back pocket. He stepped around Daisy and out of the bedroom, then made his way back toward the front door. "Let's go find out why no one over on that island is answering our calls."

SIXTY-EIGHT

THE FERRY WAS GONE. The dock where it should have been moored waiting for the first passengers of the day was empty. Decker squinted out across the bay toward the rays of dawn sun that were spilling across the eastern horizon, and the many islands that dotted the water. He could see the rocky sliver of land upon which CUSP had made their headquarters as a silhouetted hump against the morning sky. What he couldn't see was any sign of trouble.

"We have to get over to that island," Daisy said, standing next to him.

"Then I suggest we find someone willing to rent us a boat," Decker replied. He looked around at the fishing vessels, yachts, and tourist charters tied to their moorings in the harbor. "Can't be too hard."

"There's somewhere I need to go first." Daisy turned and started back toward the rental car. "It's not far. I'll tell you how to get there."

They climbed back into the car and Daisy gave turn by turn directions until they arrived at a small nondescript brick building in an industrial area on the edge of town. She climbed

ANTHONY M. STRONG

out and led them to a rusty steel door sprayed with graffiti and secured by a hefty padlock. She unlocked it to reveal a square entryway. Beyond that was a second metal door, smooth and shiny with no handle or visible locking mechanism except a small oblong panel with a face of polished black glass set into the wall nearby.

Daisy leaned toward the panel and stared into it. A moment later, there was a click, and the door slid open.

"Retina scanner?" Decker asked.

Daisy nodded and stepped into the room beyond, even as concealed lighting flickered on, illuminating the space.

When Decker stepped across the threshold, he found himself in a large, windowless chamber with walls made of smooth, unblemished steel. Sturdy metal racks lined the walls. Racks that contained a veritable armory of weapons, some of which Decker recognized, like a row of AR-15 assault rifles, a selection of Glock pistols, and even a shoulder mounted rocket launcher. Other weapons were less familiar.

He stared in wonder. "What is this place?"

"It's exactly what it looks like. An armory." Daisy skirted an oblong table in the middle of the room and went to a rack containing sleek handguns that looked more like something out of a science-fiction movie than anything that existed in the real world. "Every CUSP location around the world has an off-site facility like this nearby as a precaution against hostile activity."

"Smart." Decker crossed to a matte black box with a control panel on one side that was sitting on a shelf. "If anything happens to the primary location, field operatives can still arm themselves and fight back."

"Yes." Daisy motioned for Decker to step away from the box. "You don't want to touch that. It's a localized EMP device. Activate it by accident and you will short-circuit every piece of technology within a two-mile radius."

"Okay. Leaving the box alone." Decker turned back to Daisy. "What are we here for?"

266

"These." Daisy lifted two of the futuristic handguns from their cradles, then picked up a pair of shoulder holsters. She gave one of each to Decker and kept the others for herself. "You might want to put that under your jacket until we get to the island."

"Got it." Decker took his jacket off and strapped the holster to his side before slipping the gun into it. "What exactly do these things do?"

"The same thing that every gun does," Daisy replied. "They shoot bullets. The difference is that these particular bullets act more like heat-seeking missiles, only much more sophisticated. Lock onto a target with the digital sights on the gun, and the bullet will hit its mark even if the target has moved by the time you pull the trigger. Even better, you can fire again and again without reacquiring your target so long as you don't clear the lock from the gun's memory."

"And the bullets will follow the target wherever they go?"

"Yes. The bullets are programmable. You can fire straight up into the air, and they will alter course to find their mark. Of course, it's easier just to point the gun in the direction of what you want to hit."

"Where did you get technology like this?"

"From DARPA," Daisy replied, citing the US government's Defense Advanced Research Projects Agency. "But it's still experimental and beyond top-secret, so don't expect to see these weapons on the battlefield anytime soon."

"Yet we already have them in our possession."

Daisy shrugged. "What can I say? They like us."

"What other cool stuff do you have hidden away in here?" Decker asked, looking around.

"Nothing that we need right now." Daisy went to a panel set into the far wall that turned out to be a safe and typed a code into a digital keypad to open it, then withdrew a thick wad of twenty-dollar bills secured by a rubber band. She closed the safe and tucked the money into her pocket. "To get us a boat. Cash talks."

"And it's untraceable."

"Right. That, too." Daisy was already making for the door. "Come on. We have an island to visit."

SIXTY-NINE

IT DIDN'T TAKE them long to find a charter boat captain willing to ferry them to the island, especially since Daisy paid him twice what he asked in exchange for his discretion.

As they cruised out of the harbor, Decker asked Daisy something that had been on his mind. "I've been thinking about the shapeshifter. Thomas Barringer—sorry, Nathan Bailey-must have had more in mind for him than just shooting you and stealing our jet."

"I'm assuming that he used the shapeshifter to gain access to the island and our headquarters," Daisy said. "Which is why I'm so concerned that we haven't been able to contact anyone over there for such a long time."

"I agree. But the thing is, the shapeshifter won't be able to stay looking like me forever, right?"

"That's true. If he's anything like the other shapeshifters I've encountered over the years, he will revert to his true form somewhere around twenty-four to thirty-six hours after assuming your identity. Unless he gets a fresh infusion of your DNA, that is. And since Bailey and that woman who works for him only took one small syringe of your cerebrospinal fluid, I don't think that is likely."

"Which means that we could run into him over on the island and not know it."

"In theory. But after so many hours, I would be surprised if any hostile actors are still over there."

"You can't know that for sure," Decker said. "Because we don't know with certainty what Bailey's agenda is."

"I can guess." Daisy stared over the boat's bow and out across the choppy gray waters toward the island, which was growing larger in front of them as they drew close. "His goal isn't to occupy the island, which would not be a sustainable objective. He wants revenge against Adam Hunt. He will have done his damage and fled."

"The question is, how much damage did he do?"

"I guess we're about to find out," Daisy replied as the boat reached the easternmost tip of the island and followed the shoreline until the dock came into view, and the road that led away from it toward CUSP's headquarters standing above a cliff on the opposite shore.

But instead of approaching the dock, the captain stopped his boat a couple of hundred yards distant. Because there was already a vessel there. Or at least, what remained of it. The ferry was half sunk with its stern below the water and its bow, which was blackened and charred by fire, tilted upward at an angle.

"I guess that explains why the ferry was missing," Decker said, staring at the ruined vessel with a growing sense of dread.

"We need to get ashore." Daisy turned her attention to the captain. "Can you get us there?"

"Not sure I want to risk it," he said, eying the stricken vessel and the large swells that battered it. "There's no way to get close to the dock with a boat this size."

"What about that outcrop?" Daisy said, pointing to a jagged, rocky protrusion thrusting into the ocean to the left of the dock.

"Are you crazy?" The captain shook his head. "With those waves? One wrong move and we'll slam into the wreck, or worse, have our hull ripped open by some rock hiding under the surface. Next thing you know, we'll be on the seafloor."

Daisy pulled out her ward of cash, peeled off five more twenty-dollar bills. She crossed the deck to the wheelhouse and held them out. "Will this change your mind?"

The captain took the money and counted it quickly, keeping one hand on his wheel. "Double the amount and I'll see what I can do. But if you make it ashore, you're on your own. I'm not waiting around for you to return. Not under these circumstances. It's too dangerous."

"Fair enough," Daisy said, taking several more bills from her stash and handing them to the captain.

He took the cash and pushed it deep into his pocket. "Better brace yourselves. This is going to get rough."

Daisy returned to the front of the boat where Decker was standing, then gripped the rail as the captain pointed his vessel toward the rocks and powered up the motor. They cut through the water, drawing close to the shore. At the last moment, he swung the wheel hard, bringing the boat around parallel with the outcrop so that it was five feet off their starboard side.

"If you're going, now's the time," the captain shouted over the crashing waves. "I can't hold her here like this for long."

"You want to go first?" Decker asked, looking at Daisy.

"Not really, but I will." Daisy ducked under the rail and stood on the outside, gripping it with both hands. As the boat rose, lifted by a swell, she bent her knees, waited for the wave to lift them to its apex, and launched herself toward the rocks.

For a moment, she hung in the air, and Decker was overcome by a sickening certainty that she was going to fall short and drop between the boat and the outcrop, where she would be crushed. But then, just as she started to lose altitude, her feet found a boulder with a flat top, and she was able to grab the rocks and steady herself before scrambling up and onto the shore.

"Now it's your turn," she screeched into the blustering wind.

Decker was already on the outside of the rail and anticipating the next rise, which would give him extra momentum as he jumped. And then his feet left the deck. The rocks rushed up to greet him, sharp and deadly. He aimed for the same flat boulder Daisy had landed on, but at the last moment, a sudden gust of wind twisted him in the air. He landed hard, stumbled, and almost toppled backwards into the frothy surf at the base of the outcrop, but then he felt a hand grip his arm and heave him forward to safety.

Daisy was standing atop the outcrop, a faint smirk on her face. "You jump like a girl."

"You weren't exactly a picture of grace." Decker climbed up over the rocks and joined her, even as their ride backed away from the rocks and turned its bow toward Portland. Decker watched the boat plow through the water for a moment before rubbing his hands on his jeans to dry them. "There goes our only way off this island."

"Not true. There's a causeway at low tide that connects us to the next island over where there's a small town. They have a harbor and fishing boats. If we can make it there, we can find someone to take us back."

"We couldn't have just gone there now instead of jumping off that damned boat?" Decker asked.

"No. Like I said, the causeway is only accessible during low tide, which is at least a couple of hours away. We don't have the luxury of waiting that long." She turned and started toward the dock, and the paved parking area beyond.

There would normally have been a shuttle bus waiting to pick up passengers from the ferry and drive them to the facility, but he didn't see it, which meant they would have to walk along a narrow road with trees on both sides, part of the woodland that covered the middle of the island. It was a trek of about two miles. Not a huge distance, but time-consuming when every second counted, because they had no idea what they were going to find at the other end.

Daisy must have been thinking the same thing, because she

fell silent as they started walking. No doubt her thoughts were on Adam and Mina, and what tragedy might have befallen their headquarters. But she had barely any time to dwell on the subject, because no sooner had they started walking than a gigantic shadow fell across the road ahead of them. A shadow that swept across the ground at an alarming speed.

Decker raised his eyes skyward in time to see a winged creature with brown leathery skin and a long, thin tail swoop through the air above their heads.

He ducked instinctively as the beast cut a lazy arc through the sky above the trees and turned back toward them. "What the hell is that?"

"That would be a dragon," Daisy said, her voice heavy with fear. "And now we need to run."

SEVENTY

IT WAS dawn by the time Nancy and Celine arrived back in Portland. Nancy had been so keen to return that she had given little thought to what they would actually do when they got there. Without a solid plan, they went to Celine's house and locked themselves inside. Nancy sat on the sofa while Celine went to the kitchen and made coffee, which they drank black and strong. The caffeine swept away some of Nancy's exhaustion and she could finally think straight.

"John was coming back to Maine. He probably hasn't been able to get in touch with Mina or anyone else any more than we have. He'll go straight to the island."

Celine shook her head. "That's not true. He'll go to the house first and make sure that you got out."

"And when he finds it empty, he'll go to the island, because he won't know what else to do." Nancy wished she had some way to contact her husband, but he didn't have his phone, which meant that she had no choice but to wait for him to call her. It was infuriating.

"Maybe."

"Which is why we should go there, too."

"Are you crazy?" Celine stared at Nancy, a quizzical look on her face. "Just head on over to CUSP's secret headquarters and knock on the door?"

"Do you have a better idea?"

"We should've stayed at the motel."

"But we didn't. You agreed to come back. What did you think we were going to do?"

"I don't know." Celine leaned forward and rested her elbows on her knees. "How would we even get to the island? It's not like we can just hop on the ferry. They check IDs."

"Considering that no one over there appears to be communicating, I doubt the ferry is running," Nancy said. "Something bad has happened. I can feel it."

"That still doesn't answer my question."

Nancy thought for a moment. "Easy. We get a boat of our own. The harbor is full of them, and we have a wad of cash."

Celine was silent for a long minute, presumably contemplating this course of action. Then she nodded. "Beats sitting around here and waiting for that doppelgänger to show up and kill us."

Nancy grinned. "My thoughts exactly."

Celine jumped to her feet. "Then let's go."

Fifteen minutes later, they were at the waterfront and strolling past the piers, looking for a suitable vessel. There were boats of all shapes and sizes, from the occasional luxury yacht to rowing boats with oars placed across the seats. Most of the boats were dark and empty. The only people around were fishermen who had not set out in search of a catch yet. They approached several of the men but received the same answer each time. They weren't available for hire and didn't have time to make a detour to the island.

Disheartened, Celine turned to Nancy. "This is a waste of time. We should go back to the house and sit it out until John calls."

Nancy stuck out her chin. "I'm not doing that."

"Well, what do we do now, then?"

"We keep searching for a ride."

Celine opened her mouth to reply, then slammed it shut, her gaze drifting past Nancy to the end of the pier that they were on. Her eyes widened. "Better make it fast. We have company."

Nancy followed Celine's gaze, and fear clutched at her heart. There, at the end of the pier, blocking their only way back onto solid land, was a figure she recognized too well. "The doppelgänger. He's found us."

"I told you this was a bad idea." Celine looked around, hoping for another means of escape, but none presented itself. Save for jumping in the frigid water, that was.

Nancy had come to the same conclusion. "If all else fails, we jump and swim."

"And hope that we don't freeze to death."

"It's not that far," Nancy said, looking at the next pier across. "We'll be fine."

"Screw that. I hate water." Celine reached under her jacket and drew her gun. The doppelgänger was still standing at the end of the pier watching them, and perhaps waiting for them to make the first move. "He comes any closer, I'll shoot him."

"And end up in jail for murder if anyone sees you," Nancy said, shaking her head. She looked around, watching a dinghy of the kind used by larger boats for its occupants to reach shore. It was cutting through the water and approaching at a fast clip, guided by a single male occupant wearing a thick cable-knit sweater. She prayed it wouldn't keep going past the pier.

It didn't.

The small vessel made straight for an empty slip and pulled in.

Nancy's heart leaped. She raced toward the slip and looked down at the boat's occupant, a burly man with a scraggly salt and pepper beard that seemed to run unchecked across his face.

"We need your help," she shouted over the gusting wind. "That man at the end of the pier has been following us. I think he wants to harm us. We need your boat. My husband is on an island across the bay. Will you take us there?"

For a moment, the boat's pilot just stared up at her. Then his eyes narrowed even as his gaze shifted to the figure at the end of the pier. "That man wants to do you harm?"

"Yes. Please, we need to go right now."

"We can pay you." Celine quietly slipped the gun back under her coat. "We have cash."

"I'm not taking your cash," the man said in a thick New England brogue. "And I'm not letting that fella lay so much as a finger on you."

He stood and climbed from the boat, never taking his eyes off the doppelgänger.

"Please, no," Nancy said, realizing that the sailor was going to be a hero. "Just take us to the island."

"Not before I teach that fella a lesson for harassing the two of you." The sailor stepped past them and started down the pier.

Nancy watched with growing horror as he approached the man who looked like her husband. There was a brief exchange between the pair that she could not hear, but judging by the sailor's stance, it was not friendly. Then, quick as lightning, the doppelgänger made his move. She saw a flash of steel. A knife. Moments later, the sailor's legs gave way beneath him, and he crumpled to the ground in a motionless heap. At the same time, a shout went up from somewhere further afield. A second man, who had obviously seen the altercation, was approaching at a fast pace from a bait and tackle hut situated on the wharf.

Celine reached inside her jacket again for the gun.

Nancy tore her gaze away from the dreadful scene on the other end of the pier. The doppelgänger, ignoring the man from the bait hut, started toward them.

Celine raised the gun with shaking hands and fired. The bullet whizzed harmlessly past their attacker.

Nancy reached out and put her hand on Celine's arm, trying

to force the gun down. "Stop. You're going to hit an innocent bystander."

Celine pushed back against her. "It's all we have."

"Not true," Nancy said, her gaze drifting down to the dinghy. The ignition key was still in the outboard motor, forgotten by the sailor in his haste to defend their honor. Nancy pushed Celine toward the slip, then bundled her down into the boat.

The doppelgänger was closing in on them and appeared unworried by the weapon in Celine's hand.

There wasn't much time. Nancy jumped down into the boat and started the motor. A moment later, even as the doppelgänger reached the slip, they were pulling away.

Nancy risked a glance back as they headed toward the open water. The doppelgänger was standing on the pier, glaring at them. Then he turned and strode off, even as a distant wail of sirens floated on the ocean breeze. For a moment, she relaxed. The police were on their way and would surely take him into custody. Then another thought occurred to her. He looked and sounded just like her husband, which meant that when they fingerprinted him, took his mug shot, John Decker would be a murderer. What that meant, she didn't know, given that they would already have the doppelgänger in a jail cell. But she knew one thing. It wouldn't be good.

SEVENTY-ONE

DECKER RAN for the trees with Daisy beside him as the winged creature above them swooped down. A blast of red-hot flames slammed into the ground behind them, singing the hairs on the back of his neck.

"Really?" he said in a breathless voice as they reached the safety of the woods. "It breathes fire, too?"

"It's a dragon." Daisy took shelter behind a tall birch tree. "What do you expect?"

"I wasn't expecting to get roasted." Decker risked a glance back toward the road. A black scorch mark scarred the asphalt. Curls of smoke rose into the morning air. "How do we even have a dragon, anyway?"

"George has been with us since the fifties after farmers complained of their sheep going missing. Found him living in a cave in the Scottish Highlands. Last of his kind, as far as we know."

"You called that beast George?" Decker peered up through the trees and toward the sky, but the dragon was nowhere in sight now.

"Sure. Like in George and the Dragon."

"Wasn't George the one who slayed the dragon in that story?"

"Close enough. He needed a name."

"Fair enough." Decker spotted the dragon silhouetted against the sun as it flew overhead for a second time. "Where were you keeping a creature that large? There's no way you had it locked up in The Zoo."

"We have a special enclosure on the north end of the island, where it has plenty of room to live out its life in comfort."

"Well, it's got a bunch more room now." Decker pulled his gun from its holster. The fancy weapon with the high-tech bullets that he had taken from the armory.

Daisy glared at him. "You're not shooting at George."

"Have you got a better idea?" Decker asked. "Because in case you hadn't noticed, your pet dragon is trying to kill us."

"Which is his nature. Once we get to our destination, we'll get him safely back into the enclosure."

"I guess it's George's lucky day." Decker reluctantly returned the gun to its holster. "How the hell did that thing even get loose?"

"My money is on the doppelgänger. All the animal enclosures on the island, including The Zoo, are monitored from a central control room. Your double must have gained access and released the dragon."

"What better way to sow chaos," Decker said.

"Exactly. But he couldn't have done it alone. Someone must have provided him with the security codes necessary to unlock the enclosure."

"Which confirms that Barringer—a.k.a. Bailey—still has someone on the inside."

"Yes. Someone with access to sensitive information." Daisy glanced up at the sky. "The question is, if they released the dragon, how many other creatures did they set free from other enclosures or even from The Zoo?"

"That's a question that will have to wait until we reach

headquarters," Decker said. "But I know one thing. We can't keep walking along the road with that creature up there."

As if to prove him right, the dragon gave a screeching cry from high above their heads. This was swiftly followed by a thin but deadly jet of fire that set the trees near the road alight.

Daisy scurried back, away from the searing flames. "We'll have to go through the woods instead. It will be slower, but safer."

"If we're lucky, the dragon will keep looking for us here."

Daisy nodded, even as she turned and started through the woods toward the other side of the island, picking her way through the dense undergrowth. "Dragons aren't the smartest of beasts. They also tend to obsess once they get something in their head. It won't give up easily, but it probably won't widen its search field, either. It will just circle up there, waiting for us to reappear until it eventually loses interest."

Decker pushed the branches of a prickly bush aside, ignoring the thorns that scratched his skin. "That's another thing. Why didn't the dragon just fly off and escape? Leave the island behind?"

"Because it can't. We have a secondary security system that protects the outside world if something catastrophic happens. The island has an invisible dome over it. An electromagnetic barrier. Every creature we bring here is implanted with a chip that stops them from crossing through that barrier. If they try, the chip will induce a reaction in their brain that temporarily disables them. It's completely harmless and doesn't hurt the creature, but it does mean that they can't leave the island even if they escape their enclosure."

"Well, that's good to know, at least." Decker glanced over his shoulder as another cry split the air, but this time it sounded further away. Daisy was right. The creature had stayed right where it was, looking for them. But now another thought occurred to him. If the dragon had gotten loose, what else was out here in these woods? "Not counting The Zoo, how many other enclosures do you have on the island?"

Daisy was silent for a moment, as if she didn't want to answer, then she said: "Fourteen. All on the north end of the island."

"Dare I ask what you have in them?"

"I'm not sure that you want to know, under the circumstances."

"Maybe not. But I also don't want to get eaten by something I don't see coming."

Daisy nodded. "We have a smilodon—that's a saber-toothed cat—and a pair of bigfoots. We also have an ogre. Those are probably the most dangerous of the island's permanent residents. Excluding the creatures that we keep in The Zoo, of course."

"And any one of them could be roaming these woods right now."

"It's probably best if you don't think about it," Daisy said. "Let's just focus on the job at hand and worry about the smilodon if it finds us. And anyway, we don't even know if any of the other creatures escaped."

Decker was about to tell Daisy that she was a hopeless optimist. If Bailey had released the dragon, he had also surely released other monsters. But he never got the chance, because at that moment there was a noise off to their left. Something large moving through the underbrush toward them.

Daisy had heard it, too. She took her gun from its holster. "We have company."

"Yeah." Decker scanned the surrounding woods but saw nothing. "Maybe it's just a deer."

Daisy was on full alert. "Hate to burst your bubble, but there are no deer on the island. In fact, there isn't anything larger than a squirrel."

"Except for the smilodon and his pals."

"Yes. Except for them."

Another sound off to the left.

The sharp snap of the twig.

Daisy raised her gun.

Decker reached for his own weapon. But there was no time.

The bushes parted. A dark shape appeared. Then all hell broke loose.

SEVENTY-TWO

THEY CRUISED out across the bay with Nancy steering the boat and Celine sitting in the bow. Ahead of them, a couple of miles distant, was their destination. CUSP's island headquarters. Beyond that, rolling across the ocean from the horizon, was a thick bank of winter fog.

At first, Nancy relaxed. They had escaped from the doppelgänger, who by now would surely be in police custody for assaulting the man whose boat they now occupied. She hoped he was not dead, but suspected he might be. That thought filled her with remorse. If only she hadn't involved him, the man might still be alive. On the other hand, she had done all that she could to stop him from engaging with the shapeshifter.

Then there was her husband. She was sure that he would have made his way straight to the island after arriving back in Maine. Once they got there, she would be reunited with him. The emotions swirled within her, a strange mix of anticipation and sorrow.

It was short-lived.

They were halfway across the bay when Celine gave a strangled shout. "There's a boat. It's coming right toward us."

Nancy turned to see a small speedboat cutting across the

water in their direction. It was more powerful than the dinghy, with twin outboard motors that left a frothy wake in its trail. And at the helm, the doppelgänger.

"What the hell?" Nancy turned the tiller, trying to weave away from the approaching danger, but it was a pointless endeavor. No sooner had she altered course than the speedboat did the same. Worse, it was gaining on them with remarkable speed, its bow aimed directly at their midsection.

"He's going to ram us," Celine said, her voice cracking. "What are we going to do?"

"Shoot him," Nancy replied. "Shoot at the boat. Shoot anything."

Celine fumbled with the gun, raised it. She pulled the trigger. The sharp crack echoed across the bay and was soon swept up into the wind.

The boat kept coming. If Celine had scored a hit, it wasn't evident.

"I thought Colum taught you how to fire that thing," Nancy said, glancing quickly toward her companion.

"He did. On a range. I wasn't shooting at moving targets and people." Celine aimed the gun and fired again.

The boat veered to the left, but soon resumed its course, closing the gap between them.

Nancy made one last frantic attempt to evade the oncoming threat, but it was no use. The speedboat had them outmatched and outpaced. It flew through the water, bow lifting, and crashed into them, slicing through the middle of the dinghy.

At the last moment before impact, Nancy gave up on the tiller, and dove into the water. She went under, sucking in a mouthful of icy water before surfacing with a sputtering cough.

To her dismay, she saw the dinghy, now partially deflated, slip beneath the waves and sink. Further afield, the speedboat was turning for another pass.

A sudden panic gripped Nancy. Where was Celine? Had the speedboat hit and killed her as it rammed them? Had the vessel's twin outboard motors sliced her to pieces on its way through?

Nancy looked around, frantic to find her friend. And there she was, several feet away, surfacing with a splash.

When she saw Nancy, she swam toward her. But at that moment, the speedboat arrived back on the scene, positioning itself between the pair. Treading water to stay afloat, Nancy watched the doppelgänger lean over the side and haul Celine into the boat. There was a brief struggle as Celine fought back, but then the doppelgänger delivered a powerful punch to her face. Celine went limp in his arms before he lowered her onto the deck of the boat. Then he turned his attention to Nancy, steering the speedboat close enough to grab her by the lapel of her coat and heave her up over the side of the boat and out of the water before flinging her down onto the deck.

"You were more trouble than I anticipated," said the doppelgänger in a voice that sounded less like her husband with each word. "But now it's time to finish this."

The knife appeared again, still slick with the sailor's blood. Or maybe it was that of whoever owned the speedboat, because Nancy was sure the doppelgänger had not rented it.

She shrank back, pushing away from him with her feet. He raised the knife and took a step toward her. And then she noticed something curious. His face was undulating as if it were made of some pliable material that couldn't hold its form. One moment, he was John Decker. The next, he was a man with heavy brows and a wide jaw that she didn't recognize.

She stared in horror as the twin faces merged to become a third countenance, part Decker and part stranger, before that face fell away as well. Then, as they watched, the man's face puckered and stretched, almost as if it were being kneaded like bread by invisible hands.

The man staggered forward, determined to complete his task even though he was clearly undergoing a painful metamorphosis and returning to his true form. He gripped the knife tightly in one hand and reached toward her with the other.

Nancy had scooted back as far as she could. There was nowhere else to go. She closed her eyes, waiting for the cold bite of steel and the inevitable slide into death that would follow.

But then, just as she thought it was over, a gunshot.

She opened her eyes in time to see the shapeshifter spin around as a second gunshot split the air. His shirt, once white, was swiftly turning a dark shade of crimson, even as Celine fired one last deadly shot.

The doppelgänger staggered backwards with a look of surprise mixed with anger on his face. The knife fell from his hand and clattered harmlessly onto the deck.

Then his feet hit the side of the boat and he pitched overboard, landing in the water with a mighty splash.

Nancy scrambled to her feet, half expecting the man to climb back in and finish what he started. But instead, she saw the doppelgänger's lifeless body floating face down in a widening pool of blood that stained the sea around it an angry red.

She looked at Celine. "You did it. You saved us."

Celine grinned wearily. "I guess Colum taught me how to shoot, after all." Then she added, "even if it was at point-blank range."

"Who cares?" Nancy said, watching the body as it floated further from the boat. "He's gone, and we are safe."

"And freezing, too," Celine said, wrapping her arms around her torso and glancing over her shoulder toward the island that was still a good mile or more away. "You think you can drive this boat?"

"I'll give it a try," said Nancy, turning toward the twin outboard motors and inspecting them. "And if worse comes to worst we're floating in that direction, anyway."

SEVENTY-THREE

DAISY TOOK a diving roll to the left, bringing her gun up at the same time. Decker finally freed his gun from its holster and threw himself to the right, landing hard before rising to a kneeling position and bringing his weapon to bear.

They had the creature outflanked. It could only go after one of them, leaving the other with a clear shot. Except that it wasn't a smilodon. Nor was it a bigfoot. Instead, a man carrying a rifle and wearing a camouflage uniform stood there, looking startled. There was a Ghost Team patch on his sleeve. The name sewn onto his uniform identified him as Corporal Tony Shaw.

No sooner had his eyes settled upon Decker than he raised his gun. "Stay right there. Place your weapon on the ground and don't move."

A second man appeared from between the trees. He wore the same uniform as his colleague, except that his rank was private first class. He leveled his weapon on Decker. "Do what the corporal says. Drop the weapon."

Decker placed his weapon on the ground and raised his arms. "I don't know what's going on here, but I'm not a threat."

The corporal scowled. "That's not what it looks like from where I'm standing. You killed a lot of people today."

"Perhaps you would care to explain that comment," Daisy said, rising to her feet.

The corporal whirled around. When he saw Daisy, his eyes widened with surprise. "Ma'am? What are you doing here with this traitor?"

"Mr. Decker is not a traitor. Now explain yourself."

The soldier glanced between Daisy and Decker. "This man led an attack on the facility. He betrayed us."

"That is not true," Daisy said in a firm voice. "Would I be with him if Mr. Decker was a traitor?"

"Well, I…" Shaw looked confused.

"The answer you're looking for is no."

"Ma'am, I beg to differ. I saw Mr. Decker kill one of my men. Dropped him in cold blood."

Daisy took a step forward. "The man you saw was a doppelgänger. A shapeshifter who assumed Mr. Decker's identity. Now lower your weapons. These woods aren't safe for any of us."

Shaw finally lowered his weapon and motioned for his colleague to do the same.

"Thank you," Daisy breathed a sigh of relief. "You had us worried there for a moment. I thought you might shoot Mr. Decker before I could stop you."

"Sorry, ma'am," replied the corporal. "We were making a final sweep through the woods on the side of the island and heard someone moving through the woods. Figured it must be an escapee from The Zoo. Then we saw Mr. Decker here, and, well…"

"It's fine," said Decker. "I would have done the same thing in your position."

"I'm glad you're not a traitor." Corporal Shaw smiled. "We've met before. A couple of years ago in Ireland when you captured Grendel. I was part of the extraction team that brought him and his mother to The Zoo."

Decker racked his brain, but couldn't recall the man's face.

"A lot has happened since then."

"Yes sir, it has." Shaw turned to Daisy. "You should know that The Zoo has been compromised. At least half the residents escaped. We've rounded a few of them up, but most are still on the loose."

"What about Adam Hunt and my mother?" Daisy asked, although the look on her face told Decker that she was dreading the answer. "The rest of the people who work here?"

"Most of them are safe. They made it to the secure bunker. Your mother is there."

"Thank heavens." Daisy's shoulders slumped. "I was so worried when I couldn't get through to her."

"The hostiles took out the cellphone tower and radio mast. They also disabled the undersea fiberoptic lines. We haven't had any communication with the outside world since the attack." Corporal Shaw hesitated. "There is one more thing that you should know."

"What?" The fear had returned to Daisy's face.

"Adam Hunt. He's gone. We searched the entire facility after the attack." Shaw took a deep breath, his Adam's apple bobbing up and down. "They took him."

SEVENTY-FOUR

THE CORPORAL WASTED no time in calling for transportation, and soon they were all heading back to CUSP's headquarters. As they drove, Shaw radioed ahead and explained the situation to avoid any more misunderstandings that might have gotten Decker shot. When they arrived, he escorted them straight to the secure bunker within which pretty much everyone except the Ghost Team had taken refuge during the attack.

Decker was horrified at the damage their headquarters had sustained. Furniture was overturned. Glass was shattered. Bullet holes riddled the walls. The power was out, reducing visibility in the building to the weak glow of emergency lighting. Here and there, he saw streaks of blood. A testament to the violence that had recently occurred.

CUSP's headquarters comprised an eighteenth-century mansion once owned by a wealthy railroad magnate, and a newer, much larger wing that had been added when the organization took over the island. The bunker was on a subterranean level beneath the addition and had everything needed to protect and sustain the facility's staff for up to a month in case of an emergency. There were sleeping quarters, a commercial kitchen, medical facilities, a control room that connected to The Zoo and CUSP's other locations around the world—at least when hostile actors had not taken communications out—and a common area large enough for everyone to gather comfortably.

When they entered, Mina ran up to them. She threw her arms around Decker. "I knew you hadn't betrayed us."

"Never." Decker was relieved to see so many familiar faces, but there was one person he knew would not be there. "They took Adam."

"Yes. The attack on our island appears to have been planned for just that purpose," Mina said. She motioned for Daisy and Decker to follow her, then made her way to a secure briefing room where they wouldn't be overheard. Once they were all inside, she turned to them. "Just a precaution. At this point, I don't know who to trust. Present company excepted, of course."

"Of course." Decker took a seat at an oval table in the middle of the room and waited for the others to do the same before he turned his attention to Mina and spoke again. "Thomas Barringer is responsible for what happened in Louisiana. He lured me there by making it look like the loup-garou had returned, but in reality, it was a regular werewolf. He's also the one behind the attack on the island."

"Barringer." Mina didn't look surprised. "Or rather, Nathan Bailey. I should have known. Clearly, we underestimated him."

"Apparently. And now he has Adam Hunt," Decker said.

"I take it Daisy told you what happened between the two of them all those years ago?"

"Yes, she did." Decker leaned forward and rested his elbows on the table. "How did Bailey pull this off? How did he manage to abduct Hunt from a facility with more state-of-the-art security than the Pentagon?"

"I'm sure we can't compete with the Pentagon," Mina said. "But it should have been impossible."

"Which is why they needed to have their own John Decker," Daisy said.

"Yes. Someone we trusted implicitly who could get through our security and disable it. We were taken completely by surprise. By the time we realized our defenses were down, it was too late. There were hostiles on the island. At least twenty of them. A highly trained strike force that acted with military precision. And then, to make it worse, Decker overrode the security protocols and released every creature in The Zoo, which should have been impossible."

"Not me," Decker said. "A shapeshifter, and he must have had help, probably from the inside. The Watchers had infiltrated The Order of St. George way back in 1911." Decker looked at Mina. "That's how they were able to abduct *you*."

"Don't remind me," Mina said with a shudder.

"I wasn't trying to bring up bad memories," Decker replied. "But who knows how many double agents they've had in The Order and CUSP since that time? They certainly wouldn't have launched an attack on this facility if they weren't sure they would succeed."

"Agreed," Mina said. "And I have every intention of finding and punishing anyone who helped to do this, but right now, we have a more immediate concern. Adam Hunt. We have to get him back before it's too late."

"And how do you plan to do that?" Daisy asked. "We have no idea where they took him, or even if he's still alive."

"He's alive. I can feel it."

"I hope you're right." Decker didn't share Mina's optimism. He was about to say more, but at that moment, there was a knock at the door.

It was Tony Shaw, the Ghost Team corporal they had encountered in the woods. "Sorry to interrupt, but I just thought you would like to know that the cell phone tower is now back up and running."

"Thank heaven for that," Daisy said.

"We're still working on the fiber-optic cable and the radio mast. Those suffered more extensive damage and might take a little longer."

"Thank you, corporal," Mina said, dismissing the man.

He nodded and retreated, closing the door.

When they were alone again, Decker turned to Mina. "I need a phone. A secure handset."

Mina nodded. "I can arrange that."

Daisy looked at him. "You're worried about Nancy?"

"Yes." Decker wished they hadn't left Daisy's phone behind in Louisiana, but there had been no choice. Bailey might have been able to trace it, and he didn't want to tip their hand that Daisy was still alive and that he had escaped from the holding cell they had put him in.

Mina was already moving toward the door. She exited the room, but she wasn't gone long. After less than ten minutes, she returned with a phone in one hand, which she offered to Decker.

"Here," she said, turning back toward the door, motioning for Daisy to follow her. "We'll give you some privacy."

"Thank you." Decker took the phone and waited until he was alone, before dialing the number of the burner phone, which he had committed to memory back when they had first moved to Portland, and he began working for CUSP.

It only rang once before Nancy answered. The relief in her voice was evident. "John. Thank goodness. I've been waiting for you to call."

Decker's anxiety fell away in an instant. "I've been worried about you. I saw the door at the house was open."

"The doppelgänger came after me, but I escaped," Nancy said. "I went to Celine's house. We took Colum's car and found a motel in the middle of nowhere. Somewhere that the shapeshifter couldn't find us."

"Good. Stay there until I tell you it's safe to come back."

There was a heavy silence on the other end of the phone before Nancy spoke again. "We're not there anymore. I couldn't take it, just sitting in that hotel room and hiding like a scared mouse, so we came back to Portland."

"You did what?" The fear lurched back.

"Please don't be mad. I wanted to face this thing head-on. You would have done the same thing."

"Because it's my job." Decker tried to keep the frustration from his voice, wasn't sure that he managed it. "You need to turn around right now and get back to that hotel."

"It's too late for that. We're on our way to the island."

"What?" Decker's fear inched to terror. The Ghost Team were rounding up creatures released by his doppelgänger, but they hadn't completed the task. "You can't come here. It's not safe."

"I'm not turning around, especially if you're on the island. We're almost at the dock. There's a sunken boat there, but our boat is small. I can probably maneuver around it and get ashore." Nancy paused again. "There's something else."

Decker was afraid to hear what Nancy was going to say next. The conversation was going from bad to worse. He waited for her to talk, the open phone line between them pregnant with expectation.

Nancy took a deep breath. "The doppelgänger. He found us after we came back. Got a boat of his own and chased us."

Decker's worst fears were confirmed. "Where is he now?"

Another pause. "He's dead. We killed him."

Decker gave this a moment to sink in, then he composed himself. There was no point insisting that Nancy turn around and go back to Portland. He could tell from the tone of her voice that she was determined to reach him. "When you get to the dock, don't come ashore. I'll have people meet you there and bring you to the facility. Soldiers who work for us. Do you understand?"

"John?"

"Just do as I say. It's important. The island isn't safe."

"Okay. Fine. We'll wait for the men with guns."

"Thank you." Decker didn't want to hang up, but knew he had no choice. He told her that he loved her, then ended the call. After that, he sprinted from the room to find Mina. He only hoped that Nancy would be safe until the Ghost Team got there.

SEVENTY-FIVE

DECKER WAITED for Nancy in a set of private sleeping quarters arranged for him by Mina and Daisy. The room was sparse, since it was in an emergency bunker and not meant for permanent habitation. There was an iron framed bed that didn't look wide enough for two people, a metal dresser painted a drab shade of gray, and a nightstand made of the same metal. The furniture looked like it had come from an army barracks, or perhaps a decommissioned fallout shelter.

He sat on the edge of the bed, leaning forward and staring at the phone Mina had given to him, but barely seeing it. A thousand thoughts swirled through his mind, not the least of which was that Nancy and Celine had killed the doppelgänger. How they had achieved that feat remained to be seen since Nancy had not elaborated. But that wasn't what Decker was thinking about. Bailey had abducted Adam Hunt and taken him somewhere, leaving behind the shapeshifter to go after Nancy. Presumably, he did not know that Daisy was alive, and that Decker had escaped captivity back in Louisiana. Those two facts came together in Decker's mind and a plan was forming.

Under normal circumstances, he would never get close enough to Bailey to rescue Adam Hunt, even if he knew where they had gone. The man was a master tactician who had clearly risen within the ranks of The Watchers since leaving CUSP. He would surely have operatives ready to defend him to their last breath. But with the doppelgänger dead and Bailey unaware of his passing, an opportunity presented itself. All Decker had to do was pass himself off as the shapeshifter, which shouldn't be too hard, considering they both wore the same face.

There was only one problem. Bailey could have taken Adam Hunt anywhere on the planet, given his extreme head start. Yet Decker didn't think he had gone anywhere near that far. Bailey was hell bent on revenge for the death of his girlfriend all those years ago. He was probably planning to kill Hunt, but if that were his only goal, he could have done so right here on the island. Instead, he had put an elaborate plan in place, killed innocent people in both Louisiana and Maine, just to make a point. And where better to do that than the place where his vendetta started?

Decker thought about this a moment longer, weighing the validity of his conclusion, and decided that even if he was wrong, he would lose nothing by pursuing it. If Bailey had not taken Adam Hunt to the scene of the event that started everything—the cave in northern Maine where they had encountered the Wendigo—then he could think of nowhere else to look. He rose from the bed, intending to look for Mina and tell her his theory, but at that moment the door opened, and Nancy walked in, wrapped in a blanket, flanked by Corporal Shaw.

"John!" She ran forward and threw her arms around him in a tight embrace. After a few seconds passed, she released him. "I'm starting to rethink you coming back to CUSP."

"Me too," Decker said, brushing a strand of hair from her forehead and kissing her. "We can talk about that later, but right now, there's something I need to do."

Nancy slumped visibly. "I know that look in your eyes. Please tell me you're not putting yourself in more danger."

"I don't have a choice. The people who lured me to

Louisiana, and attacked this facility, tried to murder you and Celine, also abducted Adam Hunt. If I don't go after them, get him back, they will surely kill him."

"No." Nancy shook her head. "They can find someone else to get Adam Hunt back. You've done enough. I won't allow it."

"It's not that simple." Decker understood Nancy's fear. But he could see only one viable way to save Hunt's life. He led Nancy to the bed and sat with her, then explained his plan.

She listened quietly; her face growing ashen. "Why does it always come down to you?"

"It doesn't," Decker said softly. "Plenty of the men and women who work for CUSP put their lives in danger every day. It's the job."

"Fine. Then send one of them."

"You know I can't, and you know why."

"That doesn't make me feel any better." Nancy stared across the room at the far wall, as if making eye contact with her husband would somehow make things worse. "What if Barringer, or Bailey, or whatever his name is, sees through your ruse? What if he knows that you're not the doppelgänger?"

"That's a chance I'll have to take," Decker said. "But he won't, because the shapeshifter is dead. You and Celine saw to that."

"I'm scared, John."

"Me too," Decker admitted. After everything that had happened over the last several days, he knew only too well not to underestimate Bailey. The man had already gotten the drop on him once, had locked him in a cell and stolen his DNA. Despite his assurances to the contrary, Decker could not be certain that Bailey would accept him as the doppelgänger. But he had to try, because the alternative was too grim to contemplate. He sat there for a moment longer, holding Nancy's hand, then he stood up. "I need to find Mina."

Nancy looked up at him, her eyes brimming with tears. "Go do what you need to. Just don't get yourself killed."

"I never have before," Decker said, instantly regretting the joviality of his reply. When Nancy said nothing else, he turned and walked from the room.

Corporal Shaw and Celine were standing in the corridor, a discrete distance from the door. But it was obvious they had overheard the entire conversation, because Shaw snapped to attention upon seeing Decker.

"Mina is in the control room. I'll take you to her," he volunteered before Decker even said a word. "And just so you know, I think your plan is genius. That bastard won't even see you coming."

"I hope so," Decker replied, following the corporal toward the control room. Because the alternative was too dire to contemplate.

SEVENTY-SIX

THE HELICOPTER FLEW low over the treetops. Decker, sitting in the back of the small cabin, watched the landscape zip by below with only faint interest. It wasn't until the small city of Caribou, in the far north of Maine a stone's throw from the Canadian border, came into view beneath them, that he sat up and noted their surroundings. Despite its remote location, he had been to the city once before, albeit briefly, to investigate a Bigfoot that had attacked a group of campers. After hiking out into the wilderness, Decker and the rest of his team had discovered that the Bigfoot was nothing the sort. It was, instead, a tulpa. A creature materialized from the thoughts of its creator. Now, though, he was here for a much different reason. Caribou was the closest he could get by air to the cave where Adam Hunt and his companions had faced off with the Wendigo. A tragic encounter that had left one person dead and driven another to hatch a plan for revenge that had taken a decade to ferment.

Next to Decker, occupying the other half of the helicopter's back bench seat, was Corporal Shaw, whom Mina had insisted accompany him for backup and support, despite Decker's protestations that his plan would work better if he went alone. Eventually, they reached a compromise. Shaw would ride along but stay out of sight and only intervene if the situation got out of hand. How that would work exactly, Decker didn't know, but it wasn't worth the argument. He agreed with one caveat—that the corporal follow his orders implicitly and refrain from interfering unless absolutely necessary.

There was a rugged four-wheel-drive Jeep waiting for them after the helicopter landed at the city's municipal airport. Shaw took the wheel and drove out of the city into the densely wooded terrain beyond. They continued for two hours, heading toward the coordinates of the cave, provided by Mina from the original incident report Adam Hunt had filed many years before. They rode mostly in silence, with Decker consumed by thoughts of the task which lay ahead, and his new wife that he had left behind in Portland. Every so often, his hand went to the gun under his jacket. The weapon that Daisy had given him from the secret armory. It was all he had dared to bring along, figuring that Bailey was more likely to accept him as the doppelgänger if he wasn't an obvious threat. Still, Decker worried it might not be enough. Bailey had proved to be a more than competent foe in the past, and if he saw through Decker's subterfuge, the situation would turn deadly in a heartbeat.

"We're about as close to the coordinates as I can get us by road," Shaw said eventually, breaking the silence. "From here, it's a good mile hike to the cave entrance."

Decker waited until the corporal had pulled the Jeep to the side of the road before replying. "I'll go alone from here. Wait with the Jeep. If I'm not back in two hours, it probably means I'm dead. Notify Mina of the situation and return to Caribou. Under no circumstances are you to follow me. There's no point in both of us dying today."

"Sir?" The look on Shaw's face told Decker that he didn't approve of the plan. "Those aren't my orders. I'm to stay out of sight but provide backup should you need it."

"Your orders were to do as I say. If it goes pear-shaped up at that cave, someone needs to alert CUSP. That won't happen if we're both dead. Regardless of what happens to me, Bailey cannot be allowed to disappear into the ether like he's done so many times before."

"I don't like this," Shaw said.

Decker met the corporal's gaze. "I know."

When it became clear that the stoic Ghost Team operative had nothing more to say, Decker pushed the Jeep's passenger door open and climbed out, pulling his coat closed against the sudden biting chill. He stood for a moment, surveying his surroundings —the dense woodland that appeared practically impenetrable, and the freezing wisps of fog that curled around the trees and bleached the landscape of color. The sky was a pale shade of gray above him, devoid of the circling hawks and other avian residents that made the woods their home during the warmer months.

Decker glanced back toward the Jeep, acknowledging Corporal Shaw with a nod as their eyes met, then pulled a handheld GPS unit from his pocket and stepped into the woods to cover the last mile to his destination on foot. He only hoped his hunch was correct about Bailey, or this entire journey was for nothing. But somehow, deep down, Decker knew he was right. Because, with his warped sense of karma, this was the only place Bailey would conceivably bring Adam Hunt to quench the thirst for revenge that had begun precisely eight years earlier.

SEVENTY-SEVEN

ADAM HUNT SAT on the frozen floor of the cave, his arms secured behind his back by handcuffs cinched just a little too tightly and feet bound by a coarse rope that cut into the skin of his ankles. He glared up at his captor. It had been almost twenty-four hours since the attack on CUSP's headquarters that had resulted in his abduction, and he'd spent most of that time wondering why Nathan Bailey had taken him instead of just putting a bullet in his head there and then. Yet despite his attempts to gain some insight into his old colleague's motives, the man had remained stubbornly unresponsive.

At least, until now.

"You really don't remember, do you?" Bailey said, standing over Hunt with a gun in his hand and a placid expression on his face that belied the obvious rage simmering within.

"Of course I remember," Hunt said. "This is the cave where Kate died eight years ago."

"Not just eight years ago," Bailey said, a hint of expression finally passing across his features. A brief flash of sorrow that quickly faded. "This is the day, the exact date, that you killed her."

"I didn't kill Kate. The Wendigo did that, and you know it."

"She wouldn't have been anywhere near this cave when the wendigo attacked if it weren't for you. You're the one who insisted we split up. You're the one who led her here. If she had been with me that day, none of this would be happening. Kate would still be alive."

"You can't possibly know that." Hunt shifted on the uncomfortable ground where a jutting rock was pressing into his leg. "Besides, Kate knew the risks just like we all did. She accepted them, even to the end. If she were here, she would tell you as much."

"But she's not here. She's dead." Bailey glanced at his watch. "And in a little under fourteen minutes, you will join her."

"I don't get it," Hunt said. He was happy for an extra fourteen minutes. The longer he was alive, the more chance he had to turn his predicament around. But that didn't mean he understood Bailey's strange desire to kill him at such a specific time. "Why fourteen minutes?"

"2:07 PM. That ring a bell?"

Hunt shook his head. "Should it?"

Bailey observed him for a few seconds, as if he simply couldn't believe that Adam Hunt could be so clueless. Then he cleared his throat, perhaps fighting back against a glimmer of emotion. "That's when she died. The exact time that you let the Wendigo kill her."

Now Hunt understood. "And you think that murdering me on the anniversary of her death, at the same time and place, will bring you some sort of peace?" He couldn't help a small laugh despite his situation. "You always had a flair for the dramatic. You could have killed me at any time over the last eight years. Sent one of your operatives to put a bullet in me or sink a knife into my back. Hell, there's a thousand ways you could have done it. It would've been so easy. But instead, you obsessed and schemed and plotted. You held onto the date and time of Kate's death, never moving on from the past, just so you could bring me to this place in a pathetic effort to lay her ghost at rest. Well, guess what? It won't work. Do what you want to me. Kill me. Leave my body here as some sort of crazy retribution. But it won't stop the pain. The only way to do that is to accept what happened, honor her memory the right way, otherwise you'll spend the rest of your life living in the shadow of her death."

"Shut up!" Bailey's eyes glinted with anger. He waved the gun at Hunt. "You don't understand. You never understood. The two of us, me and Kate, we were…" His voice trailed off into a choked sob.

"You were in love," Hunt said. "It wasn't hard to see. That doesn't mean you need to commit atrocities in her name. Come on, Nathan. We used to be friends. You, me, and Kate. All three of us. Do you really think she would want you to do all of this, hurt so many people, just because she isn't here?"

"That's just it. She isn't here. She doesn't have the luxury of an opinion. And it's all because of you." Bailey looked at his watch again. "Five minutes. If you want to make your peace with this life, now is the time."

Hunt fell silent. There was no use in wasting the last few precious minutes of his life arguing with a madman. Nathan Bailey had spent eight long years thinking of nothing but this moment. If there was ever a chance of reasoning with him, making the man see the error of his ways, it had long passed. In a few minutes, Bailey would exact his final revenge and there was nothing that Hunt—handcuffed and bound—could do to stop him. Instead, he closed his eyes, took a couple of deep, calming breaths, and waited for the inevitable.

SEVENTY-EIGHT

DECKER FOLLOWED the handheld GPS for almost a mile, pushing through dense undergrowth, navigating a stream swollen by rain, climbing over large boulders, and scrambling up granite ledges. It was tough going, even without snow on the ground. It would have been even worse tracking a bloodthirsty wendigo through this terrain in a blizzard and battling subarctic temperatures. No wonder the creature had prevailed. Unlike Hunt and his companions, the wendigo thrived in hostile environments such as the one they had found themselves in that day. The weather wasn't nearly as bad now, but Decker was tracking an equally deadly foe. Which was why, as he approached the cave, he slipped the GPS unit back into his pocket, checked that his gun was concealed but within reach, and stepped confidently toward his destination.

The cave was located on a steep rise that jutted up out of the forest floor. The entrance was narrow, nothing more than a jagged, dark slit against the lighter rock surrounding it. But this was the place.

Decker stopped and looked around, surprised that he saw no one else. Nathan Bailey would surely be inside the cave with Adam Hunt, plotting his final revenge. But he was not a lone wolf. He had the backing of an entire organization and would surely not have brought Hunt here on his own. At the very least, Decker would have expected someone to be guarding the cave entrance. But the woods were eerily empty. He resisted pulling the GPS out to check his coordinates. There was probably more than one cave dotting this landscape and it was possible, if unlikely, that he had strayed from the coordinates Mina had given him. But then, from somewhere to his rear, came a faint footfall.

Decker spun around, lifting his hand instinctively for the gun under his coat, but stopping himself at the last moment, even before he saw a stocky man wearing camouflage pants and a jacket step from between the trees with a pistol in his hand. Decker recognized him as the same individual who had stood at the end of his path back in Wolf Haven while an associate crept up from behind and drugged him.

A flicker of recognition passed across his face before he lowered the gun. "Holy crap, Gabriel. What are you doing sneaking around the woods like that? You trying to get yourself shot?"

Decker cleared his throat, hoping that he could do as good a job impersonating the shapeshifter—who apparently went by the misleadingly angelic moniker of Gabriel—as the doppelgänger had done pretending to be him. "I need to speak with Nathan. I have important information about CUSP."

"What kind of information?"

Decker hesitated before answering. The man standing before him clearly knew the shapeshifter. The question was, in what capacity? Were the pair friends or simply coworkers? And if the latter, how did they fit into the hierarchy of The Watchers? Decker had two choices. Be bold and decisive, or humble in the presence of a man who might be his superior. If he took the wrong attitude, it might cost him his life. Deciding that it was unlikely that anyone in a position of power within the organization would be skulking around the woods acting as a bodyguard, he made his choice. "The kind of information I'm not willing to share with you. Now, unless you have anything else to say, I'm going inside that cave."

"The boss said he wasn't to be disturbed. You go in there and it's your funeral."

"He'll want to hear what I have to say, so I'll take my chances." Decker didn't wait for a response. Instead, he turned and walked toward the cave, expecting to feel the sting of a bullet in his back at any moment. But he didn't, and soon he was stepping out of the woods and into the cool, dark gash between the rocks.

SEVENTY-NINE

DECKER MADE his way into the cave, moving slowly. The entrance was narrow with little headroom, but it soon widened into a much larger chamber. Up ahead, he heard voices, one of which he recognized instantly.

Relief flooded over Decker. Adam Hunt was still alive. At least, for now. Because, judging by the conversation, Bailey was mere seconds away from completing his plan and getting his final revenge upon Hunt and CUSP.

He stopped momentarily behind a large outcrop. There wasn't much time, and he hadn't come up with a strategy for dealing with Bailey beyond impersonating the doppelgänger, because he hadn't known what the situation would be when he reached the cave. Now, though, he only had moments before his journey was for naught. Pulling his jacket closed to hide the gun concealed beneath, Decker took the only option available to him. He stepped out from behind the rock and approached Bailey.

The cave was deceptively large, rising from a little over five feet at the entrance to at least twice that height. A couple of battery-operated LED lanterns lit the cavern with pale, white light. The walls were slick and wet. The sandy floor was strewn with rocks, most of which had probably fallen from the ceiling overhead. Nathan Bailey stood in the center of the space with a gun in his hand. Further back, sitting on the floor, bound by his hands and feet, was Adam Hunt. When he saw Decker, his eyes widened momentarily, perhaps in recognition, or maybe in anger, assuming it was the doppelgänger who had walked into the cave.

It was enough to alert Bailey of the presence behind him.

He spun around, gun raised, then half lowered it. "What the hell are you doing here? I told you to stay in Portland and take care of the woman."

Decker had expected this reaction. "Already done. Nancy Decker is dead."

"Excellent. I hope you left enough fingerprints around to tie her husband to the crime."

"It will be an open and shut case."

Bailey nodded thoughtfully. "Once this is over, we'll release John Decker from that cell in Louisiana and let him take his chances. Between the murders of Daisy Finch and his wife, he'll be looking at life in prison. Maybe even the death penalty. And good riddance. The man was a thorn in my side."

Decker said nothing.

"That still doesn't answer my question. What are you doing here?"

"I have information about CUSP," Decker said, biding his time and looking for an opportunity to strike and free Hunt.

"You shouldn't have come here looking like him. What if someone saw you?"

"No one saw me except your goon out front," Decker said. "And I should be changing back to my true form soon."

"Yeah, well, it was a risk." Bailey looked at his watch. "Now, get out of here. I only have a few seconds to finish this."

Decker nodded and turned as if to leave, praying that Bailey wouldn't watch him exit the cave, because he had no intention of doing so.

He didn't. Instead, he turned his attention back to Hunt and raised the gun. "It's time to end this."

Decker stopped and spun around, drawing the high-tech weapon Daisy had given him and aiming it squarely at Bailey. "Yes, it is. Drop the pistol and back away from Adam Hunt."

"What's the meaning of this?" Bailey didn't drop the pistol. Instead, he pointed it at Decker. For a moment, he looked confused, then he nodded. "You're not Gabriel."

"No."

Bailey studied Decker with a look almost like resignation. "How did you escape?"

"That's not important."

"Fair enough. There will be time to figure that out later… once you're dead."

"Enough talk." Decker was losing his patience. "Throw the pistol on the ground right now."

"I don't think so. What are you going to do, shoot me in cold blood?" A faint smile played across Bailey's lips. "That's not your style. If it was, you would have killed me back on Habitat One after I left you and all those other fools for dead on the ocean floor. Now how about *you* lower your weapon. I have the advantage here. Unlike you, I'm not averse to taking lives, even innocent ones. And besides, you're outnumbered. If I don't come out of his cave in the next few minutes, my man Harlan will come to investigate."

"I just met him. Your man Harlan isn't too bright. It didn't take much to convince him I was the shapeshifter."

"You see, that's my point. You had the upper hand. You could easily have taken him out. Shot him before he even saw you. But you didn't, did you?"

"No."

"And there's my answer. You won't shoot me either, because you're not a killer." Bailey glanced toward Hunt, who was watching the exchange with a look of frustration on his face. "Now, how about we just wait here pointing our guns at each other until Harlan shows up, and then I can get on with the business of killing Adam Hunt without further interruption."

"That won't be happening," said a voice from somewhere near the cave entrance. A moment later, Corporal Shaw appeared carrying a rifle, which he lifted and pointed at Bailey. "Harlan is currently indisposed."

Bailey observed Shaw before shifting his gaze back to Decker. "You see. That's what I'm talking about. Your soldier boy here had no compunction about killing a man."

Shaw shook his head. "I never said that I killed him."

Bailey signed. "That's the trouble with you CUSP people, always trying to do the right thing. Still, I can see when I'm at a disadvantage." He looked down at the gun in his hand, lowered his arm as if he was finally going to drop it. But then, at the last moment, he lifted the gun back up, spun around and aimed at Hunt, his finger curling on the trigger.

A sharp crack echoed through the cave, deafeningly loud.

Decker lunged forward, convinced that Bailey had killed Hunt, but instead, the man who once called himself Thomas Barringer took a faltering step, and sank to his knees. The pistol fell from his hand and landed in the dirt. Blood seeped into the fabric of his shirt. He stayed that way for a moment, a look of shock on his face, then he pitched forward onto the cave floor. Decker went to him, kicked his gun out of reach, then felt for a pulse. He found none.

"Dead." He looked up at Shaw, who was still standing with his rifle aimed at the stricken man. The acrid scent of gunpowder hung in the air.

"I had no choice," said the corporal. "He was going to shoot Mr. Hunt."

Decker climbed to his feet. "You did the right thing."

"Thank you, sir."

"Although I *did* tell you to stay with the Jeep."

"I guess that sometimes I just don't hear too well." Shaw finally lowered the gun. "I accept full responsibility for my actions. Under the circumstances, I'll happily accept a reprimand."

"I don't think that will be necessary." Decker went to Hunt. "How about we get you out of here?"

"Suits me." He met Decker's gaze. "You took your time."

"Better late than never." Decker tugged at the ropes binding Hunt's feet, but they were too tight.

Corporal Shaw withdrew a KA-BAR USMC fighting knife from a sheath on his belt. "Here, use this."

Decker took the knife and quickly sliced through the ropes. While he did that, Shaw searched Bailey's lifeless body and soon came up with the keys for the handcuffs. Once Hunt was free, he climbed to his feet. "Thank you. Both of you. I thought for certain I was a goner."

"You're welcome," said Decker.

Hunt looked down at the body of his old friend, a look of sorrow passing across his face. "It didn't need to end like this."

Decker placed a consoling hand on Hunt's shoulder. "I'm not so sure about that. Bailey was hellbent on revenge. It was all he lived for. Only one of you was coming out of this cave alive."

"Maybe. Maybe not." Hunt turned toward the cavern entrance. "I guess we'll never know."

EIGHTY

FIVE DAYS LATER

DECKER SAT in Adam Hunt's office and observed his boss and mentor across the desk. Hunt looked well considering his ordeal, and the tragedy inflicted upon his colleagues by Nathan Bailey. All told, fourteen people had lost their lives on the island, most of whom were members of one Ghost Team unit or another, but three civilian employees had also lost their lives. Decker knew that those deaths, every single one of them, weighed heavily upon him. And that didn't even account for the innocent victims of Bailey's twisted plan back in Wolf Haven.

"We've recaptured most of the creatures set free by the doppelgänger," Hunt said, leaning back in his chair. "We expect to have the last few stragglers back in their pens within twenty-four hours."

"That's good to hear," said Decker. "What about the shapeshifter? Did you find his body?"

"No. We've searched the bay and the shores of the surrounding islands, but so far haven't found a sign of him. But that's not surprising. Given the currents around here, he could wash up anywhere along a thirty-mile stretch of coastline.

Assuming he wasn't swept out into the ocean, that is." Hunt drew a breath. "You're sure he's dead?"

"Nancy was certain that he was. Celine shot him at point blank range. She said that the last time they saw him, he was floating face down in the water, surrounded by his own blood."

"Fair enough." Hunt rubbed the stubble on his chin. "There's something you should know. Astrid and her son are gone."

"Astrid." The name Decker hadn't thought about in a long time. Not since he left Ireland. "Grendel and his mother escaped the island?"

"Yes."

"I thought that was impossible with the chips you implant in residents of The Zoo."

"Astrid dug her chip out with a knife. She did the same for Grendel. If it's any consolation, the removal would have been incredibly painful."

"It's not," said Decker. The thought of Grendel and his mother unleashed upon the world again sent a shudder down his spine. "You'll recapture them?"

"We'll do our best." Hunt folded his arms. "But as you know, they have been around a long time and are very good at hiding."

"A final gift from Nathan Bailey."

"Quite. But other than that one unfortunate occurrence, everything else should be back to normal in a week. Ten days at most."

"That's good to hear." There was one more thing weighing on Decker. "The harpy in Italy. The one that killed Colum when the ghost let me glimpse the future."

"We're still monitoring the situation."

"And?"

"And we'll be sure to keep Colum far from Italy for the foreseeable future. In fact, I hoped you might head the team to deal with the harpy."

Decker had been waiting for this. He looked down towards

the floor, then back up, finally meeting Hunt's gaze. "I'm not sure... I mean... If I'm still here."

"You're reevaluating your position with CUSP."

"Do you blame me, after everything that's happened?"

"I thought you had set aside your animosity toward Mina and the organization. That you had come to terms with the way this timeline has played out."

"I have. This isn't about that. It's about me and Nancy and being newly married. I'm not sure I can put myself in danger every day while she sits at home and worries. She almost lost me once already, spent months thinking I was lost in the past, or worse, that I was dead. How can I ask her to take that risk all over again?"

Hunt studied Decker, his face expressionless. "I don't think I'm the person you should be discussing this with." "Probably not." Decker pushed his chair back and stood to leave. "I'll give you my answer as soon as I can."

"Don't be in too much of a hurry," Hunt said, opening his desk drawer and withdrawing a large manila envelope with Decker's name on the front. He pushed it across the desk. "Here."

Decker looked at the envelope. "What is this?"

"It's your honeymoon. I figure it's the least we can do after wrecking your first wedding to Nancy and almost getting you killed before you even made it a week into your second one."

"Forgive me for being suspicious," Decker said. "But the last time I accepted a gift from you, I ended up stranded over a hundred years in the past and almost went down with the Titanic."

Hunt laughed. "I assure you there are no ulterior motives behind *this* gift. If you don't believe me, you can ask Mina."

"Maybe I will," said Decker.

"In the meantime, take the envelope. You'll find two first-class airfares to Hawaii and a two-week stay in a deluxe suite with an ocean view at the Four Seasons. You'll also have the use

ANTHONY M. STRONG

of a chauffeur-driven limousine and personal valet for your entire stay. All your other expenses are on us too, naturally. There's a pair of platinum cards inside the envelope. One for each of you. No spending limits."

"For a minute, I thought you were going to say that the honeymoon is in Italy, then ask me to take care of the harpy while I'm there," Decker said with a chuckle.

"Don't think it didn't cross my mind," Hunt said, grinning. "But both Mina and Daisy were quick to point out how ungracious that would be of me."

"Those are two wise young women," Decker said, picking up the envelope.

"Not so young, either of them," Hunt pointed out.

"True." Decker looked down at the envelope. "Thank you for this. It wasn't necessary."

"I disagree," Hunt said. "Enjoy your honeymoon. Don't even think about us. Then, when you get back, I hope you'll be rested and ready to see things in a better light."

"And if I'm not?" Decker asked.

Hunt shrugged. "You can lead a horse to water..." He let the last half of the well-worn idiom hang in the air. Then, he said, "but I hope that you'll be thirsty."

"We'll see," said Decker, even though he already knew what his new wife would say, because she had said it before. There was no other job in the world he would rather be doing. And she was right. But even if he suspected what his decision regarding CUSP would be, he wasn't going to let Hunt know that. Not until he was sure.

Hunt nodded. "Don't forget to stop by and see Mina on your way out."

"I will," said Decker, then he turned and left the office with the envelope in his hand and Nancy on his mind.

ABOUT THE AUTHOR

Anthony M. Strong is a British-born writer living and working in the United States. He is the author of the popular John Decker series of supernatural adventure thrillers.

Anthony has worked as a graphic designer, newspaper writer, artist, and actor. When he was a young boy, he dreamed of becoming an Egyptologist and spent hours reading about pyramids and tombs. Until he discovered dinosaurs and decided to be a paleontologist instead. Neither career panned out, but he was left with a fascination for monsters and archaeology that serve him well in the John Decker books.

Anthony has traveled extensively across Europe and the United States, and weaves his love of travel into his novels, setting them both close to home and in far-off places.

Anthony currently resides most of the year on Florida's Space Coast where he can watch rockets launch from his balcony, and part of the year on an island in Maine, with his wife Sonya, and two furry bosses, Izzie and Hayden.

Connect with Anthony, find out about new releases, and get free books at www.anthonymstrong.com